THE CONSTABLE'S TALE

THE
CONSTABLE'S
TALE

DONALD SMITH

PEGASUS CRIME
NEW YORK LONDON

THE CONSTABLE'S TALE

Pegasus Books LLC
80 Broad Street, 5th Floor
New York, NY 10004

First Pegasus Books cloth edition September 2015

Interior design by Maria Fernandez

Library of Congress Cataloging-in-Publication Data is available.

ISBN: 978-1-60598-861-0

10 9 8 7 6 5 4 3 2 1

Printed in the United States of America
Distributed by W. W. Norton & Company

For Pat

Oh, that deceit should dwell
In such a gorgeous palace!

—WILLIAM SHAKESPEARE

THE CONSTABLE'S TALE

PROLOGUE

THE CRIES WERE THIN AND FULL OF COMPLAINT. A BABY SOMEWHERE ahead in the forest, making just enough noise to be heard above the clamor coming from Nicholas's wagon, which was filled with metal candle holders, cake stamps, spouted coffeepots, milk pails, and tools and raw materials for making and repairing such things.

The first body he came to was that of a little boy. He must have been eight or nine, lying on his side in front of a house at the edge of a cleared field. Jumbles of pine needles and small limbs and sticky green cones covered the yard except for that spot, which had been swept clean. The grainy clay ground still damp from a storm that had passed through two nights before. His head lay on a pillow. Fluffy blond hair neatly combed back, lips parted. He was in sleeping clothes, a thigh-length white linen shirt with bloused shoulders and ruffled cuffs. Fancy. English manufacture, unless the tinner missed his guess, and he was good at judging merchandise. Bending down over the body, he could see a hole the size of a rifle ball between the shoulder blades. And there was something else. Someone had placed beneath his nose a sprig of rosemary. An emblem of mourning.

Trying to ignore the chill creeping up his legs, Nicholas went back to the wagon and took out his Pennsylvania rifle. Cocked the hammer, confident it would work if needed. Earlier that day, he had used it to get a squirrel for breakfast.

The house was of moderate size and made of good sawn timber, a typical second plantation house of the sort put up after the original log shelter had served its purpose. Nicholas eased the door open and entered. In the front room, a man lay outstretched on his back. Head on another pillow, face turned to one side, as if posing for a silhouette. Throat cut. Flies busy at the edges of a thickened pool of blood. Someone had gone to the trouble of turning his stockings down over his shoes and covering him from knees to chest, just so, with a linen sheet. A dark, smeary trail led to a rear room. There, Nicholas found the body of a stabbed woman. She, too, had been positioned. Slumped over on her knees in a corner next to a chimney, hands clasped under her chin as if in prayer. Eyes open, looking into eternity.

It came to Nicholas that this might be the work of Indians. On fire-lit winter nights back in Williamsburg, the grayhairs seemed to take some twisted old people's delight in scaring children with tales of horror from the troubled times. How sometimes after one of their raids the savages would leave the dead in mocking poses. In their ignorance of enlightened behavior, their complete lack of understanding of European standards concerning the rituals of warfare and death, it seemed they imagined the white tribe might appreciate their wit, as one might concede a well-played practical joke. But such barbarities were safely in the past. Or so it was thought. In the eighteen years Nicholas had been alive, Virginia and the Carolinas had been free of native violence. Most of the southern tidewater Indians were either moldering in the ground or had moved on. Still, his father had given him a warning along with the rifle, his going-away presents. Be careful, he said. There had been upsetting news from the Carolina frontier two hundred miles to the southwest, the rolling hills and rushing streams of the Sioux and, beyond them, the Cherokee. Young men returning from the war in the North were finding British farmers had moved into their lands. Some were taking revenge.

"Well, if it was some Indian devils that killed you," he told the dead woman at his feet, "they must have been lost."

The sound of his own voice threw a new fright into him. He looked through the rest of the house and saw no one else. Deciding to ignore the crying child for a while longer, he checked on a pair of small cabins he had seen on the grounds. Both looked like they had been lived in but not for some time. Spanish moss mattresses folded up on the beds, layers of dust everywhere.

Back in the main house, a foul odor coming from the crib nearly overpowered the smell of rancid flesh in the room. He stripped off the baby's gown, wiped its bottom with a sheet, and bundled it in its little blanket. As an afterthought, he gave it some water from a half-filled washbowl he found, getting about as much into the tiny mouth as he spilled. From the increasing loudness of bawling, he guessed it was hungry. But that would have to wait.

He carried the baby to the wagon and emptied a wooden box of its slabs of tinplate recently arrived from Cornwall. Laid the baby inside, tucking in some rags to cushion its head. Then, climbing into the driver's seat, he pointed his horse in the direction of the place he had been headed. A Carolina settlement whose recent change from the haunted place it once had been to a bustling center of trade was the talk of the southern provinces. Nicholas planned to open a tinning shop there before some other journeyman got in ahead of him.

The baby settled into a monotonous drone of discontent. Strange, Nicholas thought, it was still alive. To his knowledge, Indians would never leave infant survivors. Sometimes they would carry a baby back with them, raise it as a slave. They were even known to adopt a child to take the place of one of theirs lost in battle or to sickness. But they were not in the habit of sparing little ones who might grow up to kill Indian children.

He would think on this mystery of the baby later, and the odd positions of the bodies. For now, he concentrated on driving the wagon as fast as he dared without shaking it apart. The vehicle and its metal cargo protested the unaccustomed speed with a jangling commotion. A din of alarm.

CHAPTER 1

23: When you see a Crime punished, you may be inwardly
Pleased; but always shew Pity to ye Suffering Offender.
—*Rules of Civility*

CRAVEN COUNTY ROYAL CONSTABLE JAMES HENRY WOODYARD GAVE
his horse's reins a gentle shake, just enough to remind her that they
were on official business, not a leisurely stroll through the woods.
Annie had been a gift on Harry's tenth birthday from his grandfather
and their friend Comet Elijah. A handsome foal for a rowdy boy in a
world where everything was new, and old age was not even a passing
notion. But the sad truth was her lead in animal years was showing
as they made their way along the new-cut road, which led past

1

the Woodyard family plantation and into New Bern. The roadbed, equal parts sand and hard clay, was still damp, the air fragrant with earthy smells unlocked by recent winds and rain. Annie picked her way around fallen branches with the measured care of a human approaching elderliness. Longleaf pine trees towered over them in the morning mist like spindly storybook giants. Living monuments, Grandfather Natty liked to say. Ancient before any of them were born.

"I am still upset, you know," said Toby. She was riding her chestnut mare just ahead of their Negro manservant, Martin, who was on one of the grays.

"You'll be glad you came along, I promise. The seeds can wait one more day."

"We've planted collards this late before," Martin affirmed. "They always came up just as good."

"It's not just the collards," Toby said, a fussy edge to her voice. "According to Missus Logan's almanac, in this clime we are late with our cucumbers, broccoli, French beans, radishes, and cauliflowers."

Harry turned in his saddle and looked back to get a better idea of how upset she really was. She was tall for a woman. The top of her head came to just above Harry's chin when they danced. Her figure was the kind people called "near skinny," though Harry's mother liked a term she had learned from the tutor she had hired to teach her sons: *lithe*. Toby had brown hair, light olive skin, and pretty brown eyes that she modestly told admirers were about a fingernail too wide apart. For today's courtroom outing she had chosen her good silk gown, the dark blue one she usually kept for Sunday wear. It had been a gift from her parents back in Swansea in hopes that a female indentured servant with a good Welsh upbringing, education, and a few pieces of nice clothes would be soon matrimonially indentured. The strategy had worked.

By her expression, Harry judged that her mood was more one of bother than genuine ire. He said, "I'm sure Martin would let us have a cabbage or two from the servants' garden, if the worst came to the worst." Martin nodded agreeably.

"We will not be stealing from the help," Toby said. "My father has one of the finest gardens in South Wales. And in my country, the best fruits and vegetables are the ones planted at the correct time."

"Everything is better in Wales, to hear you talk." Harry turned again and smiled, lest she think he meant this in less-than-good humor. He tried to think of one of the *Rules of Civility & Decent Behaviour In Company and Conversation* that might apply. Some courteous remark he might make to smooth over any misreading of what he meant as a jest. The judge had made him memorize the rules, 110 of them. But nine years had passed since then. Such advices were hardly ever useful around home, and Harry rarely found himself in the company of people who knew and appreciated them. Without practice, they had begun to fall away from memory.

Toby was right, of course. The ideal planting times had long since passed due to the three-week wedding holiday Harry had insisted on making. He wanted to show her what lay beyond Craven County, magical places like Roanoke Island, where Comet Elijah had taken him as a boy. Harry had recounted the story for Toby on their way over, how the first English colony in America settled 175 years earlier then disappeared, leaving behind only shreds of its existence. On his own first trip, Harry had dug around the remains of an old fort on the island and found a corroded piece of steel in the shape of a crescent. Grandfather Natty recognized it as a gorget, a bit of English body armor. Comet Elijah said he probably had known the man it belonged to.

"But how could that be?" Harry had asked. The three of them were then on a hunting trip down near Swan's Quarter, sitting around a fire, roasting a pair of rabbits. Harry was eleven.

Comet Elijah seemed not to hear. "They were running low on food as I recall," he said. "They'd sent back to England for some more supplies but after a while they decided the ship wasn't coming back, so they packed up their things and left. Run off with some of my people who lived around there at that time. We heard that a ship finally did show up, but they were long away by then." He blew into the fire to make it hotter, sending sparks into the blue darkness. "I can talk to you more about this later on, if you're interested."

Neither Harry nor Natty pressed the matter. There were things about Comet Elijah, things he would say, that they had learned not question too narrowly. Not because he would take offense, but his answers would just pose more questions. Sometimes when Harry listened to him talk he felt he was losing his ability to reason and beginning to float off the ground.

"I'll admit I am interested in how justice is served in America," Toby said. "Your reports this week have made me curious. Though they won't fill our bellies as well as a dish of beans. And that reminds me, we need to talk about your ledgers. They're a mess. You owe this person three days' use of your oxen for stump-clearing, and that person owes you a barrel of tar for something else. When I kept the books in my parents' household, we put things down in pounds sterling. I know currency is scarce here, but I can't begin to figure out where your plantation comes out in the end."

"It's our plantation now, my love."

Toby smiled. A good sign. "A pretty thing to say, but we both know that the husband is the owner."

"It's ours if we go bankrupt. Anyhow, I'm grateful for your efforts, but you shouldn't worry. Everybody in Craven County owes everybody else something. It's the way we live and get along with each other. Sooner or later, everybody gets paid back. It always works out in the end."

Toby looked like she was about to say something further, but Harry seized on the pause to change the subject. "I'm sure our courts aren't much different from yours," he said. "The lawyers are always talking about precedents in English law."

"Husband, everything is different in America."

"The trials are going at a quick pace. Olaf McLeod doesn't stand on legal ceremony. I've given up trying to guess how he'll rule on any particular thing. Or when. Sometimes he'll just decide he's heard enough, hand down a verdict, and move on."

"I am sure I'll have much to tell my journal tonight."

Harry had mostly resisted peeking into Toby's diary. She had begun it a few days after the wedding. She said she wanted their future children to know how they lived when they were young. He had looked only a few times. Her neat handwriting for the most part dealt with monotonies of everyday life, making him wonder why she even bothered. The time she got up mornings to stoke the cooking fire. The day's weather. Chores she did. The visit of a neighbor now and then.

His eyes once did land on a longer piece of writing in which she put down her thoughts about the mystery of time. How one moment flowed into the next and that into the following, and so on, making an endless chain of tiny packets that defined one's existence. How no one could know what any approaching moment might hold. How they whisper by like leaves in a stream or hurtle past with great uproar, each with the prospect of changing the lives of people and nations.

She also wrote of choices—thinking, maybe, of her own decision to put herself up for indenture. She had told Harry how the idea first had surprised and then worried her father, who, according to her, was a respected and reasonably well-to-do citizen of South Wales. Directing manager of one of the new copper smelting works. The way she explained it to Harry, she wanted to get away from what had become a humdrum life in a house shared with five brothers and four sisters.

Ye Choices wee make are bourne on each of ye tiny Fractions of Time that flow through a Needle's Eye of ye Present. Once made, Choices can not be re-called, but become Frozen, mile-markers in ye ever refeeding Paft.

Just below the last sentence she had made a little flourish with her pen, as she did at the end of each day's entry. Her words made Harry reflect but only briefly. He had animals to feed.

★

They reached the end of the woods. The first sign of a town was a badly weathered wooden rail fence that stretched out on either side as far as the eye could follow. Rails hung from posts at every angle, some fallen altogether and rotting in the weeds. The gate had been missing since Harry could remember, leaving only the rusting remains of hinges looking like broken teeth. Harry made a note in his mind to bring up the condition of the fence again at the next meeting of the town commissioners, though several earlier efforts to fix it had bogged down over this thing or that.

A short distance farther along, signs of a proper settlement came into view. Streets broad enough to allow four carriages abreast. Neatly laid-out plots with one- and two-story timber-framed houses, stores, and offices. A few burned-out hulks remained from the Tuscarora uprising, their blackened bones nearly petrified from more than forty years of exposure to rain and parching sun and the occasional snow. Most of the existing buildings had gone up within the past ten years, made with new-baked brick and fragrant, fresh-hewn lumber, some of it bought from the Woodyard plantation. Harry had acquainted Toby with the town's tragic history soon after she had arrived. How the founders had named it New Bern out of nostalgia for their Swiss homeland. How most of them were now awaiting final judgment, their torn and broken remains resting in the old cemetery.

As they entered the streets under the steadily strengthening sun, signs of storm flooding became apparent. Stains crept up clapboard sidings, musty memorials of high water. The smell of mildew was about. Doors and windows stood open to allow moisture to escape. Stray sheep and chickens investigating bits of litter scattered sullenly as they rode by.

Harry looked back again as they drew near the village center. Toby was brushing wisps of hair from her eyes with the back of her hand. Face damp in the morning heat. "I've never seen so many people in New Bern at one time," she said. "It looks like a fair."

It was all noise and bright colors, a far cry from a normal day in town. At the intersection of Broad and Pollock, a group of strolling dancers with bells on their shoes entertained onlookers in town for the court session. Nearby, a leopard rested in a cage and an elephant was tethered to a tree. Their owner, a small, middle-aged man with watery eyes and a paunch and wearing a silver peruke, was chattering about his liqueurs and powders, how they imparted the physical strength of a cat and the mental powers of a pachyderm. Farther along, a storefront sign advertised THE INVISIBLE LADY AND ACOUSTIC TEMPLE: AN INEXPLICABLE OPTICAL AND AURICULAR ILLUSION. A man named Salenka and his "Learned Dog" from Charleston had established themselves in a tavern. The illustration at the door showed a large beast with shaggy gray hair that could BEST ANYONE AT CARDS, and perform CARD TRICKS AND MATHEMATICAL EXPERIMENTS. In addition, Salenka offered fireworks each night in the garden behind the building. A full bill of entertainment for only two shillings. But the showman had strong competition. A touring company of English actors had set up a makeshift stage in an empty lot across the street. They were acting out a scene from a string of plays they had been presenting throughout the week. The evening's finale would be a double bill, the sidewalk sign proclaimed: the American premiere of the famous George Lillo's adaptation of a drama from the reign of Elizabeth, *Arden of Feversham*; and another from the same period: *Romeo and Juliet* by William Shakespeare, who recently had been enjoying a revival on the London stage.

Harry caught glimpses of Toby smiling, her expression one of wonderment and, he was relieved to see, pleasure. He had won the argument about the garden. At least gained a truce. But he knew better than to gloat, lest she find some other source of discontent. Harry had never known a woman with so many complaints.

"Here we are," he said as they came to a long, low-slung building on East Front Street. "The Court of Pleas and Quarterly Sessions."

"But this is a tavern," Toby said. "You didn't mention they were meeting in a tavern."

"The commissioners decided the old courthouse is about ready to fall down. Wonder it hasn't already happened. What I hear, old man Cogdell is getting five pounds five shillings rent for the week's use of his place during the day, and he gets it back each night. We are pledged to keep good order and not let anything get damaged too badly."

In all the evenings Harry and Toby had spent at Cogdell's, it never had looked like this. The main room had taken on a cavernous aspect. Tables gone. Chairs and benches were arranged in rows for onlookers, who were beginning to shuffle in and take seats. The raised platform used for entertainments and the occasional political harangue now served as a podium. Two tables set end to end and seven chairs awaited the arrival of the magistrates.

Toby chose a front-row seat. Martin sat next to her and helped get writing materials out of her basket so she could make notes. Harry took a position to one side of the platform. Only one other peacekeeper had arrived. Chief Town Constable John Blinn, a muscular, bald-headed blacksmith with an unexpectedly high voice, had put himself at the front door. Harry wondered if the two other officers enlisted for the week's duty would show up for the last day. Absenteeism was a continuing problem in their ranks, despite the threat of a two-shilling fine for each offense. Not everyone honored to be asked to volunteer for two or three years of constable duty or the town watch took it as earnestly as Harry and John Blinn.

The rumble of conversation quieted and all stood as the justices filed in. They were wearing their scarlet summer-season robes and freshly powdered white perukes. Chief Justice Olaf McLeod was the last to enter. Six feet, two inches tall, muscular for his age, wisps of graying red hair straying from the edges of his wig, and a large, bony face weathered from years of managing his four-thousand-acre plantation to the southwest of town. The land had been a gift from the king for financial assistance during the late invasion of England by some of McLeod's deluded Highland neighbors. George did not let such acts of fidelity go unnoticed.

McLeod rapped his gavel and said, "You may be downstanding. This court be now in session," in a raspy Scotch voice several degrees coarser than usual due to a spell of a summer cold. Harry could smell spirits of turpentine, the distilled essence of pine that worked miracles as a liniment when smeared on the chest.

Trouble broke out right away.

People were loosening their clothes to let body heat to escape into the room, already rank with humidity and lingering vapors from the floodwater. Two men began squabbling over one of the remaining seats. McLeod had barely got his words out when they were throwing clumsy punches. Blinn, the first to reach them, suffered a glancing blow to the cheek. Harry came up behind Blinn's assailant and pinned back his arms. Blinn restrained the other and they wrestled both outside.

"Get your hands off me, Henry Woodyard," said the one in Harry's grasp as soon as they were clear of the door. The smell of rum was heavy on him. Harry let him go. Suddenly finding himself without support, the man pitched face forward. He landed in the road muck, which contained a fresh line of horse droppings.

"There is no cause for roughness," he said, turning onto his side and wiping the filth away from one eye with a forefinger. "Me and Reuben was having a private argument."

"I'm sorry, Abel." Harry reached down and helped him to his feet. The man started back toward the door. Harry blocked his way.

"I can't let you back in until you're sober."

In an effort to get around, Abel slipped and fell into the sludge again.

"Look at yourself," said Harry. "Both of you. You're a disgrace."

Abel mouthed the words back with a sneer. *"Oh, you're a disgrace."*

"Really, how can you ever hope to amount to anything until you straighten yourselves up, stop acting like a couple of rapscallions?"

"Why don't you go bugger yourself," said Reuben. He reached down to help his brother to his feet, nearly getting pulled down himself.

"Now is not a good time to talk about this," Harry said. "But when you're both in a more sober frame of mind, I would like to come around and see you. I can show you some things that would improve your status in New Bern. Some very simple rules of behavior."

"You've changed, Harry," Abel said as he and Reuben turned to walk off, each bracing the other. "You've forgot your old friends. You don't even come into Speight's no more."

"Our boy prefers the company at Cogdell's nowadays," said Reuben.

They proceeded away, Abel laughing at another remark Reuben whispered in his ear. Some recollection, Harry judged, of the days when they and Harry were partners in tomfoolery.

CHAPTER 2

16: Do not Puff up the Cheeks, Loll not out the tongue rub the Hands, or beard, thrust out the lips, or bite them or keep the Lips too open or too Close.

—*RULES OF CIVILITY*

THE HOURS WENT BY QUICKLY AS MCLEOD PRESSED FORWARD THROUGH the docket, settling with a stroke of his oaken gavel matters that had been festering since the last session of the court. A man was ordered to pay recompense for killing a neighbor's hog that had wandered onto his property. A store owner was warned to stop mistreating one of his servants, a woman who had accused him of taking liberties. A fine of twenty pounds of tobacco was levied against a town resident who had failed to attend public worship—his third conviction on such an offense. A runaway servant had six months tacked onto his five-year indenture for his eleven days of freedom. Two sailors were sentenced to four hours each in stocks for public drunkenness. For the crime of slander, a woman was ordered to pay into the county coffers the handsome sum of seventy pounds' proclamation money. She had told some neighbors what she called the real reason the wife of a respected member of the General Assembly had spent two months in Charleston, claiming that while there the lady gave birth to "a Negro bastard." The magistrates did not demand proof of this statement in either direction. A slander was a slander, true or not.

The court also approved a number of administrative recommendations of the town commissioners and the vestry of Christ Church, including placement of the latest crop of orphans and illegitimate children in several different foster homes. The children, two boys and four girls from four to nine years old, huddled together to one side with expressions ranging from confused to desolate as they heard their fates read out. One of the older girls wore a defiant look, as if daring the adults to do their worst.

An odor of turpentine entered Harry's nose as he and Martin were helping Toby pack up her writing tools. Judge McLeod, now free of his robes, clapped him on the back.

"Fine work today, my boy," he said. The man standing beside him nodded in agreement. Craven County High Sheriff Randall Carruthers looked uncomfortably warm in his red hunting jacket, which he had opened halfway down his chest, exposing a dark tangle of hair. His naturally fierce aspect was enhanced today by a bandage covering one eye, the result of recent combat with a disgruntled taxpayer.

Turning to Toby with the faintest notion of a bow, McLeod said, "It is a great pleasure to see you, Mistress Woodyard. And looking so prettily done up. I hope you found our proceedings edifying, if not altogether entertaining."

"I found them fascinating," said Toby. "Although you have your share of slackers and miscreants in North Carolina, I have met enough good people here to know it is one of His Majesty's finest plantations."

McLeod's old eyes, worn from the day's work, became merry. "Mister Woodyard, you have got yourself a real prize here."

"I know," Harry said. He felt a glow inside and at the same time worried that Toby might say something further that would challenge the judge's good opinion.

"I would be glad if you would join the sheriff and me in a glass before you make your way home," McLeod said. He gestured toward one of the tables that tavern employees were noisily hauling back into the room.

"The pleasure would be ours," said Toby while Harry was trying to put together a courtly response. All he could think about at the moment was the overpowering smell of medicine. He was tempted to ask about the judge's bad cold and whether his treatment was helping but decided silence would be the safest course. The *Rules of Civility & Decent Behaviour* were very clear about avoiding frivolous remarks when conversing with a person of quality.

As they were sitting down, McLeod made a signal to two men who had been lingering near the door. Harry had noticed them earlier at court. One looked to be in his middle years, wearing the plain black cassock of an Anglican minister. The other was more remarkable in appearance. He was about ten years older than Harry and a little taller, with a trim physique and military bearing. Smooth, sun-blushed skin and hair the color gold might turn if it could be burned. He nearly glimmered in a well-tailored light blue jacket with buff facings and silver buttons. The man's only visible flaw was a scar that curved up from the corner of his mouth back to midcheek, like an extension of his mouth, forming a fixed smile. A farming accident, possibly. Or a saber cut. He looked like the sort of man who might engage in trials of honor.

"I would like you to meet my houseguests," said McLeod. "Harry, Toby, may I present Reverend Ian Fletcher and Colonel Richard Ayerdale?"

The golden man's last name made an echo in some corner of his mind, but at the moment he could not think why.

McLeod said, "The reverend has come from London on a mission for the Society for the Propagation of the Gospel in Foreign Parts. He is on his way up the seacoast, from Charleston to Boston, to evaluate the state of the church in the provinces."

The minister allowed himself a smile and a stiff bow.

McLeod said, "And Richard is from Williamsburg. He is a colonel of the Virginia militia, in our midst on behalf of the British Army to judge our readiness for the rest of this year's campaign in Canada. I am also proud to announce that he is soon to wed my granddaughter, who has just come back to me from Scotland."

McLeod supplied the part about the granddaughter in an offhanded way, as if an afterthought. When it sank in, it disrupted Harry's thinking so badly that he caught only bits of the rest. That Ayerdale was from a family of Virginia planters dating to the previous century. That one of his great-grandpaps had relocated himself and a hoard of gold, plate, and jewels from England and the civil war that was going on there. That the family's network of plantations between the York and James Rivers was one of the largest individual landholdings in British America. And so on. Finding himself awash in his own past, Harry struggled to pay attention to any of this. He was drowning in recollections of a lost and, he thought he had tricked himself into believing, forgotten love.

Maddie.

He had the impression that everyone at the table, including his wife, was staring at him but only while he was not looking. Even more nightmarish, it seemed they were guessing every thought going through his head exactly at its moment of passage. Especially Toby. Shortly after their first bedding, while Toby was still under bond, he had confessed about Maddie McLeod. At least given the general outline of the story. He had no idea how much more detail she had gathered from gossips. So far, nothing of it had made its way into Toby's diary—not as far as he knew. With time and distance, Harry had more or less forgotten about Maddie. But every so often he had to remind himself not to think about the girl with curly red hair who loved riddles.

He was trying to make this one of those times when he realized that Toby was talking. Looking cool and unfazed, she congratulated Ayerdale on his engagement and asked how he'd met his future bride. It sounded like polite conversation.

"It was last August, while I was in Scotland on some tobacco business," said Ayerdale. "We found ourselves together in Glasgow at a birthnight ball for the king. I was immediately charmed by Maddie's beauty and clever conversation."

Harry noticed that Ayerdale's smile never fully revealed his teeth. A sure sign, he took pleasure in guessing, of dental problems.

"I don't suppose we Scotch are yet allowed to resume our fashion of wearing tartan to the king's celebrations," said McLeod. "I still have my father's plaidie tucked somewhere among my things awaiting the lifting of the proscription. God willing that I live that long."

"Unfortunately, memories of the forty-five are still too fresh. The wearing of plaid is granted only to members of the king's brigades. So, too, the playing of the bagpipe. Those are the legacies of your bonnie prince."

"He ain't my bonnie prince. The man is a lunatic."

Ayerdale said, "There were rumors when I was last in London that he persists in skulking about Europe, trying to raise support for another Jacobite army. For all anyone knows, he might be plotting with the French at this very moment to cross the Channel."

Harry remembered now why he was rarely invited into the company of the judge and his friends. He knew little about the current topic and had nothing to add. But Toby seemed to be following right along. All turned toward her when she laughed.

"I am sorry," she said, "I was just imagining French soldiers sitting down to a haggis alongside tablemates with bagpipes and filibegs."

"The haggis served with a proper sprinkling of peat-bog whisky, I should hope," said McLeod.

"The French are seeing pipes and filibegs aplenty in Canada right now," said Ayerdale. "God willing, it will be the last thing many of them see on this earth. Two regiments of highlanders were with General Wolfe when they entered the Saint Lawrence River four weeks ago. I will be joining them directly. I hope to be there for the final assault on Quebec."

"I trust you are finding our poor province helpful in those efforts," said Sheriff Carruthers.

"North Carolina has done its share. Especially for a plantation so far removed from the immediate threat. Your men contributed much during the second march against Fort Duquesne. Secretary Pitt has requested that his personal thanks be conveyed to Governor Dobbs, and I intend to do so before I leave."

"Thanks be to Mister Pitt and his determination to finally rid this country of the armies of the pope," said the churchman. It was the first complete sentence Harry had heard Fletcher utter. Harry had the fleeting thought that, for a preacher, he was not overly talkative. But his words had an energizing effect on McLeod, who abruptly raised his glass and said, "Long live Pitt."

"And God save the king," said Fletcher, triggering another round.

"We must hurry off," said McLeod, bringing his empty glass down hard on the table. "I am planning a small supper at my house this evening in honor of my granddaughter's return and the forthcoming nuptials." Then, to Toby, "Unfortunately, we have run out of space at our table. Otherwise, we should be pleased to have you and your husband join us." Toby took in this blatant lie with a smile.

★

Cogdell's was filling up with some of New Bern's better people coming for an evening's eating and drinking and visiting. The menu offering was the owner's famous rendition of roast beef. The tavern served beef at least once a week, most often boiled up with potatoes and carrots and turnips and what other vegetables were ready in the garden at the time, all cooked together in the same pot. Roasting required a few extra steps and more judgment as to the amount of heat applied for the best result and generally was reserved for holidays and other special occasions, which included the last day of the Court of Pleas and Quarterly Sessions.

Harry recognized a gaunt face at a nearby table. Since his arrival in New Bern from Philadelphia two months prior, Noah Burke had been teaching reading and arithmetic to Andrew Campbell, the nine-year-old son of Edward and Anne Campbell on their small plantation to the northwest of New Bern. His wages consisted of lodging and meals. This week the family had given him leave to take a temporary paying job. In the absence of any available grandmothers, Burke was supervising children whose parents were involved in court business. Now relieved of his charges, he was free to drink.

After they had eaten, Harry ordered another round of ale. Toby declined, saying she was tired and ready to go home. Harry promised they would start back well before dark. But after his glass arrived he said he wanted to pay a social call on Constable Blinn and his wife, who had just come in. By the time he returned to their table, a half hour had passed and Toby and Martin were gone.

Harry rejoined the Blinns. He was fully drunk when a young man in tradesmen's clothes burst in, holding a wailing infant.

CHAPTER 3

20: The Gestures of the Body must be Suited to the discourse you are upon.

—*Rules of Civility*

"MY NAME IS NICHOLAS," THE MAN SAID AND THEN TRIED TO TELL his whole story in one breath. Horrible murder at a plantation. Bodies placed in strange positions. Considerable blood. Only the infant left alive.

Harry and Blinn brought Nicholas to a seat and Blinn's wife scooped up the baby. They quickly determined the victims were Noah Burke's employers. Shock upon shock. Although far from the richest family in Craven County, the Campbells were among the best liked.

Trying not to slur his words, Harry summoned Burke. "Do you understand? The family you've been working for has been killed."

The schoolmaster straightened up. Pursing his eyebrows, he said with careful enunciation, "Please, call me Noah."

"When were you last at their house?"

"I left the farm on Sunday. Everything was fine then."

The tinker, trembling and face dripping sweat, met Harry's questioning look. "I got no idea how long them bodies been there. I never seen murdered people before."

Harry started for the door. Blinn caught his arm. "Where are you going?" he said.

"Home. I need to make sure my wife is safe." He turned again to go, but Blinn held him fast.

"You are the county constable," Blinn said. "You need to ride out to the Campbell place, see what you can before the sun goes down. I'll go along, but you have to go."

"Toby comes first," Harry said, giving Blinn a severe look.

"I can ride out, check on Toby," said a man at the next table. Bledsoe was a member of the town watch and a childhood acquaintance of Harry's. Tough and reliable. "I can start out now," he said, "make sure she's all right. You go ahead and do your duty."

"We should notify the sheriff first," said Blinn. "And the judge."

"Why?" said Harry. "It'll be dark soon. If we're going out there, we need to hurry."

He tried to clear his head while he spoke. This was easily the most severe crime that had happened since he had taken up his commission. Since he could remember, in fact. He saw the value to his reputation of handling it correctly. And a little part of him welcomed the excuse to drop in on McLeod's supper.

Three other members of the watch volunteered to go along. Blinn's wife said she would look after the baby. Within minutes they, along with Noah Burke, were in their saddles and fast trotting toward the high ground near the waterfront on which McLeod's house stood.

The late afternoon light was turning golden by the time they arrived. Harry heard music inside. From previous visits he recognized the throaty drone of McLeod's viola da gamba, which the old man practiced every day. Now he was playing counternotes to a high, silvery voice singing an intricate tune. A voice Harry had not heard in a decade.

"There's been a killing," Harry said to the man wearing the family's arms on a gold neck chain who answered the door. "I need to speak with the sheriff."

"They're almost finished." The man made a hushing sound as he let them into the hallway. "Please wait here."

Harry was ready to push him aside, but Blinn grasped his arm and whispered, "Those bodies will wait another minute or two. We don't want to upset the judge."

From where he was standing, Harry could see into the parlor. Candlelight made it look even more sumptuous than he remembered. Rugs from Persia. Darkly gleaming furniture. Splashes of silver, including an ornate tea service. He recognized among the guests several large-scale planters, including two members of the Governor's Council and three legislators. The county clerk, solicitor, and surveyor. All with their ladies. One of the town's richest storekeepers, a man by the name of du Plessis, was fussing with a snuffbox, seemingly little interested in the performance. Harry also spotted Reverend Reed, the Christ Church rector who had conducted his and Toby's wedding, and beside him the visiting English minister, Fletcher. Sitting in a corner chair, looking at Maddie with an expression that made Harry think of a cat that had found an unguarded dish of cream, was Richard Ayerdale.

Maddie stood facing the company in a gown of green silk with a low bodice that displayed the pillowy contours of a now fully mature woman. Her red hair was somewhat darker than Harry recalled and done up in the French manner, high and curly. Skin as he remembered it, near as pale as Christmas eggnog, and gem-like green eyes. Her slightly breathy soprano weaved through the viola notes like silver thread in an old tapestry. Harry began to feel light-headed. The rest of the world seemed to be melting away, leaving only himself and this vision.

Applause broke his trance. Brushing past the servant, he stepped into the parlor, eyes fixed on Maddie. She gave no sign of recognition. He guessed his appearance had changed as well. He directed himself to Sheriff Carruthers, who was in the front row looking amazingly transformed from his earlier appearance in court, having traded his hunting shirt for a dark purple evening suit with white ruffling at the throat and wrists.

"I regret interrupting your evening. There is a matter that I must discuss with you."

"I hope there is a good reason for this," said the sheriff.

"The Campbell family has been attacked and killed. Only the baby survived. I and some others are on our way there, but we thought it best to stop here first."

Though he was keeping his voice low, the room had become so quiet that all could hear every word. There were sharp intakes of breath.

The judge gave permission to use his kitchen for a private conversation. On their way out Harry caught a last glimpse of Maddie, who he was sure now recognized him. Her expression was too complicated to read.

McLeod, along with Ayerdale and Reverend Fletcher, joined them at the long table and Harry summed up what he knew. "The tinner thinks it may have been Indians. But there is the question of why they would have left the baby. Also, we haven't had Indian trouble in Craven County in my lifetime."

"Were there no slaves about?" asked Ayerdale.

"The Campbells had no slaves, only two bonded servants. They died of fevers within days of each other some weeks ago. Edward had contracted to get replacements, but as far as I know they are still on the ocean."

Ayerdale said, "If this is Indian trouble, Williamsburg should be apprised. I would like to go with you."

The visiting minister also decided to come along. Curious to see how murder is dealt with in the provinces, Harry supposed.

So, actually, was Harry.

★

The sun had dipped to the tree line and clouds were drifting in by the time they reached the property. The effects of the beer were gone. Or so it felt. Noah Burke also looked more clear-eyed. The Campbell boy's body was limp under the sheriff's prodding, but Carruthers felt unqualified to judge with any certainty what that said about when the boy had died. The town's coroner and only physician had recently moved away and not yet been replaced. Maybe the stiffening had not yet set in, or maybe it had come and gone, as the bad smell coming off the body suggested.

Carruthers lit a lantern they found hanging beside the door and they entered the now-darkened house. The bodies of Edward and Anne Campbell were still in the strange positions the tinker had described. The smell of rot was nearly suffocating.

"What's on this man's cheek?" McLeod asked. Carruthers brought the lantern closer and all leaned in for a look. And then jumped back.

Worms.

Kneeling for a closer view, Noah nodded his head in recognition. *"Calliphoridae,"* he said. "They appear by their size to be in the second instar. Depending on a number of variables, like the exact species of fly and recent air temperatures, I would say the man died approximately two days ago."

Everyone looked at the tutor.

"This family of insects was one of the first my father required me to study as a boy. They are born, eat, have babies, and die, just like the rest of us. Nothing to fear."

"I know that," Carruthers said. "It just took me by surprise, is all."

"It doesn't look like anything of value was taken," said Noah, casting his eyes about. "Their dearest possession was that set of English dishware in the cupboard. It seems intact."

Carruthers gestured toward a rifle with a striped maple stock cradled on hooks over the fireplace. "That must be worth a smart penny. Whoever robbed these good people of their lives was not out to steal earthly treasures from them."

"Edward was a strong man," said Harry, "but the attack must have been so quick that he had no a chance to defend himself."

"The positioning of the bodies is demonic," said Carruthers. "I am inclined to agree with the tinker: it was savages."

"Barbaric," said Reverend Fletcher, who was holding a handkerchief to his nose.

"Without a doubt, the guilty have long since fled," said McLeod. "As much as I dislike saying this, I see no point in forming a search party."

"This news will not be well received in New Bern," said Carruthers. "It's a nightmare come to life."

With McLeod's approval, Carruthers ordered Harry, Blinn, and the watch members to stay behind and get the bodies into the ground. Reverend Reed could organize a memorial service later. With that, the sheriff and the others rode off.

Harry began going through the dead man's pockets.

"What are you doing?" said Blinn. "Leave that poor man alone."

"Just wondering if there might be something here to help us figure this out." He was making a small pile on the floor. A few coins, a painted tin soldier with its head missing, and a wrinkled ten-shilling note. Nothing more.

Blinn and the watchmen said they were going outside, away from the smell, to smoke a pipe. Then they would look for something to dig with. Harry felt reluctant to leave just yet. He sat down at the table, where only a week earlier he had been served a dinner of boiled pork, corn, greens and tomatoes with vinegar, and some of Anne Campbell's cornbread pudding.

In the mellow light his eye caught a glint of something metallic underneath the baby's crib. He carried the lantern over, got down on all fours, and pulled forth a piece of jewelry and a folded piece of paper it had been lying on. The former was a gold medal about twice the size of a Spanish dollar, inlaid with tiny blue stones.

He returned to the table to have a better look. The medal had a clasp soldered onto its back. On the front side was a miniature silver builder's square surmounted by an even tinier compass with the letter G engraved in the middle. Harry recognized it as the symbol of the Freemasons. The judge had spoken of proposing Harry for membership in the Masons' New Bern lodge, though that was something far in the future. First Harry needed to show that he was fully worthy of acceptance onto the highest rungs of New Bern society, and that would take time.

Looking again on the back of the medal, Harry saw just below the clasp the etched figure of a pine tree and beneath that a line of angular markings that reminded him of Indian writing he had seen on some of the cave walls in the hill country to the west.

"In the three months I've worked here, I've not seen this medallion," said Noah. "I didn't know Edward Campbell was a Freemason."

"He wasn't," said Harry, "though he wanted to be. What do you make of the writing?" Thinking a well-educated man from a place like Philadelphia might know what it meant.

"Some form of code, obviously. There are quite a few Masons in Pennsylvania. My father has been invited to join, but he doesn't care for secret societies. Riddles don't appeal to him."

The picture of a nine-year-old girl flashed through Harry's mind. They were sitting by a creek playing at one of Maddie's favorite games, Maddie posing a riddle and Harry trying to solve it.

"Let's say you're right about this happening two days ago," said Harry, banishing memories. "That would be around the time of the storm."

"More or less."

"Let's suppose that in the midst of the storm there was a knock at the door. Edward opened it, and there was a traveler. Wet and cold in the wind. They offered him shelter, maybe a meal. That's an old North Carolina tradition, you know."

"We do the same in Pennsylvania. You southerners aren't the only hospitable ones."

"So they are getting to know each other, and for some reason there is a falling-out. Which leads to a struggle. It comes on fast. Edward doesn't have time to get a weapon in his hand. In the commotion, this badge is torn from the traveler's clothes. Maybe Edward pulls it off. It skitters across the floor and lands underneath the crib. The traveler doesn't notice. By the time he discovers it missing, he has left the house. It's too late to come back and get it. Or maybe he just doesn't have any idea where he lost it."

"That's a lot of speculation without much known fact to go on," said Noah, leaning back in his chair.

"It's something I learned from a Tuscarora Indian. A way of looking into the past. You consider a set of conditions, just use common sense and a little imagination, and see if they start to tell you a story. Do this long enough, and you can put yourself into a kind of dream, see things happening. You'd be surprised how close you can sometimes come to what really took place."

"And the positions of the corpses?"

"The killer wants to mislead us, make it look like an Indian attack. He stays long enough to arrange the bodies. When the storm is over, he places little Andrew's body outside. Or maybe shoots him as he is trying to run away, then goes out and fixes him where he fell."

"To make it look like Indians." Noah looked skeptical.

"Yes, but to imitate Indians, the killer would have had to do away with the baby. For some reason he refuses to go that far. Maybe he feels sorry for it."

"Which suggests a degree of compassion. Unwillingness to murder an innocent."

"This was not the work of either an Indian warrior or a low-class criminal. Maybe it was done to keep a secret. Something that Edward or Anne discovered about the traveler that they were not meant to know."

"And this piece of paper?"

It was about the size of a page from a small ledger book with a pencil-drawn diagram and tiny single- and double-digit numbers here and there.

"This seems to be a nautical chart of Pamlico Sound," said Harry, bringing it closer to the lantern. "That would be Ocracoke Inlet on the right, next to the ocean, and New Bern on the left, where the Trent River comes into the Neuse. The numbers must be water depths."

"Indicating navigable channels?" said Noah.

"Looks like it. Ocracoke is the only link between most of North Carolina and the Atlantic Ocean, so this would be of interest to anyone trying to get a big ship in here."

"Of course there is a deepwater port farther south at Wilmington, but that doesn't help you up here as far as access to offshore shipping lanes."

Harry threw him a questioning look. "You seem to know a lot about the layout of North Carolina."

Noah gave a short laugh. "Don't start getting suspicious. I made a study of several colonies before choosing to come here to teach. You have a serious geographical disadvantage. The chain of sand islands along your coast form a barrier to the transatlantic trade routes that have enabled Virginia and South Carolina to thrive. You are limited to shallow-draft schooners. They are fine for coasting all the way to New England but not for crossing oceans."

By unspoken consent, they got up as they talked and walked outside, where the air was fresher.

"Well, people do complain that they'll never get as rich here as they'd hoped. Some say they were drawn in by false promises. But if you knew we had such poor prospects, why did you choose to come anyway?"

"Wealth isn't my goal. My family has a great deal of money. I searched out a place I thought could benefit from my skills as a teacher. My parents disagree with my choices. My father wanted me to follow in his footsteps."

"And where would they have led?"

"He is a student of the natural world, a collector of plants, animals, and insects. Rather famous in New England, as a matter of fact. A founding member of the American Philosophical Society. He's been proposed for election to the Royal Society."

Harry guessed that was a good thing. He now had a closer look at Noah Burke. Previously he had spoken with the young man only on occasional chance meetings in town. He was about the same age and height as Harry but thinner, with reedy fingers, hollowed-out cheeks, and eyes that looked somewhat lost in their sockets.

"What would Edward Campbell have been doing with a chart of Pamlico Sound?" said Noah.

"I'm thinking on that. Maybe it wasn't his. Maybe it was the traveler's."

"In any event, I am favorably impressed, Mister Woodyard. I've never known a constable personally, but from what I've seen in Philadelphia, if a wrongdoer isn't caught immediately after the crime, the chances of his ever being found out fall dramatically. The constabulary could use more puzzle solvers like yourself."

Blinn and the others carried out the corpses. They began digging in a fallow field a safe distance off, far enough away that harmful parts of decomposing bodies would not enter the underground water that fed the well. This would be the first cemetery on the property, Harry reflected.

Under lantern light, Harry and Noah took their turns scooping out clumps of gritty clay with a pair of iron shovels Blinn found. The night air was heavy with moisture, the moon having taken on a ghostly mien behind a veil of clouds. In the thin shadow of an oak tree a wild turkey stood watching, solemn as a sentinel.

"I wonder what will happen to the baby," Noah said, laying his shovel aside and sitting down for a rest. Blinn was balanced on a pile of earth, wiping his forehead with a handkerchief.

"The vestry will take charge, put it in a foster home, just like how little Andy wound up here," Blinn said. The story was well known, how the Campbells had taken on the child as an act of charity after his natural parents died in a fire soon after his birth. "What I'd like to know is what is to become of this plantation. I've heard the Campbells were deep in debt to du Plessis for advances on crops. I'm thinking he might be awarded the property."

Harry recalled the storekeeper's conduct at the judge's house. He was a large man with a firm build. A Freemason in good standing. He had seemed as surprised as anyone by the news of the murders. But Harry wondered where he had been two nights earlier.

As he lifted another shovelful, already setting plans for the next day, thunder sounded in the southwest. Fifteen minutes later they were spattered by fat raindrops. Blinn dropped his shovel, face contorted with what looked like fear.

"It's only water," said Harry.

"Everybody knows that if it rains on a dead body, it means the person is not at peace."

Blinn grabbed Edward Campbell under his dead arms and began dragging him back toward the house. But it was too far. He dropped the body underneath an elm, the best shelter available, and went back for the other two. Harry and Noah joined in the task.

After the heaviest part of the shower passed, they went back to digging in the clay, which was now turning to sludge. The rain looked like it was settling in for a good soak.

CHAPTER 4

15: Keep your Nails clean and Short, also your Hands and
Teeth Clean yet without Shewing any great Concern for them.
—*RULES OF CIVILITY*

A CANDLE IN THE WINDOW LET HARRY KNOW TOBY WAS STILL UP.
She brought out cloths for Harry and Noah to dry off with and
put some leftover biscuits and gravy on the table. While they were
eating she told them Bledsoe had come over to check on her but she
had sent him home, feeling wholly safe with Martin and the others
about. Harry told her about their night. He handed her the Masonic
medal for a look. Martin, who had come over from his cabin, gave it
a close going-over and pronounced it a fine piece of jewelry.

"Martin will stay close by the house tomorrow," Harry said. "Field work for the others like usual. I think whoever did this has left the county, but I want you to stay inside."

They talked about what the schoolmaster would do now that his job was at an end. Toby said it would be fine if Noah wanted stay in the barn until he got resituated. Noah said he already had been told by three different people that if he ever tired of educating young Campbell, a job everyone knew was a trial due to the fact that the boy had a quarrelsome nature, he should come and see them.

"But the truth is, I'd already decided what to do when my time with Andrew was finished. I intend to set up a school that eventually will be free for anyone who wishes their child to attend. We'll start with the orphans."

★

Later, as they lay in bed, Harry looked for words to smooth over his conduct at Cogdell's. Going off drinking with friends when he should have been thinking about how Toby might be feeling. It was something he may not have given a second thought in his previous life, before Judge McLeod exposed him to the manners practiced by the better sorts of people. Now he could see that he still had not fully caught on to what the judge had tried to get across.

She interrupted his first words by touching his lips with a finger. They had left off their nightclothes due to the day's buildup of warmth. Toby began lightly rubbing ovals on the top of one of Harry's thighs. "I have already forgotten about that," she said. "Anyway, I made my journal a promise about tonight."

Harry wondered if he would ever get over feeling that every time they made love was the first. New, exciting, and slightly disreputable. It had first happened barely two weeks after Toby first arrived in New Bern. On that day Harry had gone to the dock to collect what he thought would be a man to assist Martin in cooking and other household chores, in accordance with the contract he had signed. He was surprised to find it was a woman with a man's name. Piecing it together later, he recalled Talitha had handled the entire matter: the search, the negotiation, all but the actual signing. It was she who had convinced him in the first place that Martin needed a helper. Talitha claimed innocence. However, Harry recollected that in recent months his mother had been hinting that it was time for him to pick out a wife. For years, Harry had been satisfied—happy in fact—with random moments of bliss in bed with some townsman's daughter. Even knowing that sooner or later such a coupling was likely to have consequences. Talitha acted like she was unaware of any such larking about, but lately she had taken to mentioning how few women there were in Craven County who were both unwed and suitable as potential life partners for her son: not too far above the family's station as to be out of the question and certainly not anywhere below it. She easily could have caught word of a well-educated young woman in Wales who was looking for a position in the colonies. She might have read such an advertisement in the *North Carolina Gazette*. The misleading name could have been a bonus, serving to not get Harry's suspicions up that Talitha had on her mind something more than just hiring another servant.

When Toby got off the ship, she was brought to du Plessis's house to await Harry and the signing of the receipt. Du Plessis often made his place available for such transactions. She was wearing a sunflower-colored cotton gown that intensified the effect of her dark hair. Harry at first thought this banquet for the eyes was an out-of-town visitor or maybe a hitherto unknown niece or ward of du Plessis's. As the truth revealed itself, he felt a rush of embarrassment, sure that everyone in the room was thinking about the same possibilities he was.

During the early going they kept talking to a minimum, just what was needed to get along. He turned her over to Martin for learning what was expected of her. The original plan had been for the new servant to move into Martin's cabin. But Harry decided to build her a bed in the storage loft of his house. They took their baths separately in the metal tub in the kitchen, where Harry cobbled up a privacy curtain.

After the first week he began feeling more comfortable with the arrangement and now and then would try to make light conversation. Toby seemed to have her own sense of what was proper, which resulted in short banters. Under gentle but persistent questioning, she told him of her parents' intention to make the best of her desire for a new life, their hope that she would find a husband. But her own aim was to stay independent. At the end of the five years she would take the generous freedom dues she had negotiated: fifty acres of plantable land, some farming tools, a cow and a mule and a few chickens, a new set of clothes, and thirty pounds of proclamation money. She intended to put these resources to work to make a life all on her own.

At first Harry was satisfied with her seeming lack of interest in him. But he grew increasingly curious. No amount of polite talk could entirely ease the tension he felt when she was near. And she was often near. Twilight suppers alone together, usually consisting of leftovers from dinner, were especially hard to get through. But he looked forward to them nevertheless.

One day Harry came into the house unexpectedly just as Toby had stepped out of the tub. She had pulled the curtain back. They both froze, Harry thinking he had never seen anything so terrifyingly beautiful. His first thought was to leave. But he found he could not turn his eyes away. Toby remained where she was. She could have stepped back, drawn the curtain, waited for him to excuse himself. Instead, she padded soundlessly over, eyes locked on his. He ran his hands over her shoulders lightly, seized with the ridiculous thought that if he used any pressure at all, she might fracture. She did not resist. A moment later they were wrestling standing up.

A week later Harry told Talitha he had decided to get married. Annoyingly, she did not seem surprised.

★

Afterward, as he lay next to Toby in a pleasing haze, he turned toward her silhouette against the open window. Her eyes were open, head tilted slightly toward Harry so each set of eyelashes was visible against the night sky. She seemed to be looking at something in the space between herself and the ceiling.

"What's wrong?" he asked.

She blinked, seeming to return to the room. "I was just thinking about how I really like it here. My life with you. In North Carolina."

"Then why the unhappy look?"

"It's nothing. Just the Welsh temperament."

"Tell me."

"There is an old belief that for every moment of happiness there must be a settling-up. For every summer there is a winter. For every birth, someone dies. For every pleasure, a pain."

"That sounds like a sad accounting," Harry said.

"We can be a sad people."

Toby said a word that sounded like *heer-eth*, as nearly as Harry could make it out.

"It's from our language. It means a longing to return home, go back from wherever you are to Wales. People who've traveled to far places for long periods come back speaking of it."

"We would say you were homesick."

"It's something larger than that. It's a sense of who you are, how your bloodlines have run through the Welsh countryside from generations without number. You don't know what it is until you leave. One of my brothers felt it when he moved to London. He called it a sense of longing, like there was a string attaching him to Swansea. Now I know what he meant."

"You're not thinking of going back, are you?" Harry said in a quiet voice, fearing the answer. "I mean, other than for a visit?" As the words came out, he realized how unsettling the thought was.

She rolled onto her stomach and with a burrowing motion made a place for herself inside Harry's arm.

"No. I told you, I'm happy here."

CHAPTER 5

91: Make no Shew of taking great Delight in your Victuals, Feed not with Greediness; cut your Bread with
a Knife, lean not on the Table neither find fault with
what you Eat.

—*RULES OF CIVILITY*

WAITING IN MCLEOD'S ENTRANCE HALL TO BE ANNOUNCED, HARRY
dreaded the prospect of seeing Maddie again. What had been a vaguely
agreeable state of anticipation had given way to feelings of guilt. As if
just putting eyes on her again would be an act of disloyalty to Toby.
But Maddie was not at the breakfast table. McLeod said she was still
getting over the previous day's turmoil. As uneasy as Harry had been

about the prospect of their reunion, he now found himself disappointed in equal measure.

Taking breakfast with the judge were several others from the night before: Ayerdale, Reverends Reed and Fletcher, Carruthers, and du Plessis. To Harry's surprise, Constable Blinn also had been invited. He was sitting between the sheriff and McLeod toward the head of the table. Harry felt a prick of jealousy that Blinn had been placed in a seat of such honor.

"Won't you join us?" McLeod said. His cold seemed to have gotten better. He waved off a servant so he could serve his new guests himself. The soul of hospitality.

"We were just discussing the events of last night," he said, ladling porridge and bacon onto Harry's plate. "Randall here says word is spreading quickly. People are fearful that a killer is on the loose."

"Understandably," the sheriff confirmed. "The commissioners have called for a meeting at the church tonight. Everyone wants to hear what we're doing about this."

"What they want is for us to catch the killer," said Blinn, who was sipping on a small beer.

McLeod said, "I've sent a rider to Wilmington to advise the governor of the situation. I know he will want to stay informed."

Reed announced he had arranged for a memorial service the next day. "With God's guidance, I will find healing words."

"The more I think on it," Carruthers said, "the more I believe it was Indians. No white man would have posed them bodies like that."

"There is the matter of the baby being left alive," said McLeod.

"Times change, Olaf," said Carruthers. "Maybe they wasn't looking to add an infant to their tribe just now. Or maybe they was helping themselves to the Campbells' liquor supply and got too drunk to care. I think that little child just had luck on its side."

"I suppose prospects of catching the guilty party are poor?" This from Reverend Fletcher.

Carruthers said, "You just say the word, Judge, and I'm only too happy to be on the trail with my deputies. I'm sure the militia would be good for some men to come along with us."

Knowing glances crossed the table. Everyone was aware of Carruthers's hatred for Indians. His grandfather as a young man had been captured by a raiding party of Tuscarora. A survivor was forced to watch the gruesome execution, a process that had involved fire and had taken place in stages over several days. All knew, too, that Carruthers was up for reappointment to his post in January and recently had been going out of his way to demonstrate devotion to his duties.

"Believe me," said McLeod, "I'd be all for you setting out if I thought there was any chance of catching up with 'em. But they could be all the way into the mountains by now. Or who knows where, blended in with the other savages. To have any chance of success, we'd need an army."

"It might not have been Indians," said Harry. Heads swung in his direction. "I found something interesting at the house last night after you gentlemen left."

He passed around the chart of Pamlico Sound and watched closely when it came to du Plessis. The merchant barely looked at it, saying only that such a document obviously would be of interest to someone in the maritime business.

Blinn put in, "Could it be Edward was looking for a channel big enough for a ship hired by his own self? Small as my farm is, if I could find a way to get my tobacco straight to London, why . . ." He paused, seeming to search for a witty way to sum it up. He settled on "I could be as rich as a Virginian" and aimed a grin at Ayerdale.

McLeod shook his head. "I knew Edward Campbell pretty well, and as fine a man as he was, such a grand scheme would never enter his head. Edward was a farmer, not a businessman."

"I agree," said Harry. Turning to du Plessis he said, "Can you think of any reason this chart would have been in the Campbells' home?"

"And why would I know such a thing?" the storekeeper answered with a polite smile.

"I understand the Campbells have made considerable purchases from you. Much of it on credit."

At this, the naturally ruddy color of McLeod's face noticeably deepened. "How dare you, young man?" he said. "What the devil are you implying?"

Lost in his quest for information, Harry suddenly realized how unfriendly the question sounded. "Nothing at all against Mister du Plessis," he said, thinking fast. "I just thought he might know something of the Campbells' affairs that could shed some light on the matter."

The storekeeper waved off McLeod with a placating gesture. "I take no offense. But allow me to speak frankly, and go ahead to the place where this line of reasoning could conceivably lead. It is true the Campbells were in debt to my trading house. But so is a good portion of Craven County." He paused to look around the table. With the exception of Ayerdale and the minister Fletcher, no one met his eyes. The judge himself found it convenient to fiddle with his napkin. Harry felt suddenly awkward, as he was on du Plessis's list of debtors as well. "If I were to go around killing off everyone who owed me money," he concluded, "I should have but very few customers left."

Laughter broke the tension.

Harry produced the Masonic badge and passed it around. Holding the object daintily between a thumb tip and index finger, McLeod said, "I invoke the du Plessis precedent. If we are to hold suspect every Freemason in the province, we would quickly run out of jail space."

More laughter from the guests. The exception was Carruthers, who, as everyone knew was not easily given to mirth. He said, "As one privileged to have taken the vows myself, I can tell you that no Freemason would have been capable of such a horror."

"I can think of an explanation for the badge," said du Plessis. "In my dealings with Edward, he expressed many times his admiration for our lodge. I think he wanted me to nominate him for membership when the time was right. So, might he not have bought such a lovely ornament from a traveling peddler in hopeful anticipation?"

"The most likely explanation is Indians," the sheriff said on a chuffing breath.

"I can tell you this," said Ayerdale, who had been following the discussion with a look of detached interest. "The Cherokee and Sioux filtering back from Canada are unhappy people. Before I left Williamsburg, I heard numerous reports of thievery and arson in the Virginia foothills. So I would not rule out the possibility that some young hotheads with murderous intent might have strayed into Craven County."

"Why are they so angry?" asked Reverend Reed. "I thought they went voluntarily to help fight the French and their savages."

Carruthers said, "Who knows what will set off these brutes?"

"My information is sketchy," said Ayerdale, "but I gather they found life difficult under British military discipline. General Amherst has little use for men who will not obey his every command on the instant it is given. Unquestioning obedience is something simply not to be found in the Indian character."

"So they just pulled down their lodgings and stole away?" McLeod shook his head in disgust.

"Yes. And I've heard they took along all the long rifles, ammunition, blankets, and trade axes the army had given them."

"But how should any of that engender hostility against the likes of us in North Carolina?" Reverend Reed wondered.

"If I may," said Reverend Fletcher, "I imagine finding British settlers moving onto one's properties and building houses on them would upset anyone." He said something else, but it was in a foreign tongue. Some smart Latin saying, Harry guessed.

"With all respect, Reverend," said Ayerdale, "such is the tide of history. Once we rid our continent of the French horde, the savages will be the only thing standing in the way of our flag's march westward. The Indians were slitting one another's throats over territory long before we arrived, so this won't be anything new to their experience."

"I am not necessarily defending them," said Fletcher, his tone more one of irritation than apology. "Merely offering a possible explanation for their behavior."

To Harry's dismay, the conversation began to shift away from what had happened to the Campbell family. As if finished with the subject of murder, they spoke of things Harry knew of only vaguely: the early string of British defeats, some incomprehensible, including the massacre of redcoats and Virginia militia at the Monongahela four years earlier. They talked admiringly of Pitt's subsequent rise at Whitehall, and, at his behest, the flooding of America with soldiers, along with hundreds of thousands of pounds sterling for their feeding and housing on American soil, and to pay for recruitment of additional native militia. As Harry picked at his now-cold oatmeal, the group traded opinions about the three-pronged assault then under way against Canada, with General Amherst coming up Lake Champlain, General Prideaux by way of Fort Niagara, and General Wolfe moving his army onto the Saint Lawrence River to directly attack Quebec.

"I myself will be leaving tomorrow by schooner to get my things in order at home," said Ayerdale, "and then on to Louisbourg, and thence up the Saint Lawrence to catch up with Wolfe. I am pleased to report that my fiancée has agreed to accompany me as far as Williamsburg. It seems Maddie has never seen our Virginia capital."

Harry's interest quickened. As far as he knew, no wedding date had been set. Knowing McLeod's devotion to good form, he wondered if the judge approved of this arrangement, the betrothed couple traveling together in such close quarters as would be available aboard a schooner. But Harry guessed that if Maddie wanted to go, McLeod would be hard-pressed to say otherwise.

As the conversation continued on military and political matters, Harry's thoughts wandered to his feelings about Ayerdale. They were muddled. Ayerdale was a person of substance in one of the most important provinces in the British Atlantic. Possibly he was destined for greatness. Harry envied the man's winsome looks, a gift of the gods of ancestry, the scar on the side of his jaw only calling attention to the perfection of the rest of his face. Harry wondered if he would ever find out the story behind the wound. The unavoidable fact, he had to concede, was that the prince of Virginia made a far more suitable husband for Maddie than the constable from North Carolina.

The discussion shifted to the condition of world tobacco markets and the European economy in general, subjects directly pertinent to Harry's livelihood. Ayerdale let slip a remark about the Scotch being the "Jews of Britain." Remembering the origins of his host and future grandfather-in-law, he quickly added, "Of course, some of my very dearest friends, including the late governor of Virginia, are Scotchmen."

Harry's innards warmed at Ayerdale's awkward attempt to smooth over his blunder. He imagined how Ayerdale's handsomely thin lips, which gave such pleasing shape to his words, could excuse so much.

CHAPTER 6

53: Run not in the Streets, neither go too slowly nor with
Mouth open go not Shaking yr Arms kick not the earth
with yr feet, go not upon the Toes, nor in a Dancing
fashion.

—*RULES OF CIVILITY*

HARRY WAS MAKING UP AN EXCUSE TO TAKE LEAVE FROM THE TABLE
when McLeod brought the breakfast to an abrupt end, announcing he
had to check on some late summer planting at one of his enterprises.
Blinn followed Harry and Noah out the door.

"They should of just killed them all back in '11," Blinn said as they
mounted their horses.

"I wonder if it could have anything to do with the Indian old Scroggins was talking about," said Noah.

"What?" said Harry.

"Last night at the tavern, Scroggins was going on about some Indian he'd seen lurking in the woods around his place. He was talking so loud, I thought everybody heard."

Scroggins was a small-scale planter of unknown age who lived by himself not far from the Campbell place. Harry turned and looked at Noah. "After all our discussion about Indians, you just remembered this?"

"The way Carruthers was going on at the table, I was afraid he'd go right out, find the poor man, and hang him on the spot."

"What exactly did Scroggins say?"

"Just that he'd caught peeks of a half-naked red-skinned person prowling about. From the way he was talking it might have been his imagination. He'd caught only glimpses. It was almost like he was describing a ghost. But some of his chickens have gone missing. He's got his pique up about that."

"He's never said anything to me about Indians," said Harry.

"Well," said Noah, "maybe that's because he didn't think anything would come of it. Since I've been living here I've had the impression people don't take old Scroggins all that seriously."

"Your territory again, Woodyard," said Blinn. "But I'll go along. Been a long time since I seen a live Indian."

Noah said, "I've never seen one at all."

★

On their way out of town, they passed the lot recently vacated by the acting company. The militia was drilling there, marching up and down and making turns and flanking movements to the tempo set by New Bern's fife-and-drum corps. Six boys and men were playing a recently learned tune, "The Roast Beef of Old England," reminding

Harry of the excellent food he had eaten at Cogdell's the previous evening. The song was a sentimental favorite of Governor Dobbs, who only a few weeks past had left his rented home in New Bern and moved to Wilmington. Tired, he had let it be known, of New Bern's weather and general climate, which he said was hurting his health, and also weary of the disrespectful way he felt he was being treated. The more responsible citizens of New Bern, including McLeod, had since started a campaign to get him back, fearing a downturn in their personal fortunes if the capital of the colony permanently relocated. Flattering Dobbs with a piece of music was one small part of a larger strategy to regain his favor. The militia just hoped they would get a chance to play it for him.

Harry saluted his friends, but they were busy with a right-flank turnabout, wheeling their triple marching column to form a line of skirmishers. The movement was not precise. In fact, it was painfully ragged. But everyone wound up in the correct position at the end, some by running the last few steps.

"I'm excused from militia duty as long as I'm serving as constable," Harry told Noah as they continued, the music receding in the distance.

"This constable business seems a great deal of work for a job that doesn't pay anything. Not that tutoring pays much better."

Something about Noah's friendly manner made Harry feel at ease speaking openly. "I don't have to pay taxes during my term of service, either. But there's more." He lowered his voice enough so the town constable, riding ahead, could not overhear. "I think John just likes the bit of power that goes along with the office. Carrying out orders of the court, assisting justices, escorting prisoners, serving writs, rounding up drunkards, that sort of thing. Ordering people around appeals to him. I don't care about any of that. For me, serving a few years as a constable is a way to get the attention of the kind of people we just had breakfast with. They were born into their world of comfort and privilege. I need to make my own way into it."

"I can see that is important to you."

"Judge McLeod says the next step, after a period of honorable service doing this, would be a church wardenship. Then, in due course, other offices and eventually entry into the Freemasons. All the best men in the Pamlico belong. But that step lies far in the future. For one thing, the initiation fee is more than I took in from my whole plantation last year. To get to the top around here, you need to be rich. But I have every intention of getting rich."

"I had no idea I was in the company of one with such ambitions."

"It's not just for me. My mother has worked all her life to see her family at the top of this little patch of Britain. God willing, one day she will."

He added silently to himself: *And one day, maybe a child of mine will be worthy of marrying a grandchild of a chief justice.*

★

As they rode along, Harry could not free his mind of the jaunty tune the militia had been practicing. Pastor Reed had gone so far as to add it to their regular Sunday worship service along with the regular hymns, so the congregation would be ready to perform in case Governor Dobbs were to drop in.

> *When mighty roast beef was the Englishman's food,*
> *It ennobled our brains and enriched our blood.*
> *Our soldiers were brave and our courtiers were good*
> *O, the roast beef of old England,*
> *And O, the old English roast beef!*

There were more stanzas, but Harry had yet to learn them all. Something about how stout old English traditions in the current day were being brushed aside for the macaroni fashions of Britain's old enemy, "effeminate France."

To eat their ragouts as well as to dance,
We're fed up with nothing but vain complaisance.

The tune was circling through his head when they found Scroggins, whom no one would accuse of macaroni. He was sitting underneath a tree behind his house whittling with no apparent purpose on a piece of wood. His deeply creased face a picture of concentration. His ability to hear their approach possibly diminished by tufts of hair growing out of his ears. As far as Harry could tell, he had not changed his clothes since the last time he had seen Scroggins. He stank of hogs.

"We hear you've seen an Indian," said Harry, getting right to the point.

Surprised by the sudden company, and their interest finally in his complaint, Scroggins's small eyes narrowed in what looked like suspicion.

"And what care you gentlemen for what I've been seeing?"

"Guess you haven't heard," said Blinn. "Edward and Anne Campbell and their son, Andrew, have been murdered. People are saying it might be some stray Cherokee who done it."

"I knew that red beast was up to some evil purpose. I would have shot him the first time I saw him up by Trace Creek, but I couldn't get to my rifle quick enough."

"Mister Scroggins, you can't just go around shooting people," said Noah. "This Indian you saw might be perfectly innocent of any crime."

"Well, somebody has been stealing me innocent chickens. I just found another one gone. Next time I have a chance, I'm going to put some lead in that boy's belly. See how he likes that."

"I'd hate to see you put in irons for murder," said Harry, taking a step back to get some cleaner air. "We'll have a look around. Maybe we can save you some trouble."

Following Scroggins's directions, they came to Trace Creek, then set out upstream along its northwesterly run, roughly in the direction of the Campbell house. Before long Harry noticed a downy white feather bouncing along the ground on a mild breeze. He signaled for quiet, though he knew that if there were any capable Indians with hostile intent in the vicinity, the three of them already would be either dead or seriously hurt.

First they came to what Harry recognized as a rough attempt at a longhouse in the Iroquois style. Slabs of tree bark made a haphazard covering over a framework of saplings not quite tall enough for an Englishman to stand up in. It looked flimsy and unfinished. At the entrance, a sodden pile of somebody's belongings: a blanket, woolen coat and trousers, several other scraps of cloth and animal skins, and some cooking utensils. A few yards farther upstream, they spotted the Indian.

Blinn reached for his pistol, but Harry gestured for him to leave it alone. The man looked too old to cause trouble. He was squatting in front of a blackened tin pot containing a freshly cut-up chicken in some water. The man was naked except for a greasy loincloth and turned partly away so Harry could not see his face. Slabs of withered skin flapped and quivered as he struck a fire steel against a piece of flint underneath the pot. The effort had little effect in terms of making sparks. The sparse heap of tinder looked too damp to ignite anyhow.

Either the old man was as hard of hearing as Scroggins or he was ignoring the trio. Harry stepped closer, deliberately snapping twigs under his boots. The man slowly turned his head, acknowledged their presence with a disinterested glance, and said in unaccented English, "Do you have any fresh flint?"

"Comet Elijah?" Harry ventured.

He gave the flint one more weak blow, then threw it and the fire steel to the ground. Comet Elijah had never been known for his patience.

"Do you know this man?" asked Blinn.

Certain now of his identity, Harry nodded. He wondered if his astonishment registered on his face.

"Is that chicken you're getting ready to cook?" Blinn again. Though he could see plainly that it was.

"Well, it will keep a man alive. Even though it's not as good as the roast beef of old England."

Harry, Blinn, and Noah looked at each other. They were miles from New Bern. There was no possibility the fife-and-drum corps music could have traveled that far. Or that what Cogdell had served for supper in his tavern the night before would have been reported to this location on Trace Creek.

"Why did you say that?" asked Harry.

"What did I say?"

"The roast beef of old England. Why did you use those words?"

Comet Elijah frowned, as if feeling accused of something. "I just had roast beef on my mind when you were coming up, that's all. I don't know why. I was looking at my little chicken, and roast beef came into my head."

Harry felt he needed to be on guard. He wondered what other reverberations Comet Elijah might have picked up, assuming this apparent act of mind invasion was not some colossal coincidence. It was the kind of thing that seemed a regular occurrence with him.

"Don't worry," he said, as if determining Harry's thoughts perfectly. "I can't hear anything you want to keep to yourself. Don't you remember me telling you that?"

He used his arms to help himself to his feet in the painfully slow way of old people. "Do any of you buckoes know anything of medicine? I have noticed that most white men have some doctor training."

"Not much besides what you taught me," said Harry. "You showed me there is something in the forest to cure most anything that bothers you."

Comet Elijah's features rearranged themselves into a grin. Pleased by the flattery.

"I fear that something ails my *ótkwareh*," he said, mournful again. "It seems to be slowly disappearing. It has retreated noticeably just since the end of winter. I think it is being absorbed into my body."

"What is an *ótk* . . . ?'" whispered Noah, stumbling on the word.

"It's Tuscarora for the male member." Then, to Comet Elijah, "I don't think we need to see . . ." But he was too late. With a swift motion, the loincloth slipped away from the slender waist.

"This has happened to many of my people since the arrival of the whites," he said, gesturing toward the evidence. "So far I have escaped, but now I think it is my time. My body is eating my *ótkwareh*, and I will soon die."

"There is nothing wrong with your *ótkwareh*," Harry said. In fact, it looked very healthy for a man of his age. "Now, please put that back on."

Comet Elijah obeyed, complaining as he stooped to pick up the cloth that they had not looked close enough to make an informed ruling.

"Well, I am dying, that is definite. Last night I was visited by some of the stonish clan. They asked if I had seen the Giant Head. He has been gone for a long time, but now he is in the forest again, looking for humans to eat. I know it was only a dream, but such visions come to those who are nearing the entrance to the Sky Land."

He scratched his rump, giving it a good deep dig.

"How is my old friend Natty doing these days?" he said. "And his son—what's his name? Hendry. Has Hendry returned from the war yet?"

"Natty is fine. My father is still missing. Lying in an unmarked grave on the Spanish Main, most likely."

"I am sorry to hear that. I didn't think anything good would come of him going off. He never dropped by to see me, so I didn't know if he was dead or not."

Harry's mind went back to the day everyone decided Hendry was not coming back. He had refused his family's pleadings and gone off to fight for the king at a place called Cartagena. The Spanish proved not as willing to leave their outpost on the South American continent as the British were eager to see them go. People later called it the navy's worst defeat in history. Hendry's mates in the New Bern militia said the last time they saw him, he was walking at a crouch toward the walls of Fort San Lazaro under showers of musket- and cannonballs.

The only one of them who had not thrown down his scaling ladder that fearful night and fallen back. Hardheaded to the end, they said.

Fifteen months later, at the approach of Harry's tenth birthday, Natty told Talitha he wanted to take the boy on a winter hunting trip in the mountains. It was something Natty and Hendry, along with Comet Elijah and several of their planter friends, did every year during the season when there were no crops to plant or harvest. A weeks-long excursion into the West. Talitha protested that such a trip would be too much for a ten-year-old boy. But Natty said it was time Harry began learning the things Hendry would have been teaching him were Hendry still around. In the end they left it up to Harry. Talitha said later she knew she had lost when Natty turned to Harry and said, "So, son, would you rather spend your time with the men, or stay back here with the women?"

The trip was moderately successful. More often than not they killed enough to keep themselves alive, and the times when food did run out they were welcomed into villages whose people Comet Elijah knew. But as they began making their way back, they ran into an awful storm. People would talk about it for years to come, how it was the worst outbreak of snow, wind, and freezing cold those mountains had seen in more than a hundred years.

The men had started setting up their camp earlier than usual that afternoon, knowing from how fast and hard the temperature was dropping, and from a certain uneasy feeling in the air, that they might have to stay there for a while. Harry remembered how he went walking off to investigate a sound he had heard in the forest as the first flakes came down. Before he knew it, the camp, along with the men, were gone. Lost in a grainy gray haze of wind-driven snow.

He later pieced together what had happened next. As soon as somebody noticed him missing, they fanned out to search. Each man went in a different direction. All Harry remembered was night falling around him and the snow getting thicker on the ground, the snow whipping around him so hard that he could not see beyond the closest trees. He finally lay down beside a rotted-out log for a nap and woke up an unknown time later feeling warm and safe and well under a makeshift shelter of tree branches and slabs of bark. At the entrance a small fire burned cheerily despite the wind gusts. Encircling him were the strong arms of Comet Elijah.

"I have you to thank for teaching me to be a man, Comet Elijah. You and Natty."

"You were a good learner."

"We guessed you'd gone on another of your long hunting trips, or maybe to visit your people, the ones who went to Canada. But you never said good-bye and you never came back."

"It was time to go. I had nothing more to teach my people. Or you."

Noah and Blinn had been following this exchange with looks of surprise and curiosity. Harry said to them, "I think what he means is I wasn't listening to him anymore. Or to Natty or anybody else, for that matter."

"I also wanted to see my relatives the Haudenosaunee, the ones the French call Iroquois. The Mohawk, Onondaga, Seneca, Oneida, Cayuga, and my own Tuscarora cousins who survived the uprising and went up to live with them."

"Comet Elijah was an important man," Harry said, directing himself to Blinn, who had arrived in New Bern from England only four years earlier and had shown scant interest in the town's history. Harry realized he himself knew little more than Blinn, tales from the old days just not striking him as information he needed to have. But he did know Comet Elijah's story. He had heard it over and over again from Natty.

"He was the young king of a Tuscarora band that lived north of New Bern. When the southern group attacked the Swissers, he kept his people out of the fight, and by doing so saved many lives. King George himself rewarded them with unquestioned ownership of their land. Some—the ones who didn't move away to Canada—still live on it to this day."

"The king gave them their own land?" asked Noah.

"Well, yes. It sounds strange now, but that's what happened."

"I decided I would go up to Canada for a visit," Comet Elijah said. "See if they were still angry with me for not helping them kill the whites. By the time I got up there nobody seemed to care anymore, so I was safe. I stayed for a good long time and even took a wife, but she died one winter. Then after a while I got tired of it. It's too cold up there. I wanted to come back home, see the old places again. See how you came out. Has the young warrior gained wisdom to go along with his knowledge of the tomahawk?"

"I've changed, Comet Elijah. Mostly for the better, I hope."

Blinn made an impatient noise in his throat. Curiosity satisfied, Harry guessed. "I am sure we all got a lot to talk about," Blinn said. "First, though, we need to ask you some questions."

Harry told Comet Elijah about the murders, including the peculiar poses of the bodies.

Blinn said, "It looks like it happened during the storm that came through here three nights ago. Where were you, exactly?"

"I went into my longhouse when the storm came up." He pointed in the direction of his ragged home. "It was right around dark."

"Did you see anyone?" said Harry. "Any travelers coming through here?"

"Now that I recollect, I heard hoof beats later in the night. Somebody riding by fast. The rain had stopped, but the wind was still blowing. Yes, I am sure I heard a horse. It went by too fast for me to hear what they were thinking."

"They?" said Blinn.

"The man and the horse."

Harry said, "Do you remember the direction the sound was coming from? Where they might have been headed?"

Comet Elijah made a pass through the air with a withered hand, signaling no. "I was under my blanket, trying to keep the rain off. But I may as well not have bothered. I was getting soaked. That night was not a nice time for me. We can talk more about it later on, if you'd like."

51

Harry looked back toward the ruined camp, then at the pot of uncooked chicken.

"This is no way to live. You need to come and stay at my place. You and Noah here would make fine barn mates." He introduced Noah and briefly told his story, how he had been left homeless by the murder of the Campbells.

"There's plenty room in the barn," Noah agreed. "It's better even than a tavern. You can have your own pile of hay."

"That's a fine offer, but I want to spend a few more days in the woods." He looked around. "Every one of these trees is an old friend. I see many have wounds from people draining off their life's blood."

"What about the Giant Head?" Blinn asked in a mocking tone. "Aren't you afeared of getting gobbled up?"

"I may need to battle a monster tonight," Comet Elijah said, nodding. "My ancestors would expect me to put up a good fight." Giving it another moment of thought, he added with a sly grin, "Might do my *ótkwareh* some good, too."

CHAPTER 7

57: In walking up and Down in a House, only with One
in Company if he be Greater than yourself, at ye first give
him ye Right hand and Stop not till he does and be not ye
first that turns, and when you do turn let it be with your
face towards him, if he be a Man of Great Quality, walk
not with him Cheek by Joul but Somewhat behind him;
but yet in Such a Manner that he may easily Speak to you.
—*RULES OF CIVILITY*

VAPORS FROM A SIMMERING POT GREETED HARRY AND NOAH AT
Natty's house. It was well past midday. Blinn had started back to town
to report to the sheriff the discovery of the old Indian. Natty was not

at home, but judging from the stew's rich and nearly done appearance, Harry reckoned he was not far away.

"I've never seen anything like this," said Noah, his eyes wandering around the dark interior. "It looks like something that grew out of the ground."

The way Harry had it figured, Natty so missed his former life in the Albemarle, where the dividing line between outdoors and indoors was sometimes vague, that he tried to remake it here. Over time the house had taken on a wild, shaggy look, more like a dwelling in the man's swampy homeland to the north. Thick garlands of hanging moss covered the walls inside and out. Their curling, dried-out tendrils gave the place a feeling of year-round autumn in another world. Worked into the moss were animal parts: snakeskins, antlers, turtle shells, bear and panther bones, and some other smaller, less easily identified objects, including one about the size of an apple that looked eerily like a jawless human skull.

Harry said, "Natty wanted his own place away from the main house, away from Mother, who can be a thorn in the side at times. My house is even farther away, near the edge of our family's property."

As Harry was explaining this, Natty stepped through the doorway, bending his neck to the side to clear the top. He had the rangy look of a runner. A narrow face with sharp features, pale blue eyes, and neck-length hair going raggedly gray, tied in back with a ribbon. He had on an open-throated deerskin hunting shirt and leggings. A necklace of blackened shark's teeth gleamed with moisture against his sweaty chest.

He slapped the burlap sack he was carrying down on a chair. "Coriander," he said. "I've found a wild stand of it up toward Sandy Creek."

After exchanging greetings, Harry told him the news about the murders. Natty made a frown. "The Campbells was good folks," he said, tearing apart some of the good-smelling leaves from the bag with his fingers and letting the bits fall into the stew. "I'm sorry to hear about this."

"Natty, I've seen Comet Elijah. He's come back. He has a camp a couple miles from here."

"I knew we'd not seen the last of him. How did he look?"

"Old. And smaller than I remember. But not too bad for a man that age." Harry decided not to mention the part about Comet Elijah's *ótkwareh*.

"Well, he can stay here anytime he likes."

"Mother might not care for him being so close by. I've already invited him to board with us."

"We don't want to upset Talitha. But there are a few things she's got no say in."

"Also, Maddie McLeod is back in New Bern."

"Go on. This must be the time for homecomings."

Noah threw Harry a questioning look. Harry said he would explain about Maddie later. Natty said, more or less to Noah, "I swan, I don't know which one I like better, this Harry or that boy who used to court those pretty ladies and set taverns afire."

"I saw Maddie yesterday."

"I wouldn't mind laying these old eyes on that one again myself."

"You'll have to hurry. She's leaving again tomorrow to get married."

Natty smacked his hands together. "Glad to hear it. And who might the fortunate bucko be? Anybody I know?"

"I doubt it. He's from Virginia. His name is Ayerdale."

These words had a surprising effect on Natty. His eyes went large and it looked like he stopped breathing.

"Do you know him?"

"I've heard the name." He seemed to recover himself. Got up from his chair and walked over to the hearth. "I reckon we better have some of this mess before it all boils away."

"Smells good," said Noah. "What's in it?"

"Pig brains," said Harry. "Natty's famous throughout Craven County for his pig-brain stew."

"I threw in some tongue and heart and a little liver, just to make it interesting."

Before they could put a ladle into it, someone rapped at the door. It was Maddie.

★

The fairy princess from the night before was gone. In her place was a woman in men's riding clothes, hair down and tied back with a ribbon, and a sober eye. She and Harry stood for a long moment, neither speaking, eyes locked.

Natty called out, "Is that Maddie? Come on in, girl, we was just about to eat."

Maddie nodded in his direction and said, "I need to talk to Harry. Maybe another time."

In the grayness of an increasingly dank afternoon, Maddie looked older than in the amber light of candles. Tiny lines stretched out from the corners of her eyes and around her mouth.

"I looked for you at your house, but your wife said you might be over here. Congratulations, Harry. She is beautiful. Very well-spoken for a servant."

"I suspect the whole thing was Mother's idea."

He made a quick version of the events, feeling a fresh stab of guilt at the end, realizing how much his tale of unintended romance sounded like an excuse.

"Well, you could hardly have been expected to remain faithful to me. I was off exploring Europe, having a fine time. And, Harry, I confess I was not always faithful to you."

"Ten years is a long spell."

They walked as they talked. Maddie speaking evenly, matter-of-factly, as if addressing a onetime business partner, not a lost darling.

"The purpose of my visit is simple. In light of our history together, I feel you may have questions that need answering. We need to resolve our situation so we can get on with our lives. We need not have secrets between us, nor lingering mysteries. That, Harry, is the best way."

"Suits me," he said.

She talked of how she finished her education in Edinburgh, and then Olaf agreed for her to stay in Europe, tour the Continent, with her mother as chaperone. A not-uncommon thing among those of her age and class, she explained. As it turned out, it lasted seven years. Her mother died of a fever about halfway through, and she was on her own. But whenever she ran low on money, the judge would send another note of credit to wherever she was. Venice, Avignon, Brescia. All the fashionable places.

"It makes me feel bad now to think of how much of his money I spent. But I guess it meant little to one as wealthy as my grandfather."

"I tried not to think about you," Harry said. "But I couldn't help wondering where you were, what you were doing."

"I'll confess I was curious about you as well. Mail from friends in New Bern caught up with me now and then, and I was much amazed to hear you had come under Grandfather's tutelage."

"I am in his debt for everything he's done for me. And continues to do."

She talked more about her adventures. She had befriended people whose names she seemed to think Harry should recognize, though he could not imagine why. Politicians, poets, diplomats, novelists, essayists. She had written some herself—poems, satires, even a play—under pen names. They were mostly circulated among friends, except for letters to newspaper editors touching on political issues.

She moved on to the subject of lovers as if she thought this might be something Harry would want to know about, which he did not. A middle-aged banker in Rome. A youthful artist in Geneva. A darkskinned man in Marseilles who helped unload the ship she had arrived on from Venice. In Padua, a beautiful and intense young Spaniard then visiting the courts and literary circles of Europe. A man, she implied, whose appetites did not stop at women.

Harry had nothing comparable to tell. He offered a few details about life with his mother and Natty, realizing how boring his adventures sounded. Thinking that matters involving money might impress her, he said how, two years previous, his family had made a fateful financial choice. In response to falling prices they had cut back on the amount of tobacco they were raising and were now shipping much more timber, tar, pitch, and turpentine. Gifts of the seemingly unending legions of pine trees on their property.

"Well, I don't want to prolong this any more than necessary," Maddie said when he started talking about forest products. "I just thought we should speak before we go our separate ways. It felt like unfinished business."

"You already said that."

"Yes. I wanted us to be clear about where we stand. So we can make the clean break I believe would be best for both of us. You seem happy. I hope you wish the same for me."

"Do you love him?"

Maddie stopped and turned to face him. "Richard? Of course I love him. Why would you think otherwise?"

"I'm sorry, I had no right to ask. I'm sure he has everything you want in a husband. You should be happy together."

"I have to go now." She resumed her pace. "Olaf is expecting me for supper. And I have to get ready to leave for Williamsburg. Richard has business to look after there before we leave for Canada."

"We?"

"I'm going with him. We're taking a schooner in the morning, so we don't have to go anywhere near that awful swamp. What's its name?"

"The Great Dismal."

"Yes. A good word for it."

They walked back to the railing where Maddie had fastened her horse.

"I . . ." he began, before he really knew what he wanted to say.

"I've already forgotten about you, Harry," she interrupted. "Let's leave it that way."

CHAPTER 8

40: Strive not with your Superiers in argument, but
always Submit your Judgment to others with Modesty.
                                                    —*RULES OF CIVILITY*

"AS OF YESTERDAY I'D NEVER SPOKEN TO AN INDIAN," NOAH SAID AS
he and Harry rode out the next morning to fetch Comet Elijah.
"Now I'm to be living with one. How exciting." From his way of
speaking, Harry could not decide whether he was really excited or
just making fun.

Their plan was to have him settled into the barn in time for Harry,
Noah, and Toby to proceed into New Bern for the Campbells' memorial service, which had been set for two o'clock.

"An old man like that has no business staying out in the open," Harry said as they continued along. "He'll be fine in the barn until we can figure out something else. I'm sure you'll be glad, too, when you can make other arrangements."

"Actually I'm growing rather fond of the cows. We've had some interesting conversations."

They almost missed Comet Elijah's camp in the thin morning light filtering through the pine tops. All that was left of the longhouse was a scattering of tree limbs and loose bark.

"It appears he decided to seek other accommodations," said Noah.

"I don't think so," said Harry, poking through the shapeless heap that was Comet Elijah's belongings. At the bottom was the cooking pot. Lying next to it, a trade ax. This was nothing more than a simple tool: brute, unornamented steel built for hard use. Chopping wood and dispatching small animals. Age and wear had darkened both the metal head and the handle. Harry tested its heft. Flipped it in the air one revolution, catching the wood as it came around. Showing off a little for Noah. The ax had a familiar feel. Harry allowed himself to think it could have been the very one Comet Elijah had used to teach him the customs and methods of the tomahawk.

"It's not the first thing you turn to when you need a weapon," Comet Elijah had told him when Harry first had showed curiosity. He could not have been much more than eleven. "In fact, it's the last thing you go for. You shoot first. Musket and pistol, in that order, or whichever is closest at hand. Then, if they're still coming on, use your spear if you have one. You want to take care of them before they get in too close. Only when they're right on top of you do you draw out your small blades."

Comet Elijah spent several years teaching him the surprisingly large number of offensive and defensive maneuvers possible with the ax alone and in combination with a long knife, the other object a woodsman always carried with him. He began with the foot stances available for use depending on the kind of threat posed. "Your legs are your fighting platform," he told Harry. "You have to have a good way of standing, firm and balanced, the basic one with your feet about shoulder-length apart, one foot some little ahead and the one behind turned out, just so." Then came the different ways of carrying the blades, whether both on the left or right side or one on each side, or both or just one of them in the small of the back, out of sight. Each spot had its advantages and disadvantages depending on a person's amount of skill and inclinations. The overriding idea was to get them in hand with the proper grip, and into action quickly, once the need became evident. Young Harry took in these mysteries eagerly. They were parts of the grown-up world that Comet Elijah and Natty lived in, not the tiresomely prettified world, as he thought of it then, of the Judge McLeods and the Reverend Reeds and the vestrymen and storekeepers of New Bern. Harry felt he was being brought into a secret society, a priesthood of the forest whose rites were as intricate as any Masonic ones he could imagine.

After Harry mastered the preliminaries, Comet Elijah began teaching him the various presentations to the enemy. High guard. Low guard. Middle guard. And the angles of attack. Eight in all, going around an imaginary circle with your opponent's head at the center. The thrust. The cut. The hammer blow with the back end of the ax. Special uses of the handle, fine points about how it can be employed. How, in the middle of a fight, to change your grip to best suit the way the contest was going. Methods of engaging an enemy who was close to you and one farther out. Dealing with multiple attackers. Each movement distinct, at once simple and brutal, savage in purpose, yet as graceful in its own way as a dance step. Each little piece to be practiced endlessly, both singly and along with others in different sequences. The possible combinations seemed without number.

On the first morning of this advanced instruction, Comet Elijah put on a demonstration of how the two blades could be used together against an enemy or several coming from different directions. Just to give Harry a look at the whole, he explained, before delving into the parts. Harry had to sit on a rock in a clearing and make an oath to not get up until the exhibition was finished. Comet Elijah walked a safe distance away and turned back to face him. He was standing erect but relaxed in a glow of morning sun slanting through the trees. Knife and tomahawk hanging together on his right side. No holster, the instruments just wedged in between his belt and his waist. As simple as could be. Eyes downcast, breathing easy. Seeming to draw into himself. In the next instant he was an instrument of destruction. A prolonged, flowing blur of motion, blades rising and falling, spinning, going in many directions at once, or so it seemed. Polished steel caught sunlight, which flashed bright splinters into Harry's eyes. Comet Elijah the man all but disappeared, replaced by a whirling, glittering, nearly blinding orb, making Harry want to swear he had magically grown extra arms. It seemed a fair guess that anything that came too close at that moment would be annihilated. Shredded into raw, quivering pieces.

"Comet Elijah wouldn't have left this behind," said Harry. "Not if he left this place on his own."

"Scroggins?"

Harry considered the possibility.

"I guess we ought to go see him, make sure he didn't by some accident do harm to Comet Elijah."

"I know what you're thinking," said Noah. "Blinn."

"What am I thinking about Blinn?"

"He said yesterday he was going to tell the sheriff about finding the Indian. Carruthers thinks the murders were committed by an Indian."

"Carruthers couldn't possibly believe the old man we saw yesterday could have killed the Campbells."

"Maybe not. But you heard the talk at the table yesterday. News of the murders wasn't even a day old and already the town was in a tumult. If they could arrest somebody, wouldn't that calm people down, take pressure off? I've heard that Carruthers is up for reappointment as sheriff. Maybe he wants to have this matter settled. The others, too."

"You have a suspicious mind, Mister Burke. But that is exactly what I was thinking."

★

They found Comet Elijah locked inside a run-down, otherwise empty warehouse near the waterfront. Harry had heard the town was paying a small monthly rent for its temporary use while plans went ahead for replacing the old jail, which had been judged unsafe for humans, even criminals. Comet Elijah was the only inmate.

Two or three dozen people milled about the front, trying to get a glimpse of the prisoner through a row of small barred windows. Harry muscled his way through, Noah following in his wake. The heavy wood door was latched from the inside. Despite distortions in the door's small bull's-eye glass, Harry recognized several members of the town watch on the other side. They let Harry and Noah pass through the entrance. All had scrapes and bruises, signs of recent combat.

The inside was dark, humid, and smelled of tar and pitch, ghostly leftovers from barrels once stored there awaiting shipment. The plank flooring bore a dull polish from years of ground-in grime. Lining two walls were eleven-foot-tall wooden stalls intended for storage of higher-priced items coming into New Bern: furniture and silverware and fancy clothing and the like. Each stall had its own set of lockable doors and small barred windows, making ideal cells.

Comet Elijah was sitting cross-legged on the floor of a stall, eyes closed, as if asleep. He looked poorly. Bruises on his face, one eye swollen and darkened to the color of river clay.

"Is that Harry?" he said, his good eye barely parting into a slit.

"What happened?"

"It was a great surprise. I didn't foresee them coming. They said I had to go with them. I asked where they wanted to go. They said New Bern. I asked why. They said I didn't need to know that. Then I started getting suspicious. They looked like men, but they could have been monsters disguised as men. Before I could get out my tomahawk, they were upon me."

"Looks like you put up a pretty good fight."

"I was able to knock one of them out with my fists. At least, I think I knocked him out. When I looked again he was gone. But there were too many. I don't remember much else. I woke up in here. Where am I? They won't tell me."

"You're in a warehouse on the Trent River in New Bern."

"Are you really Harry?"

"Yes."

"Can you say why I'm here?"

"It's a mistake. They think you are the person who killed the Campbells. I'm going to see if I can't get it straightened out."

"That's good. I'd like to get back home. Before dark, if I can. Some bad things are about to happen."

"Bad things?" said Noah.

"Not right away. But I need to be in a more peaceful place so I can figure it out, get a better idea of where and when they're going to take place."

"What kind of bad things?" Noah wanted to know.

"Well, a big wave coming in from the sea is going to drown thousands of people if it isn't stopped."

"Thousands? Has that ever happened here?"

"I'm not talking about North Carolina. This is going to happen somewhere in Japan. But that's not the worst. Several million people are going to starve in India because of a famine."

"You can foresee disasters in Japan and India?"

"I foretold an earthquake in China in 1555. Killed almost a million people."

"You predicted something that happened more than two centuries ago?" The confusion on Noah's face was plain.

"I might be a few of years off. Can't remember now. It was a long time ago."

"Are they feeding you all right?" asked Harry, who had heard this kind of thing from him before, to the point where he was no longer amazed.

"Eating isn't my biggest worry right now. I need to get out of here. It's killing me." He again partly opened his working eye, which had drooped shut.

"I'm working on that," said Harry.

"You'd better hurry up. No fooling, I'm dying in this place."

★

If Carruthers wanted to show New Bern he had an easier, more culti-vated side to his nature, the brick-walled flower garden in his eastern side yard could not have served better, with its cunningly thought-out sections of annuals and perennials separated by grassy stretches and walkways made of paving stones. Everything laid out with exacting symmetry. In the center was a bronze sundial mounted on a slab of blue granite that Carruthers boasted of having paid to transport all the way from South Carolina.

The sheriff was about to enter his house with a handful of hydrangea when Harry and Noah rode up. Carruthers said, "I'm afraid I haven't got time to talk just now, I'm about to dress for the service. But I do want to thank you for your fine work in chasing down the savage."

"You can't really think such an old man as Comet Elijah could have killed the Campbells," said Harry.

"You are speaking of the Indian named Tom Walker, yes? The one whose Indian name sounds like some nonsense combination of a prophet and a heavenly body?"

Harry nodded.

"Son, you weren't there when my deputies picked him up. He put up a fight. I have no doubt he is capable of murder. "

"But why would he do such a thing? You've at least heard of King Walker. He was always a friend of New Bern."

"Yes, and I'm sure we will find out what inspired him to commit murder before this is over. Now, if you will excuse me." He slammed the door behind him with more force than Harry felt was needed.

McLeod also was in a hurry. "You are going to the memorial service, aren't you?" he called from the parlor when Harry and Noah arrived. "I'll make sure you and your wife have a seat up near the front."

"Judge, you must know that forty-eight years ago Comet Elijah saved the lives of many settlers in this place by keeping his people out of the attack that destroyed it."

McLeod let out a gust of breath. "Look, Harry, he will have every opportunity to explain himself at the trial. And he'll have lots of time to get ready. The next session of Superior Court won't be until the middle of October."

"You're going to keep him locked in that little stall until October?"

"I'd rather not, of course. Feeding prisoners is expensive. But capital crimes can't be tried in a quarterly session. And I can't convene a superior court before its term just to hear one case."

McLeod's manner had been pleasant, almost fatherly. Now Harry's ear was picking up a sharper tone. Nevertheless, he pressed on.

"Judge, I will post whatever bond you think is right and guarantee Comet Elijah's presence at the trial, if you'll release him into my custody. My wife has already agreed to let him stay with us. A man of his age and state of health may not live that long in those conditions in the warehouse. I beg you to do this."

"And I beg you to remember your place," said McLeod, the last smidgen of moderation dropping off. "Constables do not question decisions of high sheriffs and magistrates. Those of us with duties to the community must look to the greater good. At this moment, the people we have the privilege of governing are living in fear. They need to see someone in jail. One of these days you may be in a position such as I, and then maybe you'll understand what I'm talking about."

Harry heard him mumble something else as he turned away. It sounded like, "Or maybe not."

CHAPTER 9

74: When Another Speaks be attentive your Self and dis-
turb not the Audience if any hesitate in his Words help
him not nor Prompt him without desired, Interrupt him
not, nor Answer him till his Speech be ended.

—*Rules of Civility*

REVEREND REED PUT A GOOD MEASURE OF ENERGY INTO HIS SERMONS,
a style of preaching Harry did not associate with other Anglican ministers he had seen, like those from the Society for the Propagation
of the Gospel in Foreign Parts who would pass through New Bern
while on tours of the colonies. Reed's style was more akin to that of
Congregationalists, Anabaptists, and adherents of other rebellious

religions whose clergy, from time to time, filled tents rigged just outside the town.

Reed was in especially lively form for the Campbells' memorial. As soon became plain, he had something new to say.

Harry had wanted to skip the whole affair. His thoughts were still occupied with Comet Elijah's dilemma, trying to decide what he should do. But Noah convinced him that as time went along he would regret not going. McLeod, true to his word, had arranged space for Harry and Toby in the third row, with just enough room for Noah to wedge in beside them. Talitha and Natty had come separately, early enough to find seats halfway back.

Now people filled every pew shoulder to shoulder, house servants and field hands of both races touching arms with the wealthy and powerful. Everyone perspiring. Throngs pooled up outside the windows, hoping to hear what Reed would say. It was the kind of affair the governor himself would have attended were he still a resident of New Bern, and his absence was yet another sad reminder of his recent adjournment to Wilmington.

Harry looked around for Maddie and Ayerdale and, not seeing them, guessed they had departed for Williamsburg.

It seemed the hearts of everyone in Craven County had been gladdened in some way by the Campbells. A testament, the preacher declared, to the generous and loving spirit of the young couple. Reed used for his text Samuel II:18, "It is the Lord, let him do what seemeth to him good." But he soon departed from the fatalistic tone of this verse and turned to a theme he had been exploring from Christ Church's high pulpit for the past several weeks: how, after a time of growth and enlarging fortune, New Bern had begun to slide into the abyss of complacency, even outright godlessness.

"Church attendance continues to slacken," Reed said in a voice louder than the usual Anglican monotone, "and along with it, the tithes that make possible the continuation of the Lord's work." Harry smirked inwardly at this, recalling that ever since Reed had arrived five years earlier he had complained endlessly about his low rate of pay, which was often late, and the living arrangements he and his wife had been afforded: a not especially handsome three-room house with a small garden, only one servant, and the vague promise of a glebe sometime in the future.

"And what is the result?" he demanded. "Public drunkenness has become all too common. As have sloth and other lascivious behavior. Not to speak of a generalized lack of respect for the Crown. I can't remember the last time I've heard of a toast being offered to our gracious king, whether in tavern or at home."

Nods of agreement greeted each one of these statements. The reverend had brought up the same concerns on previous Sabbaths. But now he entered new territory.

"As much as it pains me," he said, touching the fingers of one slender hand to his black-robed breast, "I must say that all of us as a people fall short every day in the eyes of our Lord. Landlords charge their tenants too much rent. Tenants find sly ways of deceiving landlords. Masters cheat servants and the other way around. Oh, yes, don't look away. Tavern keepers charge too dearly for drink and food. Farmers demand too much for their victuals. Merchants parade before our eyes their wondrous luxuries from across the ocean, extravagances that far exceed the plain necessities of life. And how do we respond to their lures? We borrow money to buy things we cannot afford, in hopes that such baubles will somehow give our lives value and purpose."

As he continued in this direction, his voice rising even further, the idle coughing, rustlings of clothing, and creaking of pews typical to Sabbath services ceased. Everyone now sat rigid, eyes tending downward. And Reed was far from finished.

"Blasphemies of the flesh have grown all too common, accompanied by an increase in bastardy and orphans. Husbands lie with women who are not their wives. Wives are untrue to husbands. Among the lower classes, brothers lie down with sisters, and uncles with nieces. Oh, yes, my children. All of us have sinned in some way, and now all are being punished. With the departure of our beloved governor, we have lost a faithful friend and the Christian religion an able advocate among us. Can there be any doubt that meetings of the assembly and members of the governor's council will soon follow him to Wilmington? What then shall become of our beloved city? Were we so puffed up that we could not have conceded him a better house at lower rent? Day in and day out, paid him even the simple courtesies due his royal office?"

Harry now felt the reverend was on a considerable drift from what he guessed all this was leading up to, that the Campbells' death was just another a piece of how God was scolding them for their wickedness. A familiar theme, how the Almighty would punish an entire village for the sins of just a few. In Dobbs's case it was the sins of many. It just was not in the nature of New Bernians to make reverences for anyone who had not in their opinion earned them. And Dobbs had not.

"My little children, ours is a jealous God. Who knows what more disasters will befall us?"

He was now bobbing his head and jabbing his hand to the rhythm of his words. His volume having grown to such a level that Harry was sure those standing outside could plainly hear every damning word. Those nearest shrank from his passion and from balls of spit firing from his mouth like tiny cannonballs.

"Listen well, sons and daughters of New Bern," he said, aiming a finger skyward. "As the people of Sodom and Gomorrah discovered, the Lord does not suffer a wicked people. Our own city was once destroyed by fire through the offices of satanic savages. Such destruction could rain down on us again. We are being warned."

He took a step back and fell silent. Then, mopping his brow with his kerchief, he finally turned to the subject at hand. Harry sensed relief sweeping through the pews as he began speaking of the beloved Campbells. Their unshakeable faith in the Almighty while they lived. The special challenge they had been given by the Lord in the person of Andrew, who, the reverend reminded everyone, was one of those children who would try the patience of saints.

"During his nine short years on Earth, the child suffered from a mental restlessness. A seemingly constant need to be in motion, angry and, at times, given to destructive outbursts. And the occasional vile tongue. We wondered where he had even heard such language as sometimes issued from his innocent mouth, to the point we considered the possibility of demons. But now Andy's struggles, along with those of his parents, are over. They have departed this dark vale of ours to await the final reward our blessed Savior has prepared for us, the mansions he's built in a land far away from North Carolina. Until that day of resurrection, may all three of them rest in the peace of our Lord."

Seated toward the front, Harry, Toby, and Noah were among the last to file from the church. Harry slightly sore at the back of the neck from looking upward for such a long time. And feeling drained from the scolding they all had received.

Outside, old Scroggins had set himself up in the shade of an elm, where he was loudly demanding punishment for the murderer of the Campbells. The killer who, he said, now resided in Clark's warehouse. Luckily, Scroggins was standing downwind. Harry judged that had he been inside the church during the service his odor would have made the ordeal of the sermon completely unbearable.

Scroggins was talking fast, words tumbling out as if he feared letting such a rare chance to address an audience slip by.

"This whole mess could have been headed off if Sheriff Carruthers and them other fine gentlemen had listened to me in the first place. I told them there was a savage in the woods up there, and they would be sorry if they didn't lock him up to where he couldn't do nobody no harm. They didn't pay no attention, and now you see what has happened."

Seeing some begin to drift away, he added in a still louder voice, "Did you know they found bones up where he was camped? That's right, human bones. They was all boiled up. The meat gnawed off to where they was smooth and white as eggshells."

Several who had been passing by stopped to listen.

"Oh, yes. They ain't let on nothing about that, has they? They is keeping that part quiet."

Harry could abide it no longer. "Nobody found any human bones," he said. Eyes pivoted to where he was standing on the church steps. "All that Indian was eating up there was chickens."

"That's what you say," Scroggins countered. "I went there myself. I seen pieces of arms and legs strewn about. And ribs, too. Lots of ribs. They was just scattered here and yonder, all around." He made circular motions with his arm. "See, they don't want you to know about them bones, does they?" He made a wider gesture that encompassed Harry and the church, as if to include in his accusation the whole membrane of authority in Craven County. "I seen 'em with my own eyes. Them bones was just as big and white as could be."

Scroggins paused, savoring the effect he was having. All movement of people turning away had ceased.

"You remember what Parson Reed preached in there? Jehovah is punishing this place for its low-down ways. He hath sicced that demon upon us, that Indian. It is a test. Now that we done caught up with him, God wants us to punish him in accordance to the amount of evil he has done. If we don't do what he commands, he will turn on us again, hurt us like we never been hurt before."

"We ought to just hang him now and be done with it," said somebody else. Harry recognized a boyhood mate, a small outlying plantation owner by the name of Berry. "Ain't no use in messing around with this any longer than necessary."

"That's not the way we do things in Craven County," said Harry. "I have known for years the old man they've got locked up. Many of you don't know him because you've arrived here in recent times, but he is an old and faithful friend to this town. He will be proved innocent when his trial comes up, if not before."

"I hear he's been bounded over to the Superior Court, and that don't even meet until October," said Berry.

"I wouldn't wager that Indian staying around that long," said Scroggins. "They is wily ones. They can't be held by no white man's jails." A murmur of agreement passed through the assembly. "Besides, who's to say that courthouse crowd won't just let him loose once the fuss has died down? I wouldn't put it past them. You included, Henry Woodyard."

"Yes, Woodyard," said Berry. "That Indian being an old friend of yours don't mean he didn't kill nobody."

Harry was not used to being included in the people who ran the village. He could not quickly think of a good response. And no one seemed to be waiting for one. People had begun sliding away again. In low natterings of conversation, Harry heard someone say, "It was his raising-up. He's half savage himself." Someone else said, "Gets it from his granddaddy."

Harry felt a hand on his shoulder. It was du Plessis.

"Don't pay any mind," he said. "We have some ill-informed people among us."

"Thank you for that," Harry said.

"I'm glad I caught up with you. I've been thinking about that object you were showing around at the judge's house. The brooch. I have a friend in Williamsburg who deals in Masonic jewelry. It would be long odds, but he might be able to tell you something. If he didn't sell it himself, maybe he could at least identify it, say where it was made. Maybe even translate those markings on the back."

"I thank you for your concern," said Harry. "But Williamsburg is a long ride. And I don't know that I could afford the fare for a boat to go by sea."

Du Plessis spread his hands. "Harry, you are a valued customer. I would be more than pleased to advance the funds you'd need."

"But I already owe you so much money."

"I'm sure we could work out something. Would another few pounds on the ledger really make a difference? Besides, I'm sure there would be a reward involved if you brought the real killer to justice. I would certainly argue for such." Du Plessis produced one of his calling cards and wrote down a name on the back. "This will serve as an introduction to my friend in Virginia."

Their route back to Harry's house brought them near the waterfront. He caught sight of a three-masted schooner ghosting downriver on the tide, headed toward the open sound. He pictured Maddie aboard as it picked its way through the shallows, following the winding, ever shifting channel until it reached Ocracoke and beyond that the Atlantic. A short run north along the coast, a turn into the Chesapeake Bay, and up the James to Williamsburg.

Toby and Noah had gone ahead to get the horses. Harry was glad she had not heard his conversation with du Plessis. He tried to imagine explaining that he needed to spend a week or two away during planting season so he might make a two-hundred-mile journey to another colony on the slender chance a stranger might offer some clue as to who had killed the Campbells. And, by the way, he wanted to finance the trip by borrowing more money. On the other hand, it was very likely that Comet Elijah would die without some intervention. Harry could prove his innocence only by catching the killer.

CHAPTER 10

86: In Disputes, be not So Desireous to Overcome as not
to give Liberty to each one to deliver his Opinion and
Submit to the Judgment of the Major Part especially if
they are Judges of the Dispute.

—*RULES OF CIVILITY*

"YOU HAVE TO GO, NO MATTER THE COST," TOBY SAID.

"Good on you, girl," said Natty.

They were sitting on Harry's porch in rockers and a swing the
next afternoon: Toby, Harry, Talitha, Natty, and Noah. Staying out
of the sticky heat that had built up inside. Martin and the others were
in the yard cleaning off the plank table, where all had eaten dinner.

Talitha seemed distracted. She kept looking over at them as if not entirely satisfied with the way they were stacking plates or folding table linens, despite their years of practice.

"You're the one who talks about our debts," Harry replied. "You've near about convinced me no good can come of owing people money."

"Maybe you won't have to borrow it." Toby hesitated, as if making up her mind about something. She got up from her chair and went inside, leaving Harry and the others to puzzle. When she came back, she placed in Harry's hands a heavy hemp sack.

"What is this?" he said.

"Have you never seen a guinea?"

"No. Heard of them, though." He untied the drawstring, peeked inside, and saw gold coins. From their weight he recognized they amounted to a small treasure.

"My father gave me these when I left Swansea. They were to be used for emergencies. I think this qualifies."

Overcoming a moment of speechlessness, Harry said, "This is my emergency, not yours. I can't take this."

"I didn't say you could have it all," she said with a quick laugh. "But I've heard you and Natty speak of Comet Elijah, what he means to you. I don't think I could bear the sorrow of your finding him, only to lose him again."

She retrieved the bag, counted out eight coins, and forced them into Harry's hands.

"Here in North Carolina each one is worth one pound, ten shillings, as best I can determine. Do you think that will be enough for taverns and ferries and such to Williamsburg and back?"

"With some to spare, I imagine."

"Martin and I and the others can manage the plantation until you get back. Just don't spend any more time than you need. I'll miss you."

"So it's settled," said Natty. He was using a small knife to pry scraps of pork shoulder and collards from his teeth. "As far as I know, this will be the first time a Woodyard has been in Virginia in, oh, about a hundred years." Turning to Harry he said, "If you chance to run into any more Ayerdales while you're up there, tell them that Robert Woodyard's grandson sends his greetings."

"Your grandfather knew the Ayerdales?" said Harry.

"Used to work for 'em. Grandpap was a bonded servant."

"You never told me that."

"You never took no interest in where we come from. And why should you? Why should anybody? In this country, what matters is what you do with your own life here in the right now. Not what some grandpap did with his."

"Amen to that, friend Woodyard," said Noah.

Harry said, "I guess I just kind of thought we'd always lived around here."

"In the Pamlico, with all these fancy people?" said Natty. He let out a poof of air. "Maybe it's time to enlighten you as to our origins. If you really want to go back, our people was originally border-country Scotch. Somehow we wound up in Ireland. Don't ask how, because that ain't entirely clear to me. Anyway, Grandpap was a young bucko of sixteen when he signed up to work for a big landowner in this place across the ocean called Virginia. The man had a bunch of plantations. The biggest was called Rosewood. That's all Grandpap knew when he took the contract. Turned out the Ayerdales had been gentry folk back in England, connected to the king somehow."

"Important people," Talitha said.

"That's right. Thank you, Talitha, for saying what I just said. Well, they got themselves caught on the wrong side of the civil war."

Seeing Harry had never heard of the civil war, Natty added, "That was a big scrap they had over there between the king and Parliament. But the Ayerdales, they was smart."

"Real smart," said Talitha, nodding her head.

"They'd started buying land over here in Virginia long before the shooting busted out. By the time the king and his head separated, they'd stitched together near about fifteen thousand acres. And that was just to start. Soon as they moved over here, they bought up more countryside. Probably had a good twenty-five, thirty thousand acres by the time Grandpap Robert got there."

Noah let out a low whistle.

"Now, us Woodyards, we was Scotch Presbyterian. Good hard-working folks."

"The salt of the earth that our Savior spoke of," said Talitha.

"Anyway, my great-grandpap's family owned a farm back in County Antrim. Not big but nice. But Robert had ambitions of bettering himself, and that was just not possible back in Ireland. The recruiter what signed him up painted a pretty picture of Virginia, said life there was nothing shy of a sweet dream. Animals to hunt. Fish to fish. Crops that would just about plant themselves."

"A real Garden of Eden," said Talitha.

"Turned out it weren't that easy. Especially not on a big place like Rosewood. And them Ayerdales was nasty bastards. Especially the old man."

"Treated his servants horrible."

Natty said, "Talitha, are you going to tell this story or do you want me to? You're throwing me off track."

He took Talitha's sigh as a sign for him to go ahead.

"The only thing old man Ayerdale was interested in was getting his hands on a lot of cheap labor to work all that land he had. By the time Robert came along he'd started just buying people outright, hauling up black Africans from Barbados. And he didn't treat his bondsmen much better than his blacks. Didn't feed 'em like he'd contracted to nor give them proper clothing. He'd beat you at the wink of an eye, slave or servant, man or woman, didn't make no difference. Well, young Robert didn't care for that kind of treatment. It weren't the way he'd been raised up back in Ireland. Then, on top of all that, the old man was always messing around with his girl servants. One of them happened to be somebody Grandpap had taken a liking to his own self. Truth is, they had become sweethearts."

Natty broke off long enough to look around, see if they were still following his story. Sometimes people's attention started to wander off when he talked for long periods of time. Seemingly satisfied, he continued.

"Well, one day Robert and the girl who was to become my grandmam up and ran off. Headed south, straight down the middle of the Great Dismal. Figured the swamp would put a damper on anybody coming after them. And they was right. I guess in time old man Ayerdale got over losing his best bonded field hand and his little bed warmer. Pardon the expression, Talitha."

Talitha waved her hand in the air as if to say that was not the worst thing she had heard come out of her father-in-law's mouth.

"They built them a place down toward the south end of the swamp, one of the patches of dry land after the marshland runs out and the Albemarle begins, and started having young 'uns, and they in turn had their own. One of them was me. I had a good growing-up there, did just about anything I wanted, ate and drank as I liked, chased pretty ladies, and ended up sticking with one. I met Harry's future grand-mother at a funeral. Then, when I turned forty, I made a right smart piece of money off a Spanish ship that had the bad luck to smash up in the waves out near Chickahawk. Not a proper fortune you might say but not too bad. I would of spent it all on women and rum, but my new daughter-in-law at the time"—he paused here to nod respect-fully to Talitha—"convinced me to buy us some land down here in the Pamlico."

"Where all the finer people were going," Talitha added, quickly holding up both hands to promise she would say nothing further.

"And that was that. It's old history now, but I'd say we Woodyards have done right smart well for ourselves in North Carolina. And without no slaves."

"Hurrah for the Woodyards," said Noah.

"I got no idea what kind of man this here Richard Ayerdale is," said Natty. "But you need to know, Grandson, you got no reason to doff your cap to him, no more than anybody else you see walking around on two legs."

"I don't plan to," said Harry. "Don't know that I'd even see him while I'm up there anyhow."

Talitha said, "Are you going to ask Judge McLeod if he minds you running off like this?"

"Do I need to?"

She straightened up in her chair and folded her hands in her lap, as if to give a color of importance to what she had to say. "You're not just a private citizen anymore, Harry. You are an appointee of the chief justice of the peace of Craven County. Don't you think it would be a good idea to check with him, maybe the sheriff, too, before you go off on such an errand?"

Harry looked at his grandfather. His expression had taken a disagreeable turn.

"Talitha, in my opinion, you worry too much."

"I am only trying to offer my child wise counsel."

"What if somebody says no?"

"Now, why would they do that?"

"Who knows what cockadoodle reason they might come up with? Carruthers might just want the chance to kill an Indian. Far as I'm concerned, when you decide you need to do something, you go ahead and do it."

Talitha handed Natty a stern look. But her next words had a mollifying tone.

"Son, I just would hate to see you spoil what we've worked for, you especially, how you've lifted up yourself and the Woodyard name. I'm so proud of you. Especially after the stumble you took, what has it been now? Ten years ago?"

Natty said, "If you're talking about what happened between him and that fine young girl Maddie McLeod, she had something to do with that herself."

From a corner of his eye Harry noticed another questioning glance from Noah. He guessed that before much longer he would have to talk about what had transpired, the events that had seemed so calamitous at the time but that had sent him down his current path toward respectability.

Of one thing he was sure: he had to save Comet Elijah.

★

He spent the early part of the next day getting ready to go. To burden Annie as little as possible, he packed only one extra set of clothes and little else. He left off his rifle, doubting he would need to hunt. Ordinaries were strung out along the old post road about a day's ride from one to the next. He did lay out a pair of pistols, along with his knife and tomahawk, as defense against possible bandits.

The rest of the day he devoted to looking over his forest operations, visiting every section of trees then under tap. Getting pleasantly dizzy from the smell of pine sap draining out of the living wood and pooling in tin buckets hanging from pegs. He and Martin talked over when to change the locations of the rigs in case his trip took longer than he expected.

Noah followed close behind, taking down notes. He said he wanted to write something about the longleaf pine, its phases of life and methods of harvesting sap and processing it into tar and pitch. He hoped to make it good enough to be approved by the Royal Society, the association in London he had spoken of before in connection with his father. If the head men approved, they would send his letter to members around the world through their journal. By the reverential way Noah spoke, Harry gathered this would be a great achievement.

"I want to go with you to Virginia, too," said Noah on their way back to the house. "I'd like to see what other plants and animals live between here and there. I'll pay my own board if you can furnish a horse."

"I thought you'd turned your back on your father's interest in nature."

"I just don't care for his blindness to the rest of the world. And, too, I guess things you're exposed to as a child have a way of sticking."

"I'd be glad of the company. I'm sure Martin can spare the gray for a week or two."

After another minute Noah asked if Harry was going to say anything to the judge.

"I've given it a good deal of thought. My mother has her points, but so does Natty. I'm not going to put my intentions at risk by giving anybody a chance to say no. Maybe I can even be back before they know I'm gone."

★

A packet of fresh air moved in that night and with it a light rain. Toby accepted Harry's touches hungrily in the coolness of their room. But she seemed unusually quiet afterward, turning over directly to go to sleep after they had finished. As Harry began drifting away he pondered the fact that her diary had gone missing from the place she usually kept it, a table beside the spinning wheel in the side parlor. He guessed that if she could find a place to hide a sack of gold coins, she could hide a book.

His last waking thoughts were of what she might be writing in it now.

CHAPTER 11

49: Use no Reproachfull Language against any one neither Curse nor Revile.

—*Rules of Civility*

THE RIDE TOOK FIVE AND A HALF DAYS. HARRY LED THEM SOME MILES
out of their way to save money that would have gone to ferries. He
skirted the western side of the Great Dismal, and as the morning of
the fifth day fell they crossed the Virginia boundary. Or the place he
reckoned it to be. The exact location was a matter of disagreement,
an issue awaiting settlement in London. Harry was sure only that he
had passed into unknown country. Along the way Noah jotted down
Latin names of plants and the occasional animal. Now and then he

would point to things Harry would not otherwise have noticed: how the vegetation was steadily changing as they made their way off the tidewater flats and toward the more hilly country in the west.

By the next evening they were only a short distance from Williamsburg, but rather than pressing on and arriving after dark, they decided to have an early supper and stay the night at the ferry-landing inn on the north shore of the York. The establishment, which the owner had fancifully named Heavenly Gate, turned out to be most the luxurious they had stayed in. Their meal of boiled beef and cabbage, though cold, was pleasingly tender and cheerfully served by the owner's daughter. That night they had a whole bed to themselves.

Back on the road shortly after daybreak the next morning, they came to a pair of stone pillars marking the entrance to a plantation. Its name was etched into one of the rocks.

ROSEWOOD

LEVIUS • QUAM • AER

Harry reined in Annie and stared in silence. He had known their path would take them near Ayerdale's holdings, but he had not counted on running into the flagship property itself. His thoughts flew to a long-ago night, the one Natty had spoken of. A desperate seventeen-year-old boy stealing away with his beloved.

"Isn't that . . . ?" Noah began.

"Unless there's more than one plantation in Virginia of that name."

"The phrase below is Latin," said Noah. "It means 'lighter than air.' A family motto of the Ayerdales', I imagine."

Harry guided Annie between the pillars onto a tree-lined lane that was wide, straight, and long. Vast fields nearly flat as baking pans, some green with clover and some lying fallow, lay on either side, ending in lines of trees.

A mile farther they came to a large white house with a pillared portico. A short distance from that, Harry spotted two horsemen.

They could be seen only from their saddles up, as though standing in a shallow gulley. Both had their gazes fixed on the ground. One was Richard Ayerdale. His hair matted from exertion in the morning damp.

As Harry and Noah drew nearer, the object of their attention came into view. A dark-skinned Negro girl wearing a sack of unbleached homespun was kneeling before them. She must have been ten or eleven years old. Ayerdale got off his horse and began striking the girl across her shoulders with a strip of rawhide. He did not look to be in a temper. The blows were calm and methodical, as if it were some everyday task, like chopping wood.

"Say there," Harry called out. "Why are you whipping that girl?"

Ayerdale recognized Harry and bade him a cheerful good morning.

"My overseer and I have just come upon this young blackamoor skulking over yonder among some underbrush. She claims her father accidentally locked her in their cabin when they were leaving for this morning's field work. She further states she got out by pushing a plank off and crawling away and was just on her way to the field."

Then, returning his attention to the girl, he said, "This won't do. Now, tell me the truth. You were trying to hide out for the day, weren't you?"

The girl began to speak in a high-pitched voice, but her words were hard to make out because of her ragged breathing.

"You have not got enough yet," Ayerdale said. "Pull up your shift and lie down on your back." The girl instantly complied.

"Sir, I really must protest." This from Noah. "It would be easy enough to find her father and see if he would verify what she has said. In any case, your behavior is entirely out of bounds."

Ayerdale gave no sign of having heard. He resumed striking the girl as before, except now the blows landed not on her shoulders but on her naked loins and thighs and then her back and flanks as she twisted to avoid them. She screamed and pleaded for Ayerdale to stop. Yet she made no effort to run away.

Harry had never seen a child flogged this way. But harsh measures against Craven County's growing population of Negro slaves were not uncommon. He disliked seeing such things but had come to know they were outside his power to stop and that interference likely would result in worse punishment for the victim. But Noah lacked the benefit of this understanding. He got off his horse and took a few belligerent steps toward Ayerdale, fists clenched. At that, the overseer made a show of pulling out a pistol and aiming it at Noah's belly.

"Take just one step closer and I will make sausage meat of you," he said in a voice full of purpose.

"Get back on your horse, Noah," Harry said. "We're leaving."

They heard more screams as they made their way back toward the lane. Harry resisting the impulse to ride back and shoot them both. Finally, the cries subsided into choking sobs and groans. They looked back to see Ayerdale and the overseer cantering toward them. Ayerdale still in a jovial mood.

"She meant to cheat me out of a day's work," he said. "And she has done it, too." He looked around at the overseer, grinning as if he had just made the best joke. "But never mind that. I am surprised to see you here, Master Woodyard. And your friend. Burke, isn't it?" Ayerdale touched his forehead with his crooked index finger, as if doffing an invisible cap. Under the circumstances it seemed more a taunt than a sign of respect. "Might I inquire what brings you gentlemen to Virginia?"

"I am chasing whoever murdered the Campbells."

"And you believe you might find them here on my plantation?"

"As you recall, I found a Freemason's badge on the floor of the farm-house. One of our New Bern merchants believes an acquaintance in Williamsburg may be able to identify the owner."

"Williamsburg is that way," said Ayerdale, jabbing his finger northward.

"I recognized the name of your plantation as we rode by and thought we might pay our respects. But I see you are busy."

Ayerdale affected a warm smile. "Well, welcome to Rosewood. Since you're here, won't you stop over for a small beer and bite of breakfast? I'm afraid you've missed the delectable Miss McLeod. My fiancée took the phaeton into Williamsburg yesterday. I will be joining her there on the morrow."

If Ayerdale's aim was to aggravate Harry by calling Maddie "delectable," the shot landed true.

"I would be shy of trying the food at this place you call Rosewood," said Harry. "I'm afraid that after tenderizing one of your blacks with a whip, you might roast her for supper."

Ayerdale's handsome features took a puzzled shift as he seemed to consider whether the jest was meant in good humor or bad. He made up his mind and his face turned sour. "Here in Virginia, sir, such a remark would invite a contest of honor. Since you are a friend of my beloved, I will not press the matter. But I advise you to look after your tongue, lest you part with it in a way you would not find amusing. Now, please get off my land." He wheeled his horse roughly and galloped away, the animal protesting with a coarse whicker. The overseer gave them a backward glance as if fixing their faces in memory.

"You continue to astound me," Noah said as they continued toward the gate. "And there is nothing wrong with your tongue. It would be at home in the drollest of company."

"I've never thought of myself as being smart with words," said Harry, basking in Noah's approval.

"Maybe you just need the right inspiration. Human bondage is a powerful muse."

"I've heard Natty say he'd rather go back to living in a swamp than buy another man's life. I feel the same way."

As they regained the postal road, Harry wondered if Maddie had any idea what sort of a man she was to marry.

CHAPTER 12

37: In Speaking to men of Quality do not lean nor Look them full in the Face, nor approach too near them at lest Keep a full Pace from them.

—*RULES OF CIVILITY*

WILLIAMSBURG LOOKED MUCH LIKE NEW BERN, EXCEPT OLDER AND cleaner. No animals in the streets, which, though about the same width as the ample avenues of the North Carolina town, were better kept. Shops were shuttered and the streets nearly deserted, it being a Saturday. Harry guessed people were at home or off on diversions.

He fished from his pocket the card du Plessis had given him and looked at the name written on the back, fixing it in his mind.

Thomas Bannerman

They were passing an enormous brick building, larger than any structure Harry had ever seen and surrounded by at least an acre of lawn. A man trimming bushes said it was the governor's palace. "Bannerman's store is over there," he said, making a vague gesture toward the northeast. "But he ain't going to be in today. Most everybody is off to the horses. Excepting me, that is." He added with a smile that uncovered several missing teeth, "Me good woman hath laid down the law."

The racetrack bore only the broadest resemblance to the one in New Bern. The course itself looked about the same size, a mile loop, but fancier. The viewing stand was sheltered by a shingled roof to keep sun and rain off spectators. Banners the size of bedsheets, including a Union flag, flew at intervals, giving the place a look similar to prints Harry had seen in books about medieval times. Men and women in working clothes filled most of the seats, but a sizeable faction wore rainbows of silk-and-brocade finery and, in the case of the men, powdered wigs. Negroes mixed freely among the crowd.

A lull in the activity coincided with the arrival of Harry and Noah while jockeys, Negro boys and slightly built young whites, brought in fresh mounts for the next race. Harry asked around for Bannerman until someone pointed to a man wearing a jauntily cut jacket with white silk lace at the throat and a consternated look on his face. He was standing on the ground at an entrance to the stands with a group of other well-dressed people. Among them Harry spotted Maddie and, beside her, the Anglican minister Fletcher.

Seeing that Bannerman might be in an ill temper, Harry gave a fleeting thought to saving his business until later. But he already had been seen by Maddie, who was staring at him as if she had just seen a Chinaman. Knowing he could not escape without notice now, he nodded toward Maddie, then headed over toward Bannerman. Begging his pardon, he said, "Someone told me you might be able to identify this for me." Holding up the Masonic badge.

Barely giving the object a glance, the merchant said, "Young man, I do not conduct appraisals at the racetrack. Just now I have lost a great deal of money. If you would like me to evaluate your little gewgaw with a more dispassionate eye, I suggest you make an appointment at my shop."

"I apologize if this is an inconvenient time," said Harry, reaching deep into the bag of wordings he saved for important occasions. "But I am not seeking an appraisal. This article was found at the scene of a murder. I am told that you may be able to enlighten me as to its origins."

"A murder, you say?" The question came from a tall young man with a large pockmarked face. He was standing next to Maddie puffing on a clay pipe. "May I ask where?"

"In North Carolina."

Bannerman turned and began walking away. "Call on me on the morrow and we shall have a look," he said without bothering to turn his head. "If we haven't hanged ourselves by then."

A thin, patrician-looking sort in his midfifties stepped forward. "I am Francis Fauquier," he said with a slight bow. "I wonder if I might be of service."

"The governor of Virginia?" asked Noah.

Fauquier made another mannerly bow. "Officially speaking, my title is 'lieutenant governor,' much like that of your own Arthur Dobbs. But the gentlemen who bear the loftier titles have never set foot in America. So the good people of Virginia and North Carolina have to make do with us, the less exalted but more directly serviceable agents of the king."

While the rest of the company tittered their admiration of Fauquier's self-effacing wit, Harry raked through his memory for a Rule of Civility that could guide him. He had been brought up by his grandfather never to make any gesture of servitude toward anyone, on the ground that no one was better than a Woodyard. That was certainly not the spirit of the *Rules*, and it was all he could manage to keep his hand from rising toward his forehead of its own will. He recalled something about needless flattery and affectations of ceremony. These were to be avoided on the whole but should not be neglected when due.

"Governor Dobbs sends his compliments," he said.

Thankfully, Fauquier appeared flattered and maybe impressed by Harry's supposed connection to the North Carolina executive. It seemed a safe bet he would never find out that Dobbs had never sent any such thing.

"Sir," Harry continued, "I am looking into the murder of a British family."

"An entire family?"

"Husband, wife, and child. It happened about a week ago. I discovered this piece of jewelry on the floor. I'm sure it did not belong to the victims."

Several standing closest leaned in for a better look as Fauquier plucked it from Harry's hand.

"Here on its face is the sign of the Freemasons," the governor observed, pointing for all to see. "On the back is a pine tree. Although we have many pines in Virginia, as I am sure you do in North Carolina, I believe this is the accepted symbol for New England."

"They are a different species," Noah commented in a quiet voice, almost to himself. Then, noticing he had gained their attention, he said, "In the South you have *Pinus palustris*, longleaf pine. New England has northern white pine, or *Pinus strobus*."

Harry introduced him to the company as a schoolmaster in New Bern, originally from Pennsylvania.

"Would you by chance be related to Peter Burke of Philadelphia?" asked Fauquier.

"He is my father. Do you know him?"

"I know of him." To the company he said, "Peter Burke is one of our country's finest students of natural history. In London I sit on the Royal Society board, which has approved publication of several of his letters."

Noah's face colored. "I hope one day to be known for my own works, not those of my father."

Fauquier registered this with a single blink, then turned his attention back to the badge. "As to these markings underneath the tree, from their appearance they are a Masonic code."

"I've been told that Mister Bannerman deals in jewelry especially made for Freemasons," said Harry. "He may even have been the one who sold it to the person I seek."

"Are you a relative of the victims?"

"They were dear friends." Then, an afterthought: "I am the constable for Craven County."

A woman in the company with a pleasing French accent said, "Is it not unusual for a constable to be pursuing a killer for so long a time after the crime has been committed? In my country, if the *hu e cri* is not immediately successful, the perpetrator is rarely discovered."

She looked a few years older than Harry and was outfitted in a lavender silk taffeta gown whose tight bodice exposed a subtle swell of breast. A parasol shielded her pale features from the sun. Harry took in at a glance her small but sharply defined nose, pronounced cheekbones, and silky black hair done up in a tower of swirling curls. Her eyes nearly matched the subtle purple shade of her gown. They seemed large for the rest of her face but somehow the overall effect was perfect.

"An old Indian has been arrested and charged with the crime," Harry said, trying to make himself sound casual, as if he often treated with such unnerving beauty. "I believe him to be innocent. I am not only trying to catch a killer, I am trying to prevent a wrongful execution."

"May I present Madame Jacqueline de Contrecoeur, Baroness de la Roche?" Fauquier said. "But before you arrest her as a spy, you should know that she is a fellow Huguenot. She opposes both the popish religion and King Louis's intentions in America."

Fauquier turned to Maddie as if to introduce her, but Harry headed him off by saying that they were old friends. Maddie, who first had appeared surprised beyond measure to see Harry, now seemed just annoyed.

"You may already have met Reverend Fletcher," said Fauquier. "He has recently arrived from your city on his mission of assessing the condition of the Anglican Church in His Majesty's American plantation."

"Good day, Mister Woodyard," Fletcher said. "I must say I am finding these Virginians considerably more generous with their clergy than your countrymen in North Carolina."

"The saving of souls is a more luxurious occupation here than anyplace else on this side of the ocean, I do believe," said Fauquier. "In Virginia, Anglican clergy are potentates."

As Fauquier and Fletcher continued bantering, Harry had a closer look at the tall, thin young man with the clay pipe. He looked roughly Harry's age, regally dressed, standing at least a head above the rest of the company in an erect military fashion. Stovepipe legs encased in tight leggings. A ribbon fastened his thick dark blond hair in back. Gray-blue eyes. Other than the pits on his face, an all-too-common blemish, he was a picture of youthful, masculine vigor.

Noticing Harry's appraising look, Fauquier said, "I have the honor of presenting to you one of Virginia's most notable citizens, a distinguished war hero, now the newest member of our House of Burgesses and a newlywed besides. Messieurs Woodyard and Burke, meet Colonel George Washington."

The young colossus stuck his pipe in his mouth and seized Harry's hand with a grip that might have crushed an apple. "I hope you will forgive our friend Bannerman's contretemps," he said. "I myself am well acquainted with the pain of losing money on a horse." He waved a small ledger book in the air, grinning with the gaiety of one who has learned the value of joking at his own expense.

"The colonel was with my fiancé at the Battle of the Monongahela," said Maddie. Finally, speech.

"Quite right," said Washington. "As I recall, Richard was with the baggage train during the initial attack by the French and their savages and thus escaped injury. But he did his duty as bravely as any man there."

Fauquier resumed his introductions. The party included a Reverend Maury of Gordonsville, Virginia, and Maury's wife, and a gangly, red-haired teenaged boy who, Fauquier said, had been placed by his family under the reverend's tutelage for the year. Young Thomas Jefferson, it seemed, was a talented fiddler: he had entertained a gathering the previous evening at the governor's palace. Harry wondered if he had yet been introduced to the *Rules of Civility & Decent Behaviour*.

"We are all proud of our George for his conduct at the Monongahela," said Maury. "He had two horses shot from under him and ended the battle with several musket-ball holes in his jacket."

"It was my great fortune to escape harm," said Washington. His attention shifted back to Maddie. "Fortune has favored your gallant fiancé as well, Miss McLeod."

"I've heard that Colonel Ayerdale has been lucky indeed," said Jefferson, his raw adolescent voice eager and bright. "He was later detached to Fortress Oswego but rode out for another assignment the day before the French overran it."

Washington succumbed to a fit of coughing. By his face Harry guessed he had been Jefferson's source for this information. Oswego had been a costly defeat. Ready to believe the worst about Ayerdale anyway, Harry perceived that his having managed to avoid combat both there and at the Monongahela reflected no credit on him. Jefferson's expressive face darkened as he recognized his faux pas.

"Well, our side has been winning more than its share of victories since those early days of the war," said Fauquier, breaking the awkward stillness. "Having recently arrived on these shores myself, I can tell you that His Majesty entirely shares the commitment of his government to finally throw Louis's minions off this continent. Perhaps General Wolfe will put an end to the whole matter before the summer is out."

Nods of approval greeted his mention of Wolfe. Harry had heard only a smattering about the young British officer who had been given the task of driving the French from their stronghold at Quebec. But all the tidbits were good.

Fauquier said, "I read a dispatch only this morning that more of the general's ships have left Louisbourg and are heading for the Saint Lawrence. By now they should be well on their way, perhaps even arrived by now, depending on winds and tides. I understand Colonel Ayerdale has volunteered to catch up with them there."

"And I have decided to accompany him," said Maddie. "I shall not be content to while away my time amid the comforts of New Bern or Williamsburg, while our country is at war. I wish to share the same privations as my beloved during this difficult time."

Fauquier's eyes crinkled with good humor. "I salute your patriotism, Miss McLeod. I have observed that soldiers often perform better on the battlefield when they are well cared for."

Although Maddie already had told him of her plan, Harry felt suddenly warm, as if taken by a fever. He had heard bawdy tales of what members of the New Bern militia referred to as camp followers, unmarried women who accompanied men to war. They tended to be prostitutes and scullery servants. He thought to take Maddie aside and urge her to have the ceremony before leaving or maybe aboard their ship. Then he wondered if that would not be the greater of two evils, as it would be less easily undone. Maybe if they spent more time together before marrying, Maddie could discover for herself what Harry until now had only suspected: that Ayerdale's nature had a dark side.

"You must tell me more concerning your pursuit of criminals," said Madame Contrecoeur, turning again to Harry. "If I were to go astray, would you arrest me? I am certain I would be helpless to resist such a strong man." This drew titters from all except Harry, who was helpless to keep blood from rushing to his face. "Opposition being futile," she boldly pressed, "I would be inclined to surrender willingly to my fate."

Maddie said, "Mister Woodyard's wife back in North Carolina might have something to say about that."

This drew more laughter, though Maddie was not smiling. It took no gift of insight to see she was upset. But by what right? As one betrothed to another, she had no standing to question Harry's fidelity. Then he thought of his own position. What authority had he to question her? She had every right to do as she pleased. Should he even mention the episode at Rosewood? She might take it as an act of jealousy, a spiteful attempt to deny her whatever bit of happiness their marriage might bring.

Another question began to gnaw at him. What if he were not married? If he were free, would he have any chance of starting over with Maddie? Of winning this now grown-up, worldly wise woman? At the same moment the thought entered his mind, he felt he had sinned against Toby.

Lacking anything witty from Harry to prolong the teasing chatter, the party began breaking up. The horses were assembled at the gate and now awaited the starter pistol. Still chuckling over the Baroness's naughty remarks, Fauquier said to Harry in parting, "Beware of French intrigues."

★

She was sitting at a small table at a side window of Shields Tavern, where Harry and Noah had rented a bed. Still in her lavender gown, sipping ale with a well-dressed older man. Noah had retired early, missing supper on account of a stomach complaint. Harry spotted her at the same time he caught her eye. She beckoned him over.

"I don't want to intrude, Madame," he said.

"It is no intrusion at all. My friend was just leaving. And please, do me the honor of calling me Jacqueline."

The man, who by his age could have been her father, got to his feet in the dutiful way of one who has heard a command and bade them a good evening. Harry noted that Jacqueline did not think it necessary to introduce them.

"How do you come to be in Williamsburg?" Harry made bold to ask after they had ordered food. Feeling somewhat more relaxed, though still on edge in the presence of such unearthly beauty.

"Oh, Harry," she said, giving his name a winsome French turn. "It is such a dreary tale. My family has served royal households for centuries as chamberlains, cupbearers, masters of horse. Very honored positions. We began losing our status, then our property, and finally our very liberty when we embraced the teachings of your great philosopher John Calvin. I escaped five years ago with my life but with almost nothing of my estate. Through a fortuitous connection I found employment as household manager and personal secretary to the governor of Massachusetts, the wonderful General Shirley. His wife is French, you know. When he returned to England I found a similar position here with his friend Governor Dinwiddie. Now dear Robert is gone as well. Regrettably for me, Monsieur Fauquier has his own household staff."

She kept her eyes mostly downcast as she spoke. Giving leave for Harry to study the contours of her bare shoulders.

"So, there it is, Harry." She sighed. "I still dare not return to my estate in France. For the present, these delightful people and this enchanted land of Virginia hold me like one of Mister Gilbert's attracting stones. But this is all so tedious. You must tell me more about your mission to find this murderer."

Over more ale, along with cuts of cold salted ham, sweet potatoes, cabbage, and a curiously tasty soup made from peanuts, Harry repeated his story. He added more details about how the bodies were discovered by the tinker, their odd positions, the puzzlement of the baby, and how he found the Masonic badge. He also told her about the hand-drawn nautical chart of Pamlico Sound.

"How intriguing," she said. "May I see?"

Harry got out the paper from his coat pocket. She looked it over briefly and gave it back.

"Monsieur, you have my sympathies. It would appear you have very little to help you."

"I will keep looking for answers until every question I have is satisfied and I can go no further. Only then will I stop."

"Judging from your ardor, I have no doubt you will never give up."

"I'm hoping this fellow Bannerman might have something to say about the badge."

Jacqueline suddenly reached across the table and put her hand on Harry's.

"I just thought of something. General Shirley was a member of the Freemasons. As it happens, a box of his Masonic books found its way into my possession when he was packing to return to England. I have kept it, hoping to return it someday in person. Could one of these books contain the key to the code?"

"That would seem unlikely."

"Nevertheless, you said yourself that you will continue until all questions are answered. It could not hurt to look, isn't it so?"

Harry could not disagree.

As they talked on, Jacqueline reminiscing about her life in southern France, comparing it to the Virginia countryside, the conversation began to take on the quality of a dream. Harry had never been so far from home, never even outside of North Carolina. Now he was in the storied capital of Virginia, a far more important colony than his own. Why, just this day he had conversed with a royal governor and a war hero. And now he shared a meal with an aristocrat, a great beauty from France by way of an almost mythical place in the distant North called Massachusetts. He wondered if he might at any moment wake up and find himself back in his own straw bed with his former indentured servant, now wife, Toby. And see that all of this had been but the improbable adventure of a slumbering mind.

As he watched Jacqueline's dainty movements and listened to her musical speech, he knew that if he were dreaming, he had no choice but to face the challenges of unfolding events. Including that which was unfolding now.

★

Jacqueline's rooms turned out to be located in a handsome brick house with double chimneys only two blocks from the palace. No one else was there: the owners were away on a shopping tour of London. An elderly servant brought a decanter of brandy and two snifters into the drawing room, which was subtly perfumed by lavender-infused candles. At Jacqueline's request the man also produced a wooden packing box from her chambers, then disappeared.

"How exciting," she said as she removed the lid. "The current regime in my country views Freemasonry with a certain ambivalence, but even there it has become popular among some highborn families."

The box held a dozen books. Between large sips of the brandy—the best Harry had ever had—he held each underneath an oil lamp beside his chair. There were collected treatises on alchemy, astrology, and metaphysics. Two books dealt specifically with the history of the Freemason movement, accounts of its supposed ancient origins and of its revival and spread around the world in recent years. Harry found several pages devoted to three North Carolina entities: the New Hanover County lodge, Saint John's in Wilmington, and New Bern's Royal White Hart Lodge, which the judge had so strongly hinted, if not promised, that Harry would one day join.

But nothing of secret codes.

"I need to get up," he said after a while. But his muscles ignored him. Jacqueline, who had been sitting on a small sofa opposite his chair as he went through the books, now seemed to float over in his direction. Then she was beside his chair, below him, somehow situated on the carpet, her lovely dress spread around her like the interwoven petals of a blossom. He made another effort to get up, but realized that she was now holding him down, seemingly effortlessly, by the supernatural power of one finger pressing against his chest.

"*Chéri*, must you leave so soon?" she asked. He could not think of a good answer. He regarded her with hooded eyes, chin sinking farther into his chest, inhaling her beauty. She returned to the subject of past lives. Days spent consorting with the royal family at the Château de Versailles before her family's religious conversion and subsequent downfall. Herself in America with Governor Shirley in his Boston mansion surrounded by English hedges and junipers and birds that held singing contests in the gardens every morning. She spoke of Shirley's French-born wife, an unreasonably jealous woman who clung to her Catholic faith despite the Protestant world she had entered as Shirley's bride after his first wife died. Something about Shirley's recently having been called back to Britain to answer charges of having allowed military information to fall into the hands of the enemy. And, as a result, his household manager, Jacqueline, had once again been cast adrift, without home or country, until she made her way into the graces of His Majesty's deputy in Virginia.

As Harry was trying to make sense of this narrative, he realized that the lady was undoing his clothing. He made to get up again, but she was on top of him, her slender, busy fingers working their way down the buttons of his shirt. Breathing in the flowery scent of her breasts, he discovered his hands seemed to be moving of their own volition. Exploring the subtle transition between her slender waist and slight bulge of hips. Tracing those delicate contours as if answering commands from someone other than himself.

Her face was nuzzling the area just below Harry's belt when his passion exploded. It was sudden and ferocious. His first reaction was astonishment, followed by the briefest moment of mindless ecstasy. And then, mortification.

With a great effort, he succeeded in nudging her away. "Madame . . ." he began. She interrupted with surprised laughter.

"*Mon dieu!* I see that the dragon is disarmed. All of his fire has gone out of him."

"I have no words to say how embarrassed I am," he said. "This has never happened before."

Indeed, throughout his unmarried days, when Harry had found no shortage of friendly female companions, he had prided himself on giving pleasure before receiving it, if not arranging for both things to happen at once. Another new experience: In the short span of his marriage to Toby he had never been unfaithful. Sinful thoughts had come into his mind, especially when he found himself outside of Toby's company and in the vicinity of some lady from his rowdy past. But he had never seriously considered overturning his vows. Now, as he struggled to get free of this enchantment, he tried to imagine the consequences of what had just happened.

"It is nothing," Jacqueline said, still chuckling. "I am flattered by your passion. But do not worry. There will always be another time."

"With all deference, Madame, I sincerely hope not. I am married."

"Of course you are." She continued smiling but now seemed perplexed. As if wondering what one thing had to do with the other.

He made a concerted effort to get out of his chair and nearly toppled onto the floor. She steadied him onto his feet, then half guided, half pushed him into another room and onto a bed. The last shard of thought that passed through his conscious mind had to do with the unbelievable fairness of Jacqueline's skin. And the as-yet-unresolved mystery of what the rest of her looked like.

★

It was morning when his eyes came open again. Raw sunlight streamed through cracks in the room's tall window shutters, which had been thoughtfully closed.

Jacqueline was not to be seen. He found a folded letter on the dressing table. She had gone riding with Monsieur Fauquier and some other friends. She said how much she had enjoyed his company and looked forward to their next meeting, though she did not propose a particular time or place. Then:

> I have given more Thought to the matter of your Purfuit, and I beg of you to Defift. If your Sufpicions are correct, you could find Yourfelf in Grave Danger. The Freemasons are a Wealthy and Powerful People with tentacles everywhere. I cannot imagine why a Member would want to difpatch an apparently simple Planter's Family. In all events I believe they would not hefitate to deal in the harsheft terms with Any One seeking to bring one of their Own to Account for fuch a crime as Murder. For your own fake, and that of those who love you, return to North Carolina and refume the Contented Life I am sure you have there. Try to put the terrible Epifode out of your Mind.
>
> Yr loving Flower always,
>
> Jacqueline

CHAPTER 13

35: Let your Discourse with Men of Business be Short
and Comprehensive.

—*Rules of Civility*

BANNERMAN'S STORE WAS LARGE AND WELL STOCKED. AN ENTIRE
room contained only furniture. In an adjoining room, shelves lining
the walls displayed smaller articles that a well-found household would
need to function with grace and style: porcelain and pewter dishes,
glassware, cutlery, frying pans, saucepans, bowls, pepper boxes, and
silver and brass candlesticks. An entire section consisted of leather-
bound collections of famous sermons and other works of literature.
Next to this, sliding drawers contained necklaces, bracelets, rings, and

brooches. One tray was devoted entirely to various objects of Masonic finery.

Noah, whose gut had recovered enough to join Harry for a morning biscuit and small beer at the tavern, gravitated to the books while Harry looked over the stock of jewelry. The middle-aged woman minding the store hovered around Harry.

"We can fill any special request you may have, anything at all," she said when it seemed he was about to leave the collection without having shown any interest. "We have two jewelers here in Williamsburg who accept commissions. And, of course, we have direct ties with some of the finest houses in London." To this she added in a whisper, "Paris, too. We don't widely advertise it during these times, but if you desire something of a Gallic nature I am certain that my husband, Mister Bannerman, could make arrangements."

"I saw him at the races yesterday," said Harry. "He very kindly offered to look at this for me." Producing the brooch. "I'm hoping he can give me an opinion as to its origins."

He watched her face closely for any sign of recognition but saw none. With a flourish of compliments on Harry's good taste in possessing an object of such high quality, she begged his leave to fetch the merchant.

Bannerman was in better humor. "This is a rather fine piece," he said, holding it under his eyepiece. "An exceptional example of cloisonné. The blue of the lapis lazuli inlays beautifully complement the gold, which appears to be of the highest quality. May I ask how you happened to come by this? Did you say something about a murder?"

"It fell into my hands unexpectedly." Harry saw no advantage in going into any more detail. Either Bannerman had forgotten about what Harry had said about a murder, or had decided to ignore it.

"Do you wish to sell it? I'm sure I could make you an attractive price." Peering again through his glass, this time with the eye of a businessman, he added, "Of course, I would need to take something off for these little signs of wear."

"Thank you, but I am only the person who found it. Is it possible it passed through your hands?"

"I am afraid I have never seen this piece. I surely would recall if I had."

Harry absorbed this disappointment, then said, "Can you make any guesses as to what these markings on the back side might mean?"

"They are a Masonic code, of course. I myself have not yet attained membership here in the Williamsburg lodge, though I have been proposed, and so I could not begin to decipher it for you. Nor would I were I a member, since I would then be sworn to secrecy."

"Could you say how a person might have come to own it? Who the owner might have got it from?"

"I could make a good guess. Jacob Merkly is our foremost dealer in Masonic finery in this country. A piece of this quality almost certainly was made in England for the American trade and of equal near certainty it would have passed through the House of Merkly."

"And where might I find this place?"

Bannerman looked at Harry with the stunned expression of someone who just realized he was talking to an ignoramus.

"Why, on High Street, of course. Philadelphia."

★

"I know the place well," said Noah. They were lounging on a bench on the green in front of the capitol, the schoolmaster gnawing an apple. "Philadelphia is really not that far from here. The postal roads are much better than the ones we traveled from New Bern. I would say five days of purposeful riding, assuming no detours or stopovers. Fewer ferry crossings, too."

"I'm afraid I would run out of money," said Harry, putting into words what he had already been wrestling with. "Besides, I need to get back home. Toby needs me."

"From what I've seen of Martin, I am sure he is capable of running your plantation in your absence. And Toby seems very resourceful herself."

The two thoughts, Martin and Toby, collided in Harry's imagination. He wondered if there was any other reason he should make for home. Martin was a handsome man, his darkness adding an exotic touch to his regular features. When he was in the company of ladies, Harry had noticed, they were always taking an interest in their own appearance, touching at their faces and hair. Rumors had reached his ears about Martin's leisure activities when errands kept him in town by himself overnight.

"I suppose it depends on the importance you attach to finding the owner of this badge," said Noah.

"The money question trumps all. I just can't be sure I have enough to continue."

"I'll give you what you need."

Harry smiled. "The itinerant schoolmaster, living in a barn, offers the plantation owner a few pounds to cover his expenses. That's a good one."

"I am far from penniless." Noah hesitated, as if deciding whether to continue. "The truth is, I have a great deal of money. Some of it is in the form of paper currency hidden in my saddlebag. The rest is coinage and metal bar held in trust by my solicitor in Philadelphia. It was an inheritance from my grandfather. He didn't trust my father to conserve enough to pass along to his favorite grandson. And for good reason. My father, when he was young, spent all his money on academic pursuits that held no promise of remuneration. Grandfather had grown wealthy in the shipping and warehousing businesses and considered my father's interests in the natural world trivial and wasteful."

"I can't accept such a large amount of money."

"'Large' is a matter of comparison. You have been a good friend to me, Harry, with no prospect of compensation. I would consider it an honor to assist in bringing your killer to justice."

"I will agree only on condition it be treated as a loan. Which I may not be able to repay for a time. And maybe not in cash."

"As you wish."

"I guess you would like to go and see your family in Philadelphia."

"I won't be going with you. I'm afraid my father and I are not the best of friends. In fact, we have stopped speaking to each other."

"And how did that come about?"

"Let us just say we have fundamental differences about our purposes on Earth. Unfortunately, we are both passionate about our own points of view, and it has led to a fair amount of ugliness. When the time comes for his funeral, I will not go."

"That's a terrible thing, to be so angry with your father."

"Believe me, it's mutual."

Harry started to say how much he missed his own father and wished he knew for certain whether he was even alive. But he kept silent lest it sound like lecturing.

"I appreciate your offer of money," Harry said. "But I won't go to Philadelphia without you."

Now it was on Noah to be surprised.

"I enjoy your company," Harry said, "and I will need help along the way. I value a friendly face for support and advice in these foreign lands. I really don't think I could do it otherwise." Stretching the truth a bit to assist his case. But not by far.

"Surely that is not so. You've already proven your ability to navigate Virginia. The rest of our planet, and the people in it, are not much different from what you've already seen. And I need to return to North Carolina to resume my teaching."

"How urgent could that be? You have no actual position to go back to. If you want me to succeed in finding the killer and rescuing Comet Elijah, you'll come."

Noah took out a fresh apple and wiped it on his sleeve, a look of concentration on his face. Harry accepted his offer of a bite.

★

The attack came on their fourth day back on the road.

They had spent the previous night at a tavern in the city of Annapolis that catered to rough seafarers. A short while after ordering food, a man sat down at their table without asking. He was somewhat more fashionably dressed than the other customers but had a thuggish face and loud manner. His nose in particular had an uneven look to it. Harry introduced himself and Noah.

"You can call me Mister Rafferty," the man replied, looking around as if to find someone to take his order. Then, turning to Harry again, "I've not seen your face before. What's your hailing port?"

"North Carolina."

"Oh, that's too bad. I once had the misfortune of conducting a bit of business in North Carolina."

"And what was the exact nature of your misfortune?" asked Noah in a lighthearted vein.

"Where to begin? The climate is disgusting. Your reeking pines, your bleak barrens, your fetid swamps. Disease is everywhere. Lodgings are sparse and of low quality. If I may speak honestly, I preferred a blanket on the ground over your vermin-ridden dwellings. I believe it is actually possible to poison yourself just by breathing the air."

"Well, you are in fine company with your opinions," said Harry. He threw Noah an amused look, wondering if this was some sort of initiation Marylanders subjected strangers to. Or if the man was simply feeble of mind. "Our dear governor has done nothing but whine ever since he got there."

"But the worst are the people," Rafferty continued. "They are the vilest race of villains I have yet to see upon the earth. No honor, no religion, no morality among them. They are a perfect hotchpotch of bankrupts, pirates, and libertines. Their lack of good breeding is evident from their swinish nature, which I expect comes from their unreasonable appetite for pig flesh. Pork makes for hoggishness and inclines them to the yaws. They grunt rather than speak. And the women." Rafferty paused as if searching for words adequate to sum up his disdain. "They are ugly, ignorant, and whorish, the lot of them.

One of the local tarts in New Bern tried to bed me, but I couldn't bear her breath. It smelled of turpentine."

Seemingly finished, Rafferty fixed Harry with a bellicose stare.

Under other circumstances Harry would have been upon the man by now. He was willing to bear most any slander of his place of birth, but he could not tolerate anyone insulting North Carolina women, who, by definition, included his mother.

He already had taken a measure of Rafferty's potential for self-defense. Though stoutly built, and with evidence of past combat on his face, he seemed a bit on the elderly side. Forty-five or fifty at least. Harry judged that a swift attack, a straight-on jab with rigid fingertips to the throat, followed by a quick volley of lefts and rights to the gut, or a simple roundhouse to the jaw if Rafferty refused to stand and offer his belly, should put him on the floor with the least effort. But Harry was tired from the day on the road and had not yet begun to feel the liberating properties of the ale they had been sipping. It also played on his mind that he did not want the slightest hint of misconduct on his part making its way back home. Getting into a brawl in a Maryland tavern might call for more explanation than the satisfaction of maiming the brute was worth.

The barmaid provided a distraction by delivering their supper. Harry was relieved to remember he had not asked for pork. Rafferty waved away her offer of food.

Making plain they were finished talking, Harry and Noah began to eat in silence. Rafferty made some mutterings that Harry could not catch, then got to his feet and left the establishment.

After a few moments Noah said, "What did he say about the women?"

"Ugly, ignorant, and whorish, if I recall rightly."

"I have to disagree. I haven't found them all that ugly."

Harry shook his fork in Noah's face and resumed eating.

★

The next morning they boarded a boat to cross the Chesapeake Bay. The ferryman was about to cast off when Rafferty rode up in the company of two others. They looked like younger, more physically adept versions of their previous night's companion.

"I believe I spotted that pair last night," Noah said in a low voice. "They were seated at the table next to us and followed our fond companion out the door."

The two parties stayed at opposite ends of the vessel, ignoring each other. Harry fed Annie chunks of carrots to help keep her mind off the seagoing experience.

Upon landing, Rafferty and his friends took to their horses and rode off at a fast pace. To Harry's relief, they took a road that headed in a roughly southerly direction, not the postal road that went east and ultimately north toward Philadelphia.

"This makes me feel right at home," said Harry as they passed through another pine forest. "We have loblollies like these on our property, though most of what we have is longleaf."

"*Pinus taeda*," Noah said. "It's the Latin name that's been given the loblolly pine by our great classifier, Carl Linnaeus. The needles are somewhat shorter than those of the longleaf. I've seen many of the latter in North Carolina and Virginia, but I would guess we are now passing through their northernmost extent. They are rare in Pennsylvania."

"Is this something every educated person knows? Or just the ones in Philadelphia?"

"My father drilled into me the new names for plants and animals until I could repeat them in my sleep. I am sufficiently infused that I think I will never be free of these Latin words or the smell of small corpses drying out in trunk rooms."

"I can see value in knowing what plants can be eaten. Comet Elijah taught me about those."

"I confess I am glad to know something of the natural world. But *modus omnibus in rebus*. Moderation in everything. My father cares only for natural science. He is obsessed with the subject to the point that he feels nothing for the sufferings of ordinary specimens of mankind."

"The well-to-do have better things to think on than the plight of the lower orders," Harry said. He was tempted to add "like me" but thought it would sound too awkward.

"My faith requires concern for human sufferings. We are Quakers going back three generations. I saw a good deal of misery while growing up in Philadelphia, and I resolved to spend my life doing what I could to alleviate it. But by the time I'd finished college I had concluded that the best way was not to hand around alms to beggars but to teach people to read, write, and do computations. In the country we are fortunate to have been born in, any man can rise above his origins. Unlike the state of things in Europe. Education is the key to doing this."

"Well, in the case of the Campbells, they weren't rich, but I wouldn't say they were living in misery, either."

"I came to North Carolina in the first place because it is reputed to have the fewest people in all the Atlantic colonies who can read." Noah turned in his saddle and made a respectful bow. "I mean no offense, but that seems to be the fact. We've spoken of this before. I hope to live long enough to see a basic education free to all in America. But one must start someplace."

Harry said, "I take no offense. What little education I have, my mother paid dearly for."

"Also, I'd taken a special interest in Andrew and his peculiar state of mind. I could barely keep his attention long enough to teach him anything at all. I was studying him, looking for some pattern to his behavior that might suggest stratagems of treatment, both for his sake and that of other children who suffer the same curse. Over the past several weeks, I'd come to believe I was making progress. Patience, and rewarding them when they do well, are two of the keys to over-coming the scourge of an unsettled mind, I've come to believe. Who knows what cosmic purpose our coming-together might have served, had he lived."

"Maybe you're going too hard on your father. Maybe he is one of those in this world who are making discoveries that you will one day be teaching to new generations."

"Why, Harry, I do believe you've picked up Comet Elijah's trick of wandering into people's minds. I confess I've recently begun having the same thoughts. Especially now that it appears he and I may meet again sooner than I'd expected. Maybe we can find some common ground after the ugliness that's passed between us."

The midmorning sky had been darkening in the west as they talked, indicating an approaching thunderstorm. Now a breeze gathered. Harry was peering around for possible shelter when three men rode out of the forest not more than twenty yards ahead. It was Rafferty and his two companions, each with a pistol in hand. They must have somehow circled and gotten ahead of them.

Harry brought Annie up short. Barely taking time to rein in their own horses, the Rafferty crew fired almost in unison. Harry felt more than heard a ball whiz past his left shoulder. Noah rocked backward in his saddle. His horse reared and he fell off.

Their assailants tossed their pistols aside and reached for fresh ones. But before they could shoot again, Harry had one of his own out and cocked. Aiming toward the center of Rafferty's breast, he pulled the trigger. At that range he reckoned his chances of success were about even. Rafferty reeled back, nearly but not completely falling off his mount.

Two more balls twittered past Harry. Blinded now by billows of gunsmoke, he grabbed his other pistol and fired in the direction he had last seen Rafferty's two companions. An accusing cry let him know he had hit flesh.

He slung the second pistol aside and pulled the tomahawk from his belt. Spurring Annie forward into the cloud of smoke, which the breeze was turning back on the attackers, he collided nearly head-on with the unwounded man. This one was now holding a sword. But before he could make use of it, Harry sank the ax into his forehead.

He wrenched it free and watched as the man toppled over, eyes crossed like a simpleton.

Through the smoke Harry could see Rafferty still upright on his horse but sagging, his face turning the color of ash bark. Blood spurted from a chest wound: long, arcing geysers erupting at the steady pace of a heartbeat. He would not last much longer.

Clutching his shoulder, the third man took a last look at the chaos, his expression a blend of surprise and pain, and galloped back into the woods.

Noah was lying on his back on the ground, a hole in his chest. Pink froth forming around his nose and mouth. He peered up at Harry with a calm gaze, his large, deep-set eyes unfocused, as if under water. He made to speak but the effort brought on a choking spasm. After that he seemed content to just lie quiet. His eyes wandered, drifting here and there, and finally came back to rest on Harry as if in silent communication, sharing a mystery. He took another shallow, liquid breath. His lips moved as he exhaled. Harry bent closer to hear what he might say. The last thoughts of a man who knew he was dying.

The words were barely audible yet unmistakable. "The children," he said, and then he breathed no more.

Harry spent a long time knelt over the body, grief and disbelief cycling through his mind. Trying to accept that the friendly, gentle spirit that lived behind those intelligent eyes had stolen away. He realized more completely than before how he had been liking Noah's company and looking forward to learning more from the best-educated, and possibly smartest, person he was sure he had ever known. He thought about Noah's plans for a school for orphans, now never to come to pass. How Noah Burke might have explained what cosmic purpose could have been served by his own death right here, right now, on the swelling tide of his life.

He wrapped him in a blanket and gently placed him over his saddle, then put the other two bodies over their mounts. Still marveling over the suddenness with which it had all happened. In Harry's experience, life usually unfolded gradually. Even the onset of death generally offered a chance to prepare one's self. But sometimes life's events came with the suddenness of lightning or an earthquake or the popping of a bubble in the flow of a stream.

It also occurred to him that Comet Elijah's training had worked. Maneuvers with knives, tomahawks, pistols, and long guns had become as natural to Harry as eating or sleeping or buttoning a pair of breeches. But it all had been make-believe. He had always wondered whether, or how well, any of it would work against a real opponent. In his youthful brawling he had never been called on to resort to the intricate rules of the tomahawk. But just now he had given battle in a circumstance that was no drill. He had played a game whose stakes were life and death, and he had won.

It was also a revelation to see just how easy killing really was. He wondered if he would ever come to regret having taken two human lives. Comet Elijah had warned him on this score. Regret almost certainly would set in at some future time, he had lectured.

But in this instance, Harry doubted it.

★

The sheriff in Annapolis identified Rafferty and his dead friend. The latter was the brother of the one who had escaped. All three were tough no-accounts who had spent their lives scuttling around the bottom planes of the city, mostly the docks, committing petty thievery when opportunities arose and offering themselves for whatever odious jobs came along, usually for cash currency in advance. The sheriff theorized that their attack was a rare act of highway robbery. Rare because such business needed more planning than they were known for undertaking. He had no explanation for Rafferty's quarrelsome nature the previous evening, other than that he might have been trying to take Harry's measure as a prospective victim. Decide how formidable an adversary he might prove. When it came to the actual deed, the sheriff theorized, they had opened fire because they had lost their courage at the last minute and acted with mindless alarm. Typical of the harbor scum they were.

"I doubt we'll see again the one who got away," the sheriff said. "My guess is he'll go west, try and make a new life for himself on the frontier. Fewer inquisitive people out there."

CHAPTER 14

108: When you Speak of God or his Atributes, let it be
Seriously & wt. Reverence. Honour & Obey your Natural
Parents altho they be Poor.

—RULES OF CIVILITY

August 8, 1759
Annapolis, Maryland

My Beloved Wife,
I Pray this finds You & every One well. Noah Burke is dead. But do
not be Alarmd. I was able to fend off ye attackers that came out of
the Woods and Killt two of 'em. They were trying to rob us I guef.
 I am on my way to ye Cittie of Philadelphia to talk too Someone
who awt to no about ye Freemasons Ornament which I found at ye

Campbells House. I am forry I have not Writt'n before. Ye Sheriff shewed me a copy of Davis' North Carolina Gazette which arrived heer by Packet Ship yefterday when there was an Article about Comet Elijah's effort to efcape from ye Gaol which must have takn place a day or fo after we rode off. I wifh he had Sukfeed'd, since now he is waring irons all ye time, I fear he will be moft Uncomfortable. Noah gave me fome Money before He Died to continue my Enqwirees. I mifs Your fweet Companionship & am moft Concerned for ye Bufi-nefs of ye Plantation but I feel I Muft do all in my Powr to Prevent Comet Elijah from Hanging. Alfo I defsine to deliver ye awfull News of Noahs Death to His Familie in Philadelphia myfelf.

Yr. moft ob. & Loving Hufband & etc,

Henry Woodyard

IT WAS HIS FOURTH ATTEMPT AND, THOUGH STILL NOT PERFECT, IT would have to do. Writing was just too much of a trial. Also, Harry had found only four sheets of writing paper among Noah's belongings. Rereading the final version, he wondered if he should have mentioned his experiences in Williamsburg. The governor and his fashionable friends. He probably should have explained how it had been the storekeeper Bannerman's information that sent him off in the direction of Philadelphia.

Of course, Madame Contrecoeur's name also was missing. And he had decided against confiding his suspicion, which had been mounting, that the attack might have been related to his pursuit of the Campbells' killer. He did not want Toby to suspect he was losing his reason. Such a connection never would have even occurred to Harry had it not been for the baroness's note and her reference to the power of the Masons, with their tentacles. The threat they might pose to someone seen to be pursuing one of their members. Rather than Rafferty's taking a measure of Harry and Noah at the tavern as potential robbery victims, it seemed ever more thinkable that Rafferty had been trying to provoke Harry into a fight. One the two younger men would finish in Rafferty's favor, with Harry lying dead, or at least incapacitated, on the floor.

He hired a carpenter to nail together a coffin and scratch out a simple inscription on a slab of wood to stand as a marker until a proper marble could be put up. The rector of a local church granted permission for burial there the next day and accepted payment in advance to say some words. Harry employed the carpenter and his son to work into the night digging the hole and installing a timber plank lining.

These arrangements were costly, but Harry had discovered a way to pay for them. In Noah's saddlebag was a money belt containing a thick wad of Pennsylvania paper currency. Assuming a roughly equivalent rate of exchange in North Carolina, it was well above what a skilled tradesman in New Bern might earn in two years.

Harry reckoned he should return to Noah's family what he would not need to get to Philadelphia and back to North Carolina, which should not be much. But for now he allowed himself the burden-free, slightly drunken feeling he imagined rich people felt every day of their lives. He decided to stay the night at a more expensive tavern, one closer to the capitol.

At the cemetery the next morning, under a sky the color of dishwater, the carpenter set the coffin lid aside so Harry could have a last look. Noah was still wearing the blood-stained clothes he had died in. He looked cramped in the box, shoulders pinched together in a shrug. His eyes had come partway open again. Harry pressed them shut with his fingers, then took two coins from his pocket and placed one over each eyelid to keep them down.

It was the same last loving act he had seen his mother perform all those years ago, so Ned's soul could rest.

★

He had died at seven o'clock one morning in the middle of August. Missed his footing, got caught about the waist between two logs rushing downstream on a roiling tide. The life crushed out of him in one agonizingly long moment. Harry's older brother was in the ground before sundown the next day, still looking fresh enough in the face to have been only sleeping.

Talitha had seen a token of death earlier that week. One night a flock of pigeons flew up to her room window, waking her, and, with a great dry battering of wings and claws, nearly tore the window out. She kept this experience to herself at the time, fearing it might pertain somehow to Hendry, her husband, who was still missing in South America. She also worried that by speaking of it she might let out whatever evil it might hold. But she could not have imagined it prophesied Ned's death. She collapsed straightaway onto the ground when she got the news from the river.

Ned had been the adored one. He and Harry were the only children out of six who had lived long enough to walk. Ned was five years ahead of Harry and smarter, stronger, and more handsome. At least so Harry thought, and it seemed to him others did as well. People said Ned took after his father, who was much looked-up-to throughout Craven County. Now Talitha's hopes for the future fell wholly onto Harry. He never got over thinking he was a poor substitute.

Talitha was firm on giving Ned all he was entitled to, even in death. Every ritual had to be observed as befit the family's rising station in the community. But unlike those people of the very highest quality, she had no clothes set aside especially for mourning. She would have picked out something suitable from Soloman's, but everyone knew it was bad luck to wear new clothes to a funeral, so a neighbor made her the loan of her black Sunday gown.

The same neighbor and another friend took over the job of fixing Ned's body. They opened the window in his room to let in fresh air, changed his bed linens, and, when that was done, stretched him out on the bed for bathing and dressing. Meanwhile Natty took a wagon into New Bern and brought back a casket and black armbands for them all to wear. He and some of the other men worked the rest of the day digging a hole and putting in a liner. Talitha had them do this on a small hill across the road from the main house, where Ned would rest alongside the tiny grave markers of his four sisters.

By late afternoon, word of the disaster had traveled through Craven County. Neighbors and friends began arriving, bearing food. Doors and windows remained open, and they lit as few lamps and tapers as were absolutely necessary so as to add as little heat as possible to the day's buildup. The next time Harry saw Ned, he was inside the casket and being carried through the hall and into the front room by four sweaty men with sun-darkened faces. They set him on two tables that had been brought together and removed the coffin lid. Ned's face was pale, but, looking into it, Harry could hardly believe the life had entirely gone out of him. Natty noticed Harry staring and figured out what he was thinking. He whispered into his ear that no one could have survived such injuries as Ned had suffered, but they would keep an eye on him for any signs of life just the same.

The traffic of visitors slowed but did not stop as the evening wore on. Hushed speaking continued past midnight. Recollections of Ned. Little-boy antics. Funny, grown-up things he would say. How when he was seven he had saved Harry from a sea eagle that had dived into the yard and set its claws into the squirming two-year-old. The bird was having trouble getting back off the ground with its load. Ned beat on it with a toy musket Natty had made for him, chasing it here and there as it tried and failed to gain altitude. Finally, it let Harry go and flew off.

Natty and Harry stayed up after Talitha showed the last visitors out and took to her bed. With all the windows and doors open, somebody had to keep watch for cats, which will come to corpses if allowed. They will claw or scratch at exposed flesh or lie down inside the coffin, keeping company with the deceased. But none came by that night.

Talitha returned her borrowed gown the day after the funeral. She wore her store-bought black armband until a year had passed. On the morning of the 366th day, she made a breakfast of eggs and fried pork for Harry and Natty, then said she was going into town to buy a new metal plow for the late-summer planting. It seemed the passing seasons had brought her round the full circle of life, death, and the coming of life again. That is what Harry made of it.

It was not until much later that he realized Ned's death, hard as it was on them all at the time, had served a purpose. It made Harry tougher.

CHAPTER 15

19: Let your Countenance be pleasant but in Serious
Matters Somewhat grave.

—RULES OF CIVILITY

HE HAD NO TROUBLE FINDING NOAH'S HOUSE IN PHILADELPHIA. THE
first man he asked pointed the way, looking at Harry as if he must have
been from another country.

Peter Burke himself answered the door. He was unmistakably
Noah's father: heavier around the midsection but thin-boned, long-
fingered, and with the same hollowed-out eyes that had given Noah
the slightly somber look that suited his nature. Burke was dressed in
the plain fashion that Harry had come to associate with Quakers.

"I'm afraid I have sad news," Harry said. "I knew your son, Noah, in North Carolina."

Peter Burke made a coarse sigh and his face seemed to fall in on itself. He beckoned Harry inside and, in a tense silence, led him into a parlor on one side of the large central hall. The room was furnished with tables and chairs of simple manufacture that seemed more suited for an unassuming plantation house than a four-story brick-front mansion. One wall was given over to floor-to-ceiling shelves containing row upon row of leather-bound books. In the center of the room was a long pine table whose surface was mostly hidden by scatterings of books, large paper sheets bearing illustrations of plants and animals, and, lying on a metal dinner plate, the carcass of a small brown bird.

"Where is Noah?" Peter said.

"We were attacked by three men on a road outside of Annapolis. Robbers, I reckon. I'm sorry to say Noah was killed by a pistol shot."

Harry heard a shriek. Turning toward the door, he saw a woman he took to be Noah's mother. Peter hurried to her side to steady her.

Harry told his story, how Noah had agreed to accompany him on his search for a murderer. The proceedings that had led them first to Williamsburg, then toward Philadelphia.

"This attack," Peter said. "Did you resist?" They were all seated now, Peter still cradling his wife, whose name was Martha. For a moment Harry considered saying Noah had fallen in a gallant attempt to defeat the robbers. But he told the truth. "They shot at us at almost the same moment they came out of the woods. We didn't even have a chance to put our hands up." Deciding a small lie now would be an act of kindness, he added, "I don't think Noah even had time to understand what was happening. He was killed at once. He did not suffer."

Martha uttered another cry.

"Could this attack have had anything to do with the business you are on?" said Peter. "Your search for the person you say killed this family in North Carolina?"

"It's hard to see offhand how the two things could be connected. Though there is something else. We had seen these men before." Harry recounted their run-in at the tavern the previous night.

"Is it possible this man was trying to provoke a fight? A brawl that his friends might have joined, resulting in your death or serious injury?"

Seeming to take Harry's silence as a yes, Peter said, "Whatever may prove to be the case, I am at your disposal. I will help in any way I can."

They asked more about the attack and what Harry knew of Noah's sojourn in North Carolina. They talked of a journey to Annapolis to see the gravesite and put up a marble. After a while Peter tried to get to his feet, but his knees buckled and he nearly fell to the floor. Harry helped him back into his chair.

"He was so angry when he left," Peter said. "It will forever haunt my soul that he went to his death with these feelings toward me."

"He didn't," said Harry. "Noah told me he'd come to realize he was judging you too harshly. He was looking forward to seeing you again. I believe he wanted to make amends."

"Did he really say that?" said Martha.

"Yes." Then, to Peter, "He also spoke of how glad he was for all the things you taught him."

Peter began to speak, but his throat tightened. "His anger was justified," he finally managed. "I was too dismissive of his interests. As I've grown older, I fear I have lost some of my concern for the human struggle, the kinds of sorrow people are born into and make for themselves. I've been so preoccupied with the natural universe that I've been blind to the world at my doorstep."

Harry stayed the night, falling asleep to the muffled sounds of wailing.

★

The next day, over breakfast, they insisted that Harry keep all of what he had found in Noah's money belt. "Use every farthing to find your killer," said Martha. "And let us know if you need more. If your inquiries should bring clarity to the death of our Noah . . ." She could not finish the sentence.

After they had eaten, Peter went with Harry to the merchant's store. It looked much like Bannerman's except larger and with more of everything. A clerk went to get the owner. While they waited Harry drew a butcher's knife from a slot in a wooden block. The oak handle gleamed softly under coats of lacquer. He tested its heft and balance and the edge, its thinness as it rasped sideways against the ridges of his thumb. As sharp as any blade he had ever held.

"May I compliment you on your taste in cutlery," said Jacob Merkly as he swept through the door, still buttoning his waistcoat. "This is part of a set, the latest production of the Hunter Foundry in Sheffield, just arrived on our shore this week."

"It is a handsome thing," Harry said.

"There is nothing finer than a well-honed knife, don't you think? Just let your mind go for a moment to that first cut through a piece of freshly dressed beef or a cauliflower still crisp from your garden. How the blade glides through the flesh. As if cleaving gossamer. Following your every command even as you think to issue it. I don't know about you, sir, but I find the act of carving a good piece of meat a spiritual as well as sensual experience. It is transporting. Almost as good as a dose of laudanum and probably healthier."

Harry realized he had allowed his jaw to sag on its hinge. He had never thought of a knife in such terms.

"My usual price for something so fine would be two pounds. For my best customers it is one pound, eight shillings, and six pence. That barely covers my purchase cost, but I am a generous man. Also, I buy direct from the foundry and vouchsafe its voyage across the ocean, no factor in between to skinny-up the price." Merkly held up a forefinger as if to stave off an objection. "I can see by your dress and manner that you are a gentleman, a man of quality. And so, for an even pound-and-eight, it is yours to carry home with you this very day."

Before Harry could speak, Peter said, "Jacob, I would like you to meet a young friend of mine, Harry Woodyard."

"Well," said Merkly, his face brightening further, "since you a friend of Peter's, I would be pleased to make you an even better bargain."

Harry decided the only way to get out of the shop without buying a knife was to be direct. He said, "I wonder if you could look at this piece of jewelry and let me know if it might have been sold from your shop." He showed the badge. "I understand you specialize in this kind of thing, and it may have even come from your store."

"I do indeed conduct a brisk business in Masonic *accoutrements*." Merkly laboriously puckered his lips to give the word its French pronunciation, complete with guttural trill. "I keep them locked in a strong cabinet."

"To guard against the licentious gaze of the uninitiated, I suppose," said Peter.

"I myself am a member of our Saint John's Lodge, along with my good friend and customer Benjamin Franklin." He paused and looked at Harry as if awaiting reaction. Harry supposed that by his silence he gave away that he did not know the gentleman.

"Well, let us have a look," said Merkly.

Holding an eyepiece on it, he affirmed Bannerman's judgment. It was a piece of exceptional quality, with its artistic design and skillful execution in the cloisonné style. He also agreed the pine tree represented Massachusetts Bay Colony and that the markings were code.

"It is a cipher commonly employed by Freemasons, I can tell you that. But I could not say its meaning, even if by doing so I would not be breaking an oath. Before even beginning to unstring it, one would need to know a particular word. The author of the code would have selected that word himself. The word, quite literally, is the key that unlocks the cipher." Merkly made an unlocking motion with his hand. To help Harry understand the idea, he guessed.

"It could be any word in the English language or any other that uses our alphabet. Only the author and those to whom he has divulged it would know. Through use of this word, applied to this code, members of his circle of confederates would be able to communicate freely among themselves without fear of the messages' being discovered."

Inspecting the badge further, Merkly said, "This piece might have been commissioned by its owner as a gift to himself—an indulgence, perhaps, to proclaim his membership in the brotherhood in a stylish way. Or it could have been a presentation, something awarded in honor of some deed, some high level of service, by some person or organization with Masonic ties in New England. The inscription may be a slogan having some special meaning to the honoree."

"But the markings aren't even letters," said Harry. "They are short lines and dots."

"Ah-ha." Merkly's face arranged itself into the relieved smile of one who realizes he is finally able to make himself clear. "And therein lies the true ingenuity of our code. Each mark represents a letter of the alphabet. But to recognize the shapes, one must know not only the key word, but also the pattern into which the letters were assembled."

Harry nodded. Not because he understood but out of politeness.

"More than that I must not say, on pain of disgrace and, well, death, I suppose. I fear I may already have given away too much."

"Your standing among the Freemasons is completely safe. I have no idea what you are talking about."

"And so, back to his original question," prompted Peter. "Might you have been the one who sold this medal? Would you be able to identify its owner?"

Merkly's smile turned apologetic. "Oh, I'm afraid not. This line of jewelry is produced especially for the American trade by the House of Wykes on Threadneedle Street in London. Edward Wykes operates under the patronage of the Prince of Wales himself, who, upon the by, is his third cousin once removed. I know Edward well. Good Anglo-Saxon stock. He provisions ladies and gentlemen of the highest quality throughout the kingdom, including the royal household."

"And how might someone in America have come into possession of this particular brooch, if not through yourself?" Harry tried not to let his voice betray his impatience or growing anxiety over the possibility of having traveled so far only to have the road end at a stone wall. Or an ocean.

"I mentioned that Edward Wykes is an acquaintance. Unfortunately I have yet to persuade him that I should handle his business in the colonies. That is done exclusively through a mutual friend of ours. His name is George Johnston. No doubt you have heard of him. Illegitimate son of some English earl or other. Forced to make his living like all the rest of us not born into fortune, by his enterprise."

"I don't expect Mister Johnston might be located here in Philadelphia." Harry hated to even pose the question, so sure the answer would be disappointing.

"Oh, of course not." Merkly stopped short and gave Harry a look that was becoming familiar. He had seen the same expression on the faces of several in Williamsburg, including Bannerman. A look that meant the person was readjusting, downward, his estimation of Harry and his familiarity with the larger world.

"George conducts his business in his adopted city." Merkly pointed his finger toward the ceiling, indicating, Harry guessed, north. "Boston."

CHAPTER 16

98: Drink not nor talk with your mouth full neither Gaze
about you while you are a Drinking.

—*Rules of Civility*

My dareft wife,
I pray thif Letter finds you & ye Plantation well. I feer I will not be
back in tyme to help with the Tobacco Topping but Martin and the
others shud be abel to get all the buds off and if need bee they can
borrow tyme from one or too of the naybors. Also it is not too early
to ftart thinking about burning off ye Underbrush so that Wee may
move abowt freely among ye Pines for a feason of Turpentining. Laft
year Wee made the fires a little to airly and they got out of hand and
fome Trees were Damaged but there is not as much of a Build up
now, fo I am not Overly Worried on thif Accownt. I would like to
know how My Mother and Natty are faering? & if Judge McLeod and
Sheriff Carruthers are very much upfet over My leaving New Bern
without letting Them noe My Intentions. I noe that I have abandoned

my Dutees as Conftable for ye time being but there is not much work for Me in that Realm as Wee are between Court Seshons and there are not likely to be many Writf to be ferved or Prisoners efcorted & ye like. As far as I noe Comet Elija is ye only Prisoner of any Import bein' held at Present and it do not appear to me that He if likely to goe Anywhere until the fuperior Court convenes in Oktober. God willing I will get to the Bauttom of thif Matter well before that happens fo that Poor Old Man may be Free to go about hif Bufinef as before and I will be able to rejoin you and Martin and ye Others in looking after our Plantation. The Trees Wee have been werking are near about empteed of fap & I think they'll not laft Annuther 2 Years before Wee have to move on to ye next ftand for fome Virgin Dip, but they are probably good yet for 2 or 300 Barrels of Defent Turpentine thif Year and a fair amount of Tar & Pitch. Thif should pay off a confiderable fum of our Debt which You are fo worried of efpecially if Wee can once again find fome fmart Yankee Trader who is fkilled at getting his Ship around ye Kings Cuftoms Men.

My Attemps to find ye owner of ye Mafonic Brooch continue since I have been directed to a Merchant in Bofton who feems All But Certain to be able to tell me who ye Owner is & he might Interpret the Writing on the Back, & etc. It would confoom 8 Days of steady Riding to get there but Noahs father Peter Burke fed the Journey can be akomplish'd in about 3 Days by ship. This would alfo fave Labour for Faithful Annie Who is doing well confidering all ye Trials she has been threw. I have already rezerv'd paffage using ye money Noah gave me and expect to leave toomorow.

Yr. moft ob. & Loving Hufband, etc.,

Henry Woodyard

HAVING DELIVERED HIS MAIL TO A SOUTH-BOUND PACKET, HE LOCATED among the thicket of masts waiting at the dock the vessel that would take him north. Two other men fell in behind him in the line of people and horses waiting to board. He realized they were staring at him and then placed their faces. One he knew only as Mackay, from Bath, a portly, red-cheeked planter about the age Harry's father would have been were he still alive. Mackay's companion, a Mister Nelson, was about ten years younger and only slightly less plump. He was captain of the Edenton militia and a representative of that village in the General Assembly. They owned plantations of more or less two thousand acres apiece and were married to sisters. Harry had seen them in New Bern when they were there on business but knew them only in passing. Now it seemed he and they would be spending some time together. He made a note in his mind to get out his *Rules of Civility & Decent Behaviour*, which he had brought along in an act of foresight. There were some subtle points he needed to review regarding persons of higher quality and on which side of them one should place one's self. It varied from one situation to another.

"Gentlemen," Harry said with a bow. "Delighted to see you. Please, go ahead of Annie and me."

"We are the delighted ones and surprised to see you here," said Mackay. "You are most gracious, but, please, stay where you are. We are in no great hurry to get aboard."

Though he could not remember its number, Harry recognized, like an old friend, the principle set forth in the Rules. The less privileged person offers the position of honor. The person of higher quality graciously declines. He congratulated himself on a transaction well conducted.

"Still on the trail of wrongdoers?" asked Nelson.

"You've heard of my travels?"

"People talk of little else at home," said Mackay. "Maybe throughout the whole province. How you're trying to help an Indian cheat the hangman. But, pray, what are you doing in Philadelphia? The last we heard, you were on your way to Williamsburg." A friendly grin made dimples here and there on his puffy, sun-reddened face. "And here you're boarding a ship for Boston."

Harry kept his story short, as they were nearing the head of the queue. He said how his efforts to trace the ownership of a certain object from the Campbells' house had led him to a Williamsburg storekeeper, who had pointed him to another in Philadelphia, who had all but promised that yet another in Boston would be able to identify the owner and thus, in all likelihood, the murderer. As he was compressing these particulars into a few sentences, he realized how someone of a skeptical nature might accuse him of chasing a will-o'-the-wisp.

"Well, your sudden departure caused a stir," said Nelson. "And still does. Every day that goes by with you not at your post, it seems, Judge McLeod takes greater personal affront."

Nelson's words fell on Harry's ears like stone weights.

"What, exactly, has he said?"

"Oh, it's not all that bad," Mackay intervened. An act of kindness. "You know how that old man is. He'll get over it."

"Well, he has relieved Harry of his duties as a constable," Nelson said. He seemed about to comment further but closed his mouth after getting a sharp look from Mackay.

"No permanent damage done, I'm certain," said Mackay. "Olaf can reinstate you just as quickly as he suspended you. Young man, you have many admirers in Craven County, me among them. I hope you will do us the honor of joining us at the captain's table for supper this evening."

"The honor would be mine, gentlemen."

The words sprang to Harry's lips effortlessly, almost as if from another, better-bred person. More proof that some of the Rules had stuck. But his self-confidence had been dealt a blow. He feared that any further proper comportment might be a waste of effort. His downfall possibly was already assured.

★

It was big for a coasting vessel; Harry reckoned a hundred feet long. And it was handsome: decks freshly caulked, pine masts shiny as glass with built-up varnish, and topsides painted dark green from the waterline to the white-trimmed rails. The heady smell of tar and pitch, some of it conceivably from Harry's trees, came off the vessel. A two-masted topsail schooner, American built, Harry was informed by the crew member who helped winch Annie onto the lower deck stables. The whites of her eyes showed during the trip down in the harness, but once in her stall, with Harry giving her chunks of carrots, she seemed to shrug off the experience as just another one of life's small annoyances.

Harry made sure she had fresh hay, then went off to find his bunk. It was sited down a companionway and through a dark passageway near the fo'c'sle. Though he had the cabin to himself, it was tiny, barely enough room to stand beside the wooden bin that held his bedding. The sleeping compartment appeared an inch or so shorter than Harry was tall. He would have to lie with his legs crooked. The single port-hole was too small for a grown man to slip through in an emergency. He resolved to spend as much time on the top deck as possible.

The ship's cook personally served supper in the officers' dining cabin adjacent to the captain's quarters. Harry learned that the com-mander was retired from the British Navy. The only other passenger privileged to join him and his three senior officers was an older man from Boston whose occupation, as far as Harry could gather, had to do with arranging contracts between businessmen in America and Britain.

"You must convey my commendations to the chef," Mackay told the captain, whose name was Biggerstaff. They were doing away with tender slabs of roasted beef with stewed vegetables. The dish made Harry think of his imprisoned friend.

"This is as fine a meal as I've had in any of our best North Carolina taverns," said Nelson.

"We take full advantage of fresh victuals when in port," said Big-gerstaff. He spoke through nearly clenched teeth, a habit Harry had come to associate with certain English aristocrats on the relatively rare occasions that any passed through New Bern. A slight slur indicated he had been sipping from the table's decanter of claret ahead of his guests' arrival. "We shall reprovision again in Boston, but the fresh cuts will run out well before we reach Louisbourg."

"You are going on to Canada?" asked Nelson.

"We will be delivering foodstuffs and munitions to Wolfe's army at Quebec. They seem to have got bogged down there and are running short on supplies." Biggerstaff turned abruptly to Harry and said, "Won't you come with us, young man? The general could use every available patriot to defeat Montcalm."

"I would go if I was free to," Harry said. "But I have a wife and plantation in North Carolina that need me back as soon as possible." He added as an afterthought, "The pitch and turpentine I make this fall will be worth far more to the British Navy than whatever little service I could do for General Wolfe." He felt his face flush, realizing how deceitful he was being. He had every intention of selling that year's output of naval stores directly to Yankee captains for their own dispositions, without coming to the attention of the Crown's customs collectors.

"Our young friend is on an important mission," said Mackay, wiping greasy fingers on his napkin. "He is trying to discover who murdered a Carolina plantation family."

"Indeed?" said Biggerstaff. "Were they friends of yours?"

"Yes."

"Harry is the king's constable in Craven County. Or at least he was," Nelson began. Before he could finish the thought, Harry said, "I'm taking a short holiday while I try to discover the killer."

"And you've come here all the way from North Carolina to do this?" said the captain. "Extraordinary. I had no idea constables in this land involved themselves in such matters. In my country, a constable's duties are fairly limited."

"As they are here. The truth is, the judge I work for does not approve of what I'm doing."

"The victims of this crime must have been very good friends for you to go to such lengths," said another officer.

"There is more to it than friendship or even revenge. An old friend of my family has been falsely accused of the murders. I fear he will be hung if I fail."

Nelson said, "The one they've arrested is an old Indian who helped raise Harry when Harry's father failed to return from the siege of Cartagena."

"Cartagena, you say?" Biggerstaff's eyebrows went up. "God rest your father's soul for his service to Admiral Vernon. I was there as well. First officer aboard the *Shrewsbury*. It was an awful time. We had fifty men killed and wounded by Spanish cannon. But even more died of disease."

"Your Indian friend is not well, I am sorry to report," Mackay said to Harry. "I understand he is barely eating enough to sustain life, and his trial is still a long ways off."

"The horse bettors are making odds he'll never last until October," said Nelson.

"If I am successful, he will be a free man by then. I intend to bring the real killer up before Judge McLeod in shackles."

"I like you very much, Harry," said Mackay, "the way you have turned your life 'round in such a wholesome direction. I wish you success in saving your friend."

They all lifted their glasses to that.

★

Woozy from wine and the brandy served afterward, Harry made his way back to his cabin. He had weighed spending the night on deck but was tired and drunk enough now to think he would have no trouble sleeping below.

It was black as pitch in the passageway. The ship's steward had supplied a lit candle in a tin holder, along with strict instructions not to try to read by its light while in his bunk. There had been a recent outbreak of ship fires caused by people dozing off with candles still burning. He heeded this advice and then, keeping his clothes on for a quick exit if needed, climbed over the wooden plank that formed the inboard side of his bunk. The partition was high enough to prevent him from spilling onto the floor while on a port tack, but this added to his sense of confinement. Blessedly, the warmth of the day had abated and a light breeze was making its way through the porthole.

As his thoughts began to drift, they took on physical shapes. It seemed he could see Toby. She was sitting before a candle, hunched over their eating table, a stack of ledgers to one side, trying to make sense of the plantation's affairs. Sounding the depth of the financial pit she feared they were in. This involved judging relative values. A basket of apples lent, an apple pie due in return. Loan of an ox to fill out a stump removal team for a week in exchange for a bearskin winter coat. Each of these dealings written out in Harry's messy but, for the most part, legible hand—legible to him, at least.

Maddie had been right to turn her back on this kind of a life. Harry's house was perfectly comfortable, as far as he was concerned. It even had some of the finery that enhanced the lives of wealthier residents of Craven County. But these graceful touches were mere tastes of the full measures of luxury that cushioned the daily existence of the better sorts, made the snags and pitfalls of their lives more tolerable. Harry tried to imagine the elegant Maddie spending the rest of her days in such a house as his. Visiting and receiving visits from neighbors whose manners of dress and conversation gravitated toward the simple side of things; their practical talk of the turnings of seasons, plantings and harvests, livestock, babies, elderly parents and their bodily ailments. Art and literature, politics, new discoveries in nature; such topics as would interest Maddie rarely came up at Sunday dinners with his mother and Natty, with his shark's-tooth necklaces and irregular bathing habits. Natty's idea of entertaining conversation had to do with the old days in the swamps of Albemarle country, tales of alligators and supernaturally large mosquitoes and summer nights spent among sand dunes and their whistling grasses, on the lookout for wayward ships.

He did not realize he was asleep until he was roused by a crashing noise. It was a single, sudden violence, like something large and heavy falling against the door of his cabin.

After taking a stunned moment to come fully awake, Harry clawed his way out of the cramped bed. He half expected the door to be splintered apart. But in the darkness it seemed solid to the touch.

Carefully undoing the bolt, he opened the door a crack. It was even darker in the passageway than the cabin. Opening it a smidge further, he focused every bit of wakefulness into his ears but could detect nothing outside of the ordinary creaks and groans of a ship at sea. Whoever or whatever had caused the disturbance either was gone or lurked in the inky stillness. Waiting for Harry.

He closed and rebolted the door. Felt among his belongings until he found his knife and ax. But what then? If someone had tried to get in and found the door too substantial, what would it gain Harry to go outside and confront the threat, if such it was? Maybe someone had simply tripped and fallen, then continued on his way. Somebody big.

Returning to his bunk, he wedged his blades between the mattress and the side partition, sharp sides down. He disliked feeling trapped inside this small space, but another review of his position convinced him to stay.

After what seemed a long time, he relaxed enough to recall another dream that had come to him earlier that night. It must have been triggered by the smoky smells the ship gave off. Martin was tending a tar kiln. It was night. Hot black soup oozed off a pile of smoldering pine logs and into a graded trench, pooling in an earthen basin at its lower end. In the torch-light another servant ladled the result into steel pots to boil down for pitch.

As he felt himself slipping away again, the dream took on an aspect of reality. Toby was there. She was in distress. Running away from some-thing in the house. Running in bare feet, as if having been roused from bed. Heading toward the pit. Martin was looking away at something in the distance. Unaware or, even more frightening, unconcerned about whatever was wrong with Toby. Harry felt powerless to intervene, his muscles turned to lead. He tried to shout a warning cry for help, but his throat was paralyzed. He was strangling in his own panic.

He bolted upright.

Except for a faint glow of stars coming through the porthole, it was still dark. He had no idea what hour it was. But he knew he would not be able to fall sleep a third time that night, and he could not bear to stay in the bunk.

Tucking his blades into his belt, he unbolted the door. Stepped into the passageway, into the drenching blackness. How often Comet Elijah had lectured him about using all his senses, including the hidden ones. He did so now, inching along, one shuffling step at a time, at each step pausing like a coonhound to sample the air.

Finally, a pale light ahead. Maintaining his deliberate pace, he gained the companionway and crept up the stairs. Blades at the ready.

A fog had wrapped itself around the ship. It was so dense that neither bow nor stern was visible. The air seemed lifeless, but a whisper of water along the hull indicated they were moving. Going in the same direction of whatever wind there was, making the illusion of no wind at all. Sailing in the same direction as the drifting cloud that enclosed them.

A rustle of clothing from behind made him instinctively dodge, almost but not quite avoiding the blow. He spun around, willfully ignoring the pain filling his right shoulder.

His assailant was a big man with a square, bony face and coal-black eyes, dressed in tradesmen's clothes and a sailor's woolen cap and holding a belaying pin. It had missed Harry's head but caused enough shoulder damage to make him totter.

Harry ducked another blow, this time grabbing a gigantic arm as it went by. With a shrug, the man broke Harry's grip. But before he could have a third swing, Harry crouched and, pumping his own legs like pistons, drove forward, encircling the man's waist with both arms. The man toppled backward, his head snapping back and making a sharp report as it struck the deck.

Harry thought the fight was over. But the man was tough. With amazing agility for his size, he regained his feet and lunged, this time holding a knife. Harry whirled away, narrowly avoiding the weapon, and kicked at the hand, at the same time grabbing his own blades from his belt.

The pain in his shoulder had weakened his entire right arm to the point that he distrusted its competence, feared he would drop the ax. He jammed it back into his belt and held the knife forward in a menacing gesture with his left hand. Saying a silent thanks to Comet Elijah for teaching him to fight equally well with either.

They circled each other in the gloom, Harry steadily losing ground to the larger man until they came to the railing. Harry's back pressed against the wood, the hiss of rushing ocean in his ears. His assailant paused, as if making a final assessment before charging. Harry took advantage of the break to feint with his knife. It proved just enough distraction for Harry to boost himself up onto the top of the railing. He leapt onto a set of ratlines and began scampering up.

He felt the weight on the rope ladder as the man swung in behind. Harry looked back. His pursuer was climbing at what seemed a leisurely rate, as if certain that the end of the encounter would be to his liking. On his face, in his black-button eyes, was a look more of annoyance than anger or even excitement. He had clamped his knife between his teeth for easy access when the inevitable moment came.

Harry continued until he came to the top of the lower mast. It had been easily fifteen years since he had stood on such a structure as an adventurous boy exploring merchant ships on the New Bern docks. Back then, he had no qualms about performing the tricky maneuver required to gain the top, which involved leaning backward over the deck some forty feet below while grasping tarred rigging, literally holding on for the sake of life, and swinging one's self out and up. Now, with the investment of a few more years of living on Earth, and a deepened appreciation of the blessings that his future life promised, he hesitated. But below him, making the ratlines shiver with each step, was a man who for some reason wanted him dead.

With a passably smooth sequence of movements informed by memory, he passed the point of maximum vulnerability to a sudden muscle spasm or a sneeze or a hiccup and stepped up and onto the wooden platform that sailors called the top, or the fighting top, depending on the type of ship. He was sure that in this case the latter would be more fitting.

He barely had time to catch his breath before an enormous hand appeared beneath his feet. He gave it a stomp with the heel of his boot.

The man cried out but held on and boosted himself up, managing to dodge a kick.

Before he was fully on his feet, Harry kicked again, this time full to the man's face. There was a small explosion of blood. The man grabbed at the knife still between his jaws and pulled it away. Harry realized what had happened. His foe had not been as self-possessed as he had seemed. In a moment of haste and distraction, he had placed the knife between his teeth with the blade pointed backward. Harry's kick had driven it into flesh and the muscles on either side of the mouth that make it smile.

The weapon slipped from the big man's hands. He staggered, dripping blood, seeming to ponder his situation, then lunged. But now the scales were rebalanced. Harry grabbed him around the neck and, squeezing it in the crook of his arm, began punishing his attacker's face. He bellowed and stomped on Harry's foot. The sudden pain was just enough to loosen Harry's grip and his opponent squirmed away. Without pause, Harry, still trying to ignore the soreness afflicting his shoulder, launched a powerful upward blow to the chin. Its force was enough to lift the man slightly off his feet despite his size and drive him backward into the platform railing. Without stopping to consider whether he wanted his opponent to come out of the battle alive to answer questions, Harry grabbed him around the knees and lifted. First the torso disappeared over the rail, followed by legs and feet.

Harry looked over to see him rolling and bouncing down the ratlines and over the side of the ship, where the fog and the ocean sucked him away.

★

The purser identified him as one John Liddle, a resident of Philadelphia. At least that was what he had said when boarding only minutes before the ship loosed her lines and sailed away. A cabin search turned up a small sea bag containing toiletries and a change of clothes. No papers to confirm his identity, much less any hint as to why he should have been so intent on killing Harry. The officer theorized that he had tried to break down Harry's door with the intention of stabbing him before he could get out of bed. Failing that, the ship's interior joinery consisting of good thick American oak, he must have gone outside to bide his time. Perhaps Liddle was hoping Harry would make his way onto the deck to report the incident to the watch commander at the helm; Liddle could intercept Harry there, as the commander and the bow watch were the only others up and around. The fog that blocked the crewmen's vision of the fight was, for the attacker, a gift.

Captain Biggerstaff took a casual attitude toward the whole episode. As if it were not the strangest thing he had seen during his career at sea. He did consent to having the second officer go with Harry to the court-house when they reached Boston to report the incident. Harry wondered if he should mention to the young deputy sheriff who took down the information about the previous attempt on his life. The deputy, who looked barely out of his teens, seemed eager to hear the smallest detail about this case. But Harry decided that bringing up Annapolis might cause unwanted complications that could divert him from his purpose. All he wanted now was to find the shop of George Johnston.

It was midday by the time Harry was finished making his report. The ship he had arrived on was due to continue its voyage to Louisbourg on the next morning's tide. The process of loading supplies for Wolfe's army, along with new passengers, already had begun by the time Harry left the dock. All that remained was to return and collect Annie and his other belongings, which the steward had agreed to hold for him.

Harry ate an early dinner at the tavern where he intended to stay for the time he would be in Boston, which, he hoped, would be short. The inn-keeper gave him directions to George Johnston's shop. It was not far away, but Harry reckoned their business could wait until the following morning.

He arrived back at the ship at a little past four, just in time to see a smartly dressed couple waiting to board. Maddie McLeod and Richard Ayerdale were watching a sailor manhandle their baggage up the gang-plank. Directly behind them, looking as poorly entertained as ever, was Reverend Fletcher.

CHAPTER 17

83: When you deliver a matter do it without passion &
with discretion.

—*Rules of Civility*

NONE OF THEM LOOKED HAPPY TO SEE HARRY. BUT AYERDALE AT
least was civil. Either he had forgotten about the unpleasantness at
Rosewood or had decided to pretend it had not happened. Very much
in the spirit of the *Rules*, Harry reckoned. He wondered if Richard as
a young cadet of the Ayerdale family had been made to write them all
out in a copy book, as the judge had required Harry do, or if Ayerdale
just had somehow absorbed them as part of his general raising-up. It
also seemed possible that he was born knowing them.

"And what brings the young constable to Boston?" Ayerdale asked affably enough after all had gotten over their surprise.

"I'm still searching for the owner of the Masonic badge from the Campbells' farmhouse." Harry guessed they had not heard about his dismissal as an officeholder.

"Did you think you'd find him in New England?" asked Fletcher.

"There is a well-known seller of jewelry here who, I am told, may be able to let me know who bought it."

"You can only be referring to George Johnston," said Ayerdale. "I've never met the gentleman personally, but I've dealt with his house. It is first rate. As to whether he could identify your killer, I would give that long odds."

As he spoke, an improbable idea that had been lurking in Harry's mind rose to the surface. What if Ayerdale had killed the Campbells? He was in New Bern at the time. In fact, he must have arrived at McLeod's house within a day of the murders, which could have put him in the vicinity of the Campbell house. Was he a Freemason? Harry tried to remember if that was something he had heard or only assumed. But what reason could such a man, from such a storied family, possibly have for killing a small-scale North Carolina planter and his wife and child?

All this passed through Harry's head in an instant, like an echo of some matter he already had thought on and forgot. For now, etiquette seemed to demand he make some gracious reply. Instead, he turned to Maddie. "I would very much like to say a proper good-bye. I wonder if I might tear you away for that long."

"We need to look to the stowage of our belongings and get settled in our quarters," said Fletcher.

"The parson is correct," said Ayerdale. "I am sure we will all meet again before long, back in Carolina. My beloved and I plan to pay the judge another visit once the summer campaign is finished."

"My love," Maddie said, "I see no harm in spending a few moments with an old friend. Surely you can look after my interests aboard." Then, to Harry, "We wouldn't be long, would we?"

He shook his head. "A coffeehouse is just up the street."

Offering his arm, Harry guessed that her willingness to indulge him had as much to do with disliking being directed as it did with any pining to spend time with him. But whatever her reason, he was glad of the outcome.

★

"You do know, don't you, that women aren't supposed to be in coffeehouses?" Maddie said as they walked.

That he did not know this made Harry feel stupid, a familiar feeling whenever he was around Maddie for any length of time.

"In fact, though I've tasted coffee, I've never been in one of these places myself," he said. "We can go to a tavern if you'd rather."

"No, I want to see if they'll throw me out. They never have as of yet."

The place was filled with well-dressed men busy at loud conversations concerning business at the Merchants Exchange just up the street. Aside from a few curious stares, no one made issue of Maddie's presence. Harry caught bits of conversation about prices being asked and paid for shares of farm crops, livestock, and, of even more interest to him, timber and timber products. And of buying and selling notes of credit on such commodities. He wondered if one of these men might be talking about one of Harry's own debts then being held by factors in Glasgow and London. Playing Harry's obligations like cards in a game of loo.

When they were seated and sipping from their cups of the dark, bitter, strangely energizing brew, Harry tried not to sound like an interrogator. But he was curious as to how Maddie and Ayerdale had come to be in the company of Reverend Fletcher. "It looks like you three spend a pretty good bit of time together," he said, trying to make it sound lighthearted, knowing he was not succeeding. "First in New Bern, then Williamsburg, now Boston. About to go to Canada."

"Oh, Harry, don't see implications where none exist. I was as surprised as Richard when we ran into the reverend here in Boston. He is visiting various parishes to see about the health of the Church of England in America."

"So I've heard."

"He's decided that since he's this close, he will visit General Wolfe's troops in Quebec. They are having a difficult time of it, by all reports. Reverend Fletcher simply wishes to do what he can to improve the mood of the redcoats by showing them that Mother Church cares for their welfare."

"I hope he succeeds. He depresses me."

"He is a serious man. But he does have a jollier side. You'll see it after he knows you better. Richard and I have decided he will be the one to seal our bonds."

"So you are not yet wed?"

"If it were up to Richard, we would be by now. The captain of the ship that brought us here could have done it. But I want us to wed on land, by a parson, surrounded by a lot of people. I am sure we can find some redcoats in Canada who would be happy to oblige us. I look forward to walking arm-in-arm with Richard under a bower of crossed hangers. It will be something to tell our grandchildren."

"Maddie—"

She put her finger to his lips. "Please, Harry." Her gay aspect falling away. "Don't spoil my happiness."

This was unexpected. Harry had thought nothing he could say would have any effect one way or another.

"I have no such aim. But there is something I have to say. How well do you really know this man?"

"As well as I need to. He has many fine qualities. He is from a venerable Virginia family. That counts for something, doesn't it?" With that, she put down her coffee, folded her hands in her lap, and lowered her eyes. No longer the grown-up, purposeful woman Harry had seen ever since she had been back. She seemed vulnerable, almost childlike, her defenses against whatever Harry might say dissolving before his eyes.

He took a moment to consider the position of power he suddenly felt possessed of. He could walk back from the moment, say he only wanted them to be together alone once more to wish her, from his heart, a good future. Then escort her back, give her up to a man whose full measure of cruelty he felt sure she had never seen. Or he could say what he had seen at Rosewood. The careless brutality that, once they were married, Harry was afraid would not be limited to the Africans Ayerdale owned.

Harry had tried to imagine her life under the yoke of such a person. The fix she would be in if it became unbearable. Her dowry from her grandfather, which Harry assumed would be handsome, gone. She could be ruined both socially and financially. Could he change her mind? It would be a risky gamble considering the single piece of evidence he had, other than his instincts: an accidental encounter in a Virginia field. But at stake was the future of a person he once had loved. And maybe, being honest, still did.

He began his story. How he and Noah had surprised Ayerdale and his overseer on his plantation. The young girl on the ground taking punishment. The ugliness of Ayerdale seeming to enjoy her efforts to dodge the worst.

Before he could finish, Maddie slapped the table with the palm of her hand so hard that drops of coffee spilled from their cups, distracting several others nearby from their own business, including two men who had been noisily quarreling over the proper way of raising hogs, whether to pen them up or let them range free.

"You aren't telling me anything I haven't already suspected."

"Then why are you marrying him?

She brought her voice back down to where only he could hear. "There is something you should know. I tell you this only because I can see you really care about what happens to me. And that is sweet. But you must keep what I say a secret. Swear to tell no one."

Harry so swore.

"The judge is bankrupt."

Harry heard the words but mistrusted his ears.

"He is very close to owing more than he has income to even make payments on. He has gotten back from his own lendings as much as he can in order to make a passable dowry for Mister Ayerdale. But after we are wed, Olaf will have to rely on Richard's generosity for the rest of his life. As will I."

Harry struggled to make sense of this.

"How could the judge possibly have gone bankrupt? He is one of the wealthiest men in North Carolina."

"That's what everyone thinks. That's what I thought. The truth is, he has been living on his borrowings for years. He doesn't even know I am aware of his condition."

Maddie looked at her coffee, which was still hot enough to be sending up thin windings of steam, and took a deep breath before continuing.

"I may as well tell you everything. I discovered the truth last August when I was collecting on one of the letters of credit he sent periodically during my travels in Europe. I'd gone to Glasgow to pick up my next installment, this time through a tobacco dealer by the name of Cullen. As it happened, I had only recently met Richard at the king's birthnight ball in the same city. Richard and I had spent several entertaining days together. Opera one night, theater the next. One memorable outing to the racetrack. It seems Richard loves horses, though they don't love him. He lost a great sum of money. By the end of the week, he proposed marriage. I laughed it off. Not to his face. of course. But the idea of marrying someone, anyone, amused me no end, when I was having such a good time unattached." She looked up at Harry and said with an expression he could not decipher as to its sincerity, "If I couldn't have you, my love, I didn't want anyone."

She laughed without humor.

"Well, when I went to collect my letter of credit, this tobacco man Cullen turned out to be a rather attractive older gentleman, and, to put it politely, we struck up a friendship. We attended glittering dinners, went on horseback jaunts in the park. All the things that couples do. Late one night in his rooms before falling asleep, he let it slip about my grandfather's financial status. As it turned out, he didn't realize I didn't know. My grandfather is a proud man. He wanted people, including his own family, to think well of him. Cullen explained how this led to his downfall. When tobacco prices began dropping in '48, Olaf continued borrowing and spending so that people would not know anything was the matter. Each year he dropped deeper into the ditch. The Glasgow merchants kept the money flowing on the strength of his land holdings, not his income."

Harry remembered well the recession of 1748. Most in Craven County reacted by reining in their spending on imports of English finery. Harry's family, under Talitha's canny guidance, began shifting away from tobacco and returning to the forest goods that had sustained North Carolinians long before the rage for fire-cured leaf first migrated southward from Virginia. They still borrowed from middlemen in England and Scotland to get from one year to the next, but with Britain fighting what seemed an endless war with France and her allies on the Continent, the jack-tars' hunger for pine sap, and all the different forms it could be made into, continued without pause, keeping prices steady.

"Cullen's revelations caused me to reconsider Richard's proposal of marriage. Luckily, he was still of the same mind when I next broached it. He had gotten wind of my flirtation with Cullen, but that seemed only to whet his appetite."

"It would have angered me," Harry said, without thinking on the relevance of this information.

"Richard is at an age when even the most adventurous of your sex think of marriage and having children. I believe he sees an advantage to marrying into a prominent Carolina household. And wedding the granddaughter of one of King George's favorite Scotchmen could not hurt his position in the kingdom, either."

"Does he know of the judge's financial situation?"

"He does not. And if you care anything at all for my future and that of my grandfather, you will leave it that way. When the time comes for me to speak of it, I doubt he will chastise me for not telling him Olaf is broke. Richard is fabulously wealthy and obviously isn't marrying me for financial reasons. He will overlook this matter."

She broke off for a moment, then said, "He may even love me."

"Do you love him?"

"That's the second time you've asked me that. I am very fond of Richard. Despite his shortcomings. I will try to get him to quit beating his slaves."

"But you don't love him."

Maddie's face took on an angry shine. Harry reckoned his questioning had become too ruthless. But then she looked down, seeming to relent.

"I hope he loves me. But whatever the case, with my family's future secure, I shall be satisfied."

She pushed her chair away to get up. As Harry made to do the same, she reached out and covered his hand with hers.

"I will find my own way back. It will be easier on me if we say good-bye now. Harry, I won't say I don't envy you. You have made a good marriage, by all reports. It certainly doesn't bother me that you chose to wed one of your servants. But now you have your world, and I have mine. If you still have any feelings for me, you will let me go to do as I must. Now, I beg you to forget all of this. I am sure you have your own matters to keep you occupied."

Another twenty minutes and a second cup of coffee passed amid the clamor of the stock-share gamblers. Harry mulling over how things had turned out in Maddie's life and his.

Then he remembered he did indeed have matters to attend to. He had to get his horse.

CHAPTER 18

36: Artificers & Persons of low Degree ought not to use
many ceremonies to Lords, or Others of high Degree
but Respect and highly Honour them, and those of high
Degree ought to treat them with affibility & Courtesie,
without Arrogancy.

—*Rules of Civility*

THE HOUSE OF JOHNSTON REALLY WAS A HOUSE, A FLAT-FRONT BRICK
structure in a row of similar ones with carriage lamps and expensive-
looking curtains swooping down behind tall windows. A small plaque
beside the door was the only signal it was a place of business. By its
stillness it seemed deserted. No one answered repeated knocks. He

asked several passersby where Johnston lived, if not here. Either they had no idea or thought it odd and possibly sinister that anyone would ask. The morning breeze felt unsettling on his cheek as he resolved to wait. Knowing this same stirring of air would be carrying Maddie away to Canada and to a future of reliance on a man with a taste for cruelty.

Finally, at half past ten, a servant came and unlocked the door. Harry explained his business as briefly as he could, and after a further short wait, the proprietor came out.

Johnston lived up to his billing as a blooded aristocrat, albeit a product of his father's adventuresome habits and thus deprived of title and money. He looked to be in his fifties, with a nobly featured face and the genteel manner of one accustomed to moving in high circles. Harry had rarely seen a suit of ordinary daywear as finely turned out as the buff-colored suit he wore. Speaking in a clipped manner similar to that of Captain Biggerstaff but with softer edges, Johnston asked Harry to restate his business. Harry held up the brooch. "I've been told it's possible you might be able to identify this object. It was found at the site of a murder in North Carolina."

Johnston gave the badge a look-over, paying special attention to the emblem on its face.

"Interesting," he said, handing it back.

"Do you recognize it? I understand it was likely made by a jeweler in London by the name of Wykes."

"Before I answer, might I know more about how you came to have it?"

Once again he told his story. He had nearly committed the short version to memory word for word, so often had he repeated it now.

"A unfortunate tale," Johnston said when he was finished. "Harry— Do you mind if I call you that? Would you care for some tea?"

He could stand it no longer. "Can you tell me about this brooch?"

"It is a counterfeit. A very good one, I must say, but clearly a forgery of an authentic Wykes production. Look closely at the workmanship."

"I was told by two different dealers in jewelry that the work is first class." Harry was looking at it again and could see no imperfections.

"Which ones, if I may ask?"

"A man by the name of Bannerman in Williamsburg and the person he directed me to in Philadelphia, Jacob Merkly."

"I doubt there are two finer men in America. But I'm afraid they are not as familiar as I am with the House of Wykes, and they are mistaken. Are you sure you wouldn't care for some tea? A shipment just arrived here yesterday from Macau, and I am eager to try it out."

Harry relented, and within a few minutes the servant was pouring a potent-looking brew from a silver pot. Harry wondered if any of it would ever find its way into the McLeod household. One that could no longer afford such luxuries but kept buying them.

"This design was introduced into the market fairly recently." Johnston picked up the medal again. "I would say the piece could not be over five years old. But observe the coloring of the blue insets. They show subtle signs of glazing, indicating use of enamel made to look like lapis lazuli, not the real stones. And look here." He pointed to the tiny builder's square that formed part of the Masonic emblem. "Edward Wykes has perfected a method of inscribing these squares with extraordinarily fine foot-and-inch marks. They are all but invisible to the unaided eye. One of his prized trademarks. Only a few of his most trusted craftsmen know how he does it. Obviously the one who made this piece was not among them."

"Someone went to a lot of trouble to try to duplicate what Wykes sells," said Harry.

"A few years ago a renegade former employee—a goldsmith—showed up in New England selling objects such as this at greatly reduced prices. His handiwork found favor among those looking for a good bargain and not overly concerned with authenticity. It distresses me to say that many Americans resent the prices George charges for his creations. I have no doubt the scoundrel made a good deal of money before he was called out as a thief of Edward Wykes's designs and good name. He was arrested on some charge or another and sent back to London for trial. No one knows just how much of his work made their way into America. Or, I'm sorry to say, exactly who bought it."

Several moments passed before Johnston asked Harry if he was all right. The truth was he felt sick. Each time to have traveled so far, only to see his efforts come to naught. All he had gambled, including his reputation, lost.

"There might be one way I could help you," said Johnston. "Do you have any idea what the inscription on the back means?"

"I've been told it is a Masonic code. Something to do with a secret word and a pattern. But no Freemason true to his vows will reveal what the pattern is. Which would do me no good anyway unless I knew the word, which changes from one code to another. At least, that is as best as I understand it."

"Correct on all counts. But I could at least show you the pattern the system is based on. Then it would remain only to discover the word. At least knowing the pattern would be a step in the right direction."

"But wouldn't you be telling me a secret you are sworn to keep?"

"I am not a Freemason. I've fallen into selling these baubles because it pays well and helps finance my rambles in America. Along the way, I've learned much about the brotherhood. I don't make a habit of disclosing things I probably shouldn't, but if by doing so I might help you discover the identity of a killer, I am willing. Just promise you won't reveal the source of your information."

Over more tea and some biscuits, the titleless aristocrat engaged Harry in polite conversation. They talked about the Masons, Johnston saying how, though their membership included some of the most distinguished members of British society, their much talked-about habits of secrecy exposed them to accusations of all sorts of dark doings, including sorcery. Johnston observed that such suspicions tended to occupy the minds of people with little education or hope of ever becoming members themselves.

"Frankly, I find the whole business about ancient builders and their talk about forgotten knowledge rather boring. The Freemasons I know are all upstanding, well-intentioned men who simply enjoy a little hocus-pocus in their lives."

After some hesitation, Harry admitted his ambition to someday join the New Bern lodge. Johnston inquired into Harry's own background. Harry related a few pertinences. The Woodyards' North Carolina origins in the swampy Albemarle after his great-grandfather had run away from an abusive landowner in Virginia. The family's relocation, at Talitha's urgings, to the Pamlico, made possible by his grandfather's suddenly coming into some money. Skipping over the dubious nature of Natty's good fortune.

When he was finished, Johnston took out a sheet of drawing paper and a pencil. He sketched out a hatch pattern, as if to begin a game of tick-tack. Beside this he drew a cross of Saint Andrew of similar size.

"The letters of the key word are inserted in pairs in the first series of spaces created by the hatch-work," he said. He demonstrated by writing Harry's last name, beginning in the top row and continuing in the next, by twos:

"The rest of the spaces of both the hatch work and the cross are next filled with the other letters of the alphabet, also two by two, skipping the letters already used."

He wrote out the rest of the alphabet as he had said.

"So now you have a device that will allow you to both encode and decode messages. When writing in code, instead of writing each letter of the message, one would copy the shape of the enclosure in which the desired letter appears. Whenever the second letter in an enclosure is used, the code writer signifies so by inserting a dot in the shape of the enclosure he transcribes."

To demonstrate, he drew a square and placed a dot in the middle.

"In your code, that represents the letter *C*."

He laid down the pencil and sat back, seeming to savor the look of enlightenment that Harry guessed had come over his face.

"Of all the codes that have ever been devised, I believe this is one of the most elegantly simple, and damnably hard, to break unless one knows not only the pattern but also the key word."

To make sure he understood, Harry had Johnston write a word in the code so he could translate it. The one Johnston chose had nine letters and thus nine symbols. Harry had only to translate the first three before guessing the remaining six. The word was *FREEMASON*.

He was tempted to try on the spot to write out a new code using *Ayerdale* as the key word to see if he could translate the inscription on the badge. But he decided it better not to reveal to anyone just yet his suspicion that such a prominent citizen of British America might be involved in murder. Ayerdale might be a person Johnston knew of. Instead, Harry thanked his host profusely for his help and got up to leave.

They were standing in the hallway saying final good-byes when Johnston said, "Harry, in the brief time we've been together, and having heard your story, I have taken a great liking to you."

"You do me honor," Harry said. Wondering if a small bow would be in order.

"You are a splendid example of what some of my more enlightened countrymen have taken to calling 'natural aristocracy.' I recognize in you a sharp mind and instincts every bit as noble as the loftiest lords of the realm. Full many a flower is born to blush unseen, and waste its sweetness on the desert air."

It sounded like something from a book, but Harry had no idea which one.

"I would like you to be my guest at a ball tonight."

"You flatter me, sir, but I wouldn't want to impose."

"It is no imposition at all. I really must insist that you meet some of my friends while you are in our city. Think of it as a simple act of New England hospitality."

"I'm afraid I brought along no proper clothes for a ball." In fact, Harry owned no such clothes.

"That is of no consequence. Despite our differences in age, we are of similar size and build. I have no doubt you would look splendid in any of my suits. I'll have my man assist you in choosing something from my wardrobe before you leave."

An hour later, Harry hailed a cabriolet to take him back to his inn, taking care to hold his borrowed suit, wrapped in a muslin sheet, as flat as possible to avoid wrinkling.

As soon as he was back in his room, he took from his pocket the folded sheet of paper containing the secret pattern of the Masons and got to work.

CHAPTER 19

54: Play not the Peacock, looking every where about you,
to See if you be well Deck't, if your Shoes fit well if your
Stokings sit neatly, and Cloths handsomely.

—*RULES OF CIVILITY*

HE FIRST TRIED OUT THE CODE PATTERN WITH *AYERDALE* AS THE
unknown word. The resulting translation of the inscription on the
back of the brooch looked like gibberish. Then he tried *RICHARD*.
Same result. Then, *RICHARD AYERDALE*, and *RICHARDAYERDALE*.
Nothing.

He found himself wishing Maddie were there. With her love of
riddles, her knack for stretching her mind beyond the limits of the

apparent, maybe she could help. Of course she could, he thought sourly. She would be only too happy to prove that her betrothed was not only a cruel tyrant but a murderer as well.

Discouraged, and feeling drowsy on account of his inability to sleep soundly in recent days, he left his efforts at code breaking long enough to take a nap. He awakened with a start. The cast of light coming through the window indicated the day was drawing to a close. Soon he would need to bathe and try on his borrowed finery and make his way to the ball.

But not until he tried out one more idea.

It was something that had materialized in his mind during his nap and in fact had helped bring him back awake. He had been dreaming about Ayerdale's plantation. Trying to envision what life would be like for Maddie on the banks of the James River. Looming before him was the stone pillar bearing a name.

ROSEWOOD

It did not take him long to make a new code using Ayerdale's ancestral landholding and try it out on the inscription on the brooch.

When he was finished, he laid his pencil on the table and stared at the paper for a long time, the set of letters his effort had produced.

It was complete nonsense.

★

He arrived at the ball late and on his way to being drunk. He had stayed inside his room at the inn into the evening, taking long swigs from the rum he had purchased from the innkeeper. It was a nice rum. From a nice inn, in fact. He was sharing the bed with only one other man, a well-mannered sort from New York in town on business. The man had not yet come up, so Harry had the place to himself. No one to pass judgment on this relapse into his old liberal ways with a bottle. He had the bottom of this one in sight when it came to him that George Johnston, who had been so kindly and helpful, might be disappointed if he did not see Harry with his lent suit. It would be a terrible breach of manners in the new world Harry supposed he was becoming used to moving in.

The house was in the country, only a few miles from the center of Boston, a district called Jamaica Plain. The name having some connection to the Caribbean island that was furnishing the British colonies with sugar, rum, and slaves. Or possibly it was a misunderstanding of some old Indian name. The driver seemed to be having an argument with himself for Harry's benefit about this bit of Boston lore.

The house looked new, confirming the driver's story that it had been built only recently by a merchant who had become as rich as a mogul in the shipping trade. A proper dancing room, bright with lamps and candles, occupied most of the second floor.

"Your suit looks most well on you," said Johnston, who spotted Harry immediately despite the scrum of guests. They were all in glittering clothes, the ladies accoutered in jewels, men in lace jabots and powdered perukes. A sprinkling of British and American military uniforms among them. In fact, his borrowed suit was not a bad fit at all except around the waist of the britches, which was a little loose on Harry. But this small imperfection was covered by the rakishly cut jacket, a dramatic shade of maroon with silver brocade trimmings and buttons. Harry had indulged himself in some minutes of self-admiration in front of his room's cheval glass before leaving. He reckoned he cut quite the figure even without a wig. As a general rule, Harry preferred not to cover his full head of chestnut hair, which he fastened in back with a black ribbon.

The small orchestra was on a rest when he arrived. Johnston took him straight to the home's owner, one Elihu Pearson, an energetic-looking man on the younger side of middle age, and the handsome woman by his side, whom Johnston introduced as his wife. They were conversing with a circle of equally fetching people.

"Harry is touring New England," Johnston said, making it sound like a leisurely wander. He added, before anyone could ask further, "He owns a plantation in North Carolina."

There was the briefest silence. A touch of disappointment, Harry judged, that he could not have been from Virginia or South Carolina.

"It would seem likely some of your timber and pine pitch have found their way into the sailing vessels I build," said Pearson. To the others in the party he explained, "North Carolina is our chief supplier of such things."

"I wouldn't be surprised," said Harry. "We do most of our business through factors in Boston and New York."

"Then," said another one of the gentlemen, "my father at this very moment might be walking a deck that was made seaworthy thanks to your plantation."

"Harry," said Johnston, "may I present Joshua Loring Junior, high sheriff of Suffolk County? His father commands one of the ships now with General Wolfe on the Saint Lawrence."

"Would that I were with that brave captain this very moment," said yet another fashionably dressed worthy who had just walked up. Almost in unison, the men bowed and the ladies curtsied. He continued, "General Amherst seems to think I can be of more use here in Massachusetts Bay trying to recruit militia than actually taking part in the battle." He added with a wry smile, "All evidence to the contrary."

"Governor, may I present a friend of mine from North Carolina?" said Johnston, noticing the man noticing Harry. "This is Mister Harry Woodyard. Harry, meet Thomas Pownall."

He looked young for a governor. Maybe only eight or ten years older than Harry. Otherwise not much different in appearance, especially with Harry clothed every bit as admirably. Harry thought he even saw some resemblance between himself and the New Englander. He remembered what Johnston had said earlier about natural aristocracy: Flowers born to bloom in the desert. He had a fleeting glimpse of himself ten years hence proposing his annual budget to the General

Assembly. Being addressed as "Your Excellency" in the desert of North Carolina. Why not?

Harry bowed and remained silent. By the men's smiles, he judged he had made the correct choice of behaviors.

"I have yet to visit North Carolina," said Pownall. "But I look forward to doing so." His accent was less British than New England in Harry's ears, which were becoming attuned to the Yankee way of talking. "I've heard good reports of your militiamen. They performed yeoman service to the redcoats when we took Fort Duquesne."

"I thank you on their behalf," said Harry, the high-sounding words coming out with surprising ease.

"I'm just thankful that things are finally going our way again," said Pownall's wife. "At times it has seemed the French guess our every move in advance. It was almost as if they were employing a mind reader."

A knowing titter greeted her remark. At the same time, Harry caught the high sheriff aiming a hooded, unamused glance at another in the party, a man dressed in the uniform of a Massachusetts militia major. Browning by name, if Harry remembered his introduction correctly. Browning returned Loring's look as if in some silent communication. Harry could not guess what this meant but reckoned it was something.

The orchestra had returned to their instruments. Couples began forming, answering the leader's call for a minuet. Early in his tutelage under the judge, Harry had been made to learn this dance. He did not care for its mincing steps, which, when demonstrated by the large-bodied McLeod, seemed comical. Harry was more favorably disposed to country dancing, which he had learned as a boy from his mother. Its broad, energetic movements appealed to him. But he supposed such was beneath the dignity of high-quality people. The thought brought to mind another snippet from the *Rules*. "Associate yourself with men of good quality if you esteem your own reputation; for 'tis better to be alone than in bad company." Was his family bad company?

Two by two, the guests took their leave and headed for the dance floor. "My own companion for the evening abandoned me for the lavatorium just before you arrived," Pownall said to Harry when they found themselves alone. "I suppose for now you and I are just a pair of unattached souls."

"My wife would surely enjoy this," said Harry, watching as the couples began to move around. "She loves to dance."

"You're a fortunate man, then. So far, I am sorry to say, a permanent dancing partner has eluded me. I love the ladies, but it may be that I love them all equally."

As the governor was talking, Harry thought he caught from a corner of his eye a flash of lavender. A gown. Or so he imagined. But when he turned in that direction, it was gone.

A trick of the mind, no doubt.

He turned his attention back to the floor as the dancers began their prancing, circling steps with varying degrees of success. A remembered fragrance of minty purple flowers settled over him.

"There she is," said Pownall. "Excuse me."

The governor of Massachusetts walked toward the door where the lady was standing, now in clear view. Took her hand and escorted her onto the floor. As she followed, the Baroness de la Roche spared Harry a smile.

CHAPTER 20

99: Drink not too leisurely nor yet too hastily. Before and
after Drinking wipe your Lips breath not then or Ever
with too Great a Noise, for its uncivil.

—*Rules of Civility*

HARRY FOUND HIS WAY TO THE PUNCH BOWL. HE LADLED HIMSELF
a cup, drained it, refilled, drained again. Trying to make sense of Jacqueline's being in Massachusetts Bay. He recalled she had worked for
Governor Shirley, something having to do with his household, if he
remembered correctly. Not cleaning and dusting, but overseeing that
and keeping his social calendar. A suitable occupation for a lady with
aristocratic bloodlines, a governor's palace being about the closest

anything in America came to an actual royal setting. This man Pownall was Shirley's successor. Maybe she had come to Boston to find a new situation, the new governor of Virginia having no need for her. If they got a chance to speak privately, congratulations would be in order on her ability to find favor with important men.

Someone began vigorously poking his back. Really hammering, as if with a closed fist. He turned to see a man of advanced years in a faded yellow woolen jacket, which looked too warm for the season, and a peruke that had gone for some time without benefit of powder.

"Do you mind yielding the ladle?" he said when he was sure he had Harry's attention. Harry handed it over, realizing that he had been holding it for a good while.

"My name is Hansen," he said as he dipped out a portion of punch. "I own this place. While you are in my house, you must not hog the punch bowl."

"My apologies," said Harry. "By the way, I thought the house belonged to that man over there." He gestured toward the dance floor, where the Pearsons were expertly stepping to the music.

"Lived here most of my life," Hansen said, paying no notice. "Made my fortune in trading furs with the Indians. I treated those men like my own children, and they loved me for it. Never gave me a bit of trouble, except for the odd petty theft here and there." He shrugged, spilling a little punch on his waistcoat. "I never made any fracas, as the young-sters say. Just wrote it down as a cost of making money."

A young woman came up and in a proprietary manner began leading Hansen away. Harry returned her sad smile with an under-standing nod.

He felt the punch coming together with the rum from earlier in the evening and making common cause. Fresh air seemed called for. Something head clearing for the carriage ride back into Boston. A meeting with the baroness did not seem out of the question, either. He found himself wanting to be sober enough to put words together should that come about.

When he had arrived at the mansion, he had noticed a balcony on the third floor; as good a place as any to air out.

The climb up the staircase attested to his condition. He was all but breathless and staggering by the time he reached the top. Shadows from wall candles played about the hallway as he made his way to the door he judged led to the balcony. He knocked softly and, getting no reply, opened it and walked in.

It was a large room, also fitfully lit. The walls lined from floor to coffered ceiling with books. At one end was a hearth nearly large enough to walk into. In front of it, a reading table. A sofa and chairs occupied the middle of the room, and at the end opposite the fireplace was the balcony he had seen from the front, its opening half concealed behind partially drawn curtains.

He stepped through the veils and outside. Below, a line of carriages waited, lit by large basket-shaped torches atop poles dug into the ground at intervals. From this angle Harry could fully appreciate the grandeur of the grounds, the care with which they were laid out. A fortune's worth of plantings and labor. The air was cooler than what he was used to in North Carolina at this time of year, a season that, he realized, was quickly slipping by. It was the beginning of the third week of August. Mild ends of summers were among the rewards of living in New England, he supposed. He shuddered to think how cold it must get. But with a fireplace such as he had just seen, he imagined no one in the Pearson family suffered.

"Harry?" said a tuneful voice behind him. The second syllable of his name given the playful lilt that had charmed him once before. With a rustle of taffeta, Jacqueline stepped onto the balcony.

"I saw you leave and followed as soon as I could. It would have been terrible to miss a chance to say hello."

Harry said the first thing that came into his mind. "Where's the governor?"

"Oh, Tom is busy with some of the other men at the punch bowl. He is a dear, but the price one pays for keeping company with great men is abandonment at the drop of a glove."

"I'm surprised to see you in Boston. I thought you loved Virginia now."

"I wouldn't rule out returning there someday. But I've just been offered a position here through a friend. I'll be teaching the French language to children of a good family."

"Your friends move in high circles. How long have you known Mister Pownall?"

"I met Tom when I was part of the Shirley household. He and William were political enemies. But William is gone now." She said something in French, then translated, "Life continues."

Harry felt a stab of jealousy and in the next instant realized how mistaken it was. He had no more claim to Jacqueline's affections than to Maddie's.

"I suppose this might grow into something more?" he could not resist asking. "With the governor, I mean? Or maybe it already has?"

"Tom is a sweet man. And I won't be shy: we've had our moments, even before William left. But I doubt Tom will ever be interested in anything permanent. He's too much the sport."

She sat down on the balcony's sole piece of furniture, a rattan sofa with overstuffed cushions. Giving Harry a tantalizing glimpse of the swell of breasts. She took Harry's hand and pulled him down beside her. "Now, tell me how you have fared since Williamsburg. Have you found your killer?"

He summed up his activities since leaving Williamsburg, how his search had led him to Philadelphia, then Boston. The road seeming to end here. Except he now knew something about the inscription on the brooch.

"I feel I'm very near to figuring out its meaning. I grasp the way the code was made. It's only left to learn a secret word that is the key to unlocking it, but so far I've had no success. The truth is I may be no closer to finding the Campbells' killer than the day I rode out from New Bern."

She turned and looked directly into his eyes. "Here is what I think, Harry. I fear that as close as you are to learning that secret, you are just that close to terrible danger."

"You may be right. People have tried to kill me twice now. Once in Maryland and again aboard my ship to Boston."

Jacqueline inhaled sharply. "I knew it. Did you recognize your attackers? Have you any idea who sent them?"

"Robbery can't be ruled out as a reason the first time. My friend Noah Burke—you met him in Williamsburg—was with me. He was carrying a great deal of money, something I didn't even know until later. He was killed, but they got no money. The second attack—the one on the ship—is a complete mystery."

As he spoke he wondered how closely Jacqueline was listening. Her eyes seemed preoccupied with his lips. Following their movements. Her eyes dark and liquid in the moonlight. Reflections from the torches below playing over them.

"Harry," she said when he was finished, "I won't pretend. I've thought of you often since we parted. Have you thought of me?"

Without waiting for an answer, she touched his hand. Her breath was warm on his neck. Suddenly it seemed the world beyond the balcony was falling away, leaving him and this strangely beautiful woman slowly tumbling through a void. Adrift in a universe far from New England, America, the earth itself. A world where he was unmarried and had no responsibilities, no concern other than satisfying his hunger to run his hands over Jacqueline's unclothed body. Feel her pressing against him. In this new world, he had the power to keep this rare prize for himself, to will it so that she would never again know the touch of another man.

They kissed, more furiously than lovingly. Bumping, squeezing, grappling. The sleeves of Jacqueline's gown slipping farther down her shoulders as the struggle went on. He fumbled with the buttons at her back. She seemed to be trying to wriggle away, which only increased his determination to hold her fast. Suddenly she somehow managed to bring her hands together at his chest and push him back. Hard. It seemed she was strong as well as lovely.

"No, Harry," she said, more a breathy plea than a command. He retreated, the reality of who he was and what he was doing intruding into his dream.

"I am so sorry," he began. But she put her hand to his lips.

"My love, there is a way we can be together without betraying your wife. Do you remember how?"

Before he could answer, she was unbuttoning his breeches.

CHAPTER 21

81: Be not Curious to Know the Affairs of Others neither
approach those that Speak in Private.

—*Rules of Civility*

HE WOKE UP TO VOICES. HUSHED CONVERSATION. MEN. TWO OR THREE
of them from the sound of it, talking in low tones inside the great
room. Plainly unaware of anyone on the balcony. Harry lay sprawled
on the sofa, clothes in disarray, his now-flaccid manhood in full view
of the starry sky. It was becoming a habit. Forbidden pleasure, the
slumber of the sinful, then abandoned.

Taking care not to make a stirring of the sofa's rattan weavings, he
got up and rebuttoned himself and straightened out his waistcoat.

His borrowed jacket, which he had taken such care not to crease, lay crumpled on the floor. He slipped into it.

His first thought was to announce himself to whomever was there, then just walk in. But he had no idea how long they had been there. If he suddenly appeared now, they might assume he had been eavesdropping the whole time they had been talking. A natural assumption and hard to disprove. None of the rules he could think of came close to covering this situation. He tried to imagine Judge McLeod's reaction if news reached him that his renegade constable had been caught spying on somebody.

While thinking on his next move, he could not help but pick up snatches of the conversation, which was increasing in volume. Probably a sign they were just settling into it. Something about the war in Canada. General Wolfe and the troubles he was having with the French. Overcome by curiosity, he squatted on his haunches and peeked around the curtain. A trick Comet Elijah had taught him. Stay low to the ground and motionless when surveying from hiding. Most people do not look below eye level unless movement draws their attention.

In the candlelight he could see Governor Pownall, High Sheriff Loring, and the militia officer, Browning. Loring was standing with his back turned, facing the sofa, where the other two were sitting. Harry took this tableau back with him as he returned his head to behind the curtain.

"Marie may well have been the one who enabled Montcalm's lucky guesses," the militia major was saying. There was a pause, a rustling of fabric. Then Pownall said, "I've long thought Shirley himself incompetent and seldom miss an opportunity to say so, but I've never believed he was an outright traitor. That is inconceivable."

"But his little Parisian whore might be another story," said Browning.

"Wife," corrected Loring.

"A tawdry substitute for Lady Frances." Browning again. "God rest her soul."

Pownall said, "If Montcalm did indeed have an agent in our midst, we can't disallow the possibility it was Marie. As far as I know, she remains a practicing papist to this day."

"Well, with the Shirleys tucked away in London, there's not much harm the woman can do now," said the sheriff.

"There's talk he is to be posted off to Nassau," said Pownall. "God willing, he can do little further damage to British interests there other than bugger up passports."

"I suspect we yet have a turncoat in our midst," said Browning. "Amherst should have driven off the French by now, what with all the redcoats and cannonballs he has at his disposal."

"Montcalm has spies everywhere," said Loring. "Me and my boys are ever on the watch for doubtful sorts lurking about the docks and billets."

Browning said, "One can go only so far guessing the enemy's aims just by watching movements of troops and ships. The best information comes from someone with entrée to high levels."

"It is certainly possible, even likely, there was a spy at some point," said Pownall, "but I have the impression Whitehall believes the issue has been dealt with. My latest communications with the Leader indicate no continuing concern about any high-ranking traitor."

"At three thousand miles' remove from Canada, Mister Pitt can more easily afford disconcern," said Browning. "A front-line soldier may be forgiven his suspicions."

After a moment Pownall said, "Are you still leaving tomorrow?"

"I sail on the tide aboard a mail packet. I just missed a supply ship, so the packet will have to do, though it is smaller and makes several stops along the way. With any luck, though, I should be in Louisbourg within a week, then another week to Quebec. Either the citadel will have fallen by then or I will have the honor of joining in the final attack."

"Are you sure your leg has mended well enough?"

"By the time I'm on the Saint Lawrence, I am certain my poor abused leg will be fit and ready for a scrap," said the major with a ruffling laugh.

There were clinking sounds of glasses being refilled. At length Loring said, "How fares the lady Jacqueline?"

"She fares well indeed," said Pownall.

Another lull, then Pownall's voice again. "I know what you've all been thinking, and I forgive you. She is French, and she was in the Shirley household much of the time he was governor. But I assure you, gentlemen, Madame Contrecoeur is above reproach. I have made inquiries in London as to her background, and it is well known that her family long ago rejected the Catholic faith. They are staunch Calvinists and enemies of Louis. And they have suffered for it. Anyway, she is not part of my circle of confidants, and I share nothing with her during our moments alone. We are on friendly terms socially. That is the extent of it."

"Our earlier defeats may have been simply a matter of British bungling," said Loring. "For all their high-handed manners, these jackanapes in red coats can be complete idiots."

Laughter relieved the tension that Harry sensed when Loring mentioned the baroness. But it could not chase away Harry's jealousy, the thought that Pownall no doubt had unfettered access to the whole of Jacqueline's tantalizing body, with its provocative smell of flowers. Alarmingly, Harry felt a new stirring in his breeches.

"We shouldn't take such delight in deriding our cousins," said Pownall. Then, solemn again. "If there is some highly placed agent still active on our shores, that person could give them just the advantage they need to hold out in Canada until the fighting season ends. We have them boxed in for now, but if they are still there when the snows come, it could change the entire proposition. Wolfe would have to leave to avoid having his ships frozen in. Giving His Gallic Majesty the opportunity to get resupply and troop ships through our blockade once the ice melts come spring."

"The very thought haunts my dreams," said Browning.

Pownall said, "Conceivably it could turn the tide of the war. Britain can withstand only so much more drain on its pocketbook, not to mention loss of life. I've seen reports of recruiting officers' being set upon in the streets of London and Liverpool. Nothing to worry over unduly for now. But if this war lasts much longer . . ."

If Pownall finished his sentence, Harry did not hear it. Only sounds of more liquor being decanted. Then a renewal of hushed words. The lowering of voices must have been instinctive, possibly signaling that they feared being overheard. Harry looked around for a place he might hide in case one thought to come out and look or just for some air. There was nothing but the sofa, which would not stand much scrutiny. Nevertheless, he crept behind it and hunkered as close to the floor as he could. It was the best he could do, and it put him farther away from the conversation.

In the hum of talking he thought he picked out a familiar name. At first he dismissed it as a misunderstanding of a word not well caught. He redoubled his concentration.

"may be nothing to it whatsoever," he made out from what Browning was saying. "hesitate to bring it up . . . plan to keep an eye on him when I get to Quebec."

Loring's voice. "met the gentleman on a number of occasions . . . passing through on military business."

Browning said in a more normal tone, "I confess I took a dislike to him at the outset. It was at a planning session with General Amherst and some other senior officers, and he just made a bit of a sour impression on me. I began making inquiries and discovered that he was in the vicinity of a string of defeats we suffered early in the war. In each case he was supposedly on some errand for the governor of Virginia. Checking on the strength of the garrison, status of supplies, readiness to fight, that sort of thing."

"Of course, Dinwiddie wanted to have his own reports as to the conduct of the war," said Pownall. "As does the current officeholder, Fauquier."

"But here's the interesting part. In each case, he managed to leave just ahead of the French attack. Not just once or twice but at least four times. At the Monongahela, Fort Bull, Fort Granville, and the fortress Oswego."

"Very curious," said Loring.

"At the Monongahela he was toward the rear when the Indians fell upon Braddock's vanguard. Our man got away without a scratch, unless you count the little fuss he got into with a British officer before the fighting started."

"Little fuss?" Pownall.

"As I've heard it, he and some grenadier captain had gotten off on a bad footing to begin with. I guess the captain was something of a jackass and not at all fond of provincials. He wouldn't allow his men to help out in the road-building work, which would have meant associating with Americans. He even ordered them to set separate camps with their own passwords. Well, the proud Virginian is not used to being looked down on, especially by people he would outrank were they not regular British Army. The flash point came when the captain ordered him at swordpoint to pick up a shovel and move some dirt. Our man told him to bugger himself, at which point the officer struck him broadside across the face with the flat of his hanger. The colonel still carries the mark where the edge dug into his flesh."

"We all have chafed under British arrogance," said Loring, "but I've not heard of more insufferable provocation."

"Still, he is from one of the Dominion's oldest and richest families and one of the best connected," said Pownall. "I've entertained him at my own table several times, both before and after I became governor. My predecessor even threw a banquet for him, honoring his service to the Crown. How could such a man as Richard Ayerdale betray his country?"

Although he already had guessed who they were talking about, Harry felt his pulse quicken. There was another pause in the discussion. Then, in a voice so low that Harry had to strain to hear, Browning said, "I know a secret."

Harry wished he dared look around the curtain again. If he could not entirely make the words out, he might guess from the shapes of Browning's lips as he spoke. He settled for cupping both ears.

"learned from a friend . . . moneylenders in London . . . reluctant to tell . . . violate a confidence."

"For heaven's sake, man, what is it?" said Loring.

Another pause. Suddenly through the wicker weavings he saw a pair of shoes stepping onto the deck. He lowered his eyes. Comet Elijah once had told him that the whites of eyes reflecting starlight were as good as signal lanterns to a trained eye. Whoever it was paused, as if having a quick look around. Harry offered up a prayer of thanks for the dark shade of his coat, while searching his mind for a believable explanation for his presence crouching behind a sofa. But the shoes turned and retreated into the great room.

In a clearly audible voice, Browning said, "Richard Ayerdale is flat broke."

Silence. Of a stunned nature, if Harry read it correctly. Reflecting his own reaction.

"But how could that be?" Pownall again. "To my understanding, he owns one of the largest assemblages of land in America. And hundreds of enslaved Africans to go with it."

"It seems that Mister Ayerdale is not immune to the economic tides that affect us all," said Browning. "Especially our countrymen in the South, vulnerable as they are to agricultural markets. Falling tobacco prices, combined with the demands of a lavish way of life, have hurt Ayerdale on a scale commensurate with his wealth. In addition, it seems he is addicted to gambling. My information is that in recent years he's lost heavily at cards and racing tracks in a number of cities here and abroad. It seems the worse off he became, the more recklessly he risked what he had left."

After another moment Browning said, "I have no reason to doubt the truth of my information, even though my London friend was drunk at the time. Perhaps all the more reason to believe him, since he was speaking unguardedly. Of course it would be pure speculation to go further, link Ayerdale's financial condition to suspicion of traitorous conduct. But we all know the French pay well and concoct elaborate schemes to gain information. I cannot see how the possibility of such a connection can be ignored. Especially now, when the man is on his way to the scene of what could be a decisive battle. A victory, we hope—or else a debacle that could have the direst consequences for the future of Britain on this continent."

"This information is astonishing," said Loring. The sofa creaked; then, measured footfalls. Pacing. "But how could anyone publicly point a finger at such a man without proof? Lacking evidence, the accuser might face the ruin of his own good name. Not to mention the ill effects it would have on Ayerdale, were he proved innocent."

"Precisely why I have not already made my information public," said Browning.

"I agree with the sheriff: any such allegations would require unchallengeable evidence," said Pownall, sounding like he was announcing his conclusions as he formed them. "The case would need to be shown beyond dispute, well enough to stand up in a good Massachusetts Bay court."

"Governor," Browning said, "you and Joshua are the only ones I've spoken to on this matter. In all candor, you are among the few people I feel I can trust. I'm not inclined to share it with any redcoat, no matter how high up. If we are being deceived, who knows who else might be in on it. In my opinion, the fewer who know of my suspicions, the safer our country."

"That being the case," said Pownall, "your course seems clear. When you get up with Wolfe, seek out Ayerdale. Watch him as close as you can. It appears that watching and waiting is all that can be done for now."

Harry was trying to steady his breathing lest the noise of it give him away. Richard Ayerdale, a traitor. Ever since the disappointing outcome of Harry's meeting with George Johnston, Harry had been steeling himself for his return to North Carolina with nothing to show for his efforts. Ruination assured. Whatever small edge of grace he had gotten a fingerhold on, lost. Now, suddenly, the world had rearranged itself.

He needed time to reflect on this new order. He would have preferred to do this someplace else, but the party in the great room seemed to be laying in for another round of drinks. Their talk turning to some local political matter. Once again satisfying himself that he was as well hidden as he could be, Harry let his thoughts wander.

At first impression, Comet Elijah's prospects did not seem improved by this new turn. Additionally, Harry felt he had to reconsider why he ever thought Ayerdale might have killed the Campbells, other than the fact that he might have been in the vicinity of the farmhouse at the time. The crime of betraying one's country, rather than the murder of an obscure farm family, seemed a more appropriate fit with Ayerdale's standing in the world.

On the other hand, all was far from lost. What if Harry followed Ayerdale into Canada and there proved, or helped prove, that he was a spy? Even if he could not save his old friend, at least Harry himself would be vindicated, his reputation not only salvaged but advanced. Surely he would be hailed as a hero, his name toasted in the households of New Bern. In fact, in every important city from Boston to Charleston. Surely in that case he could intervene in Comet Elijah's case, at least enough to save his old friend's life.

But what of Maddie? Even if Harry fell short of exposing Ayerdale as a turncoat, Harry certainly could inform her about Ayerdale's finances. What reason could remain for marrying him? If Harry acted in time, he might spare her from coming under the thumb of one who not only was a beast, but penniless as well. She could do with the information as she wished, beginning with confronting Ayerdale. Preferably in the company of someone who could defend her in case the conversation turned violent. An outcome Harry suspected possible.

He imagined himself facing off against the princeling of Virginia. Beating a confession out of him if need be. It might end with Ayerdale's suffering more damage to his handsome face than the lone scar that now ran along one side of it. Harry might not escape injury himself. But he was no cringing slave child, but rather a full-grown man trained in the art of killing and maiming, combat in the style of some of America's most fearsome peoples, the Tuscarora Indian nation.

The discussion seemed to be breaking up. Harry was all but done convincing himself that his way forward lacked only details to be worked out. But a new complication disrupted his thinking. The single reason he might reconsider everything. The trip to Quebec, warning Maddie, exposing Ayerdale. Why he might turn around and head back for North Carolina on the first ship south. Leave it to Major Browning and his friends in Boston to unmask the enemy. And hope such a thing would happen before the wedding.

The single reason was Toby.

CHAPTER 22

13: Kill no Vermin as Fleas, lice ticks & etc in ye Sight of Others, if you See any filth or thick Spittle put your foot Dexteriously upon it if it be upon ye Cloths of your Companions, Put it off privately, and if it be upon your own Cloths return Thanks to him who puts it off.

—*Rules of Civility*

August 18, 1759
Boston, Massachusetts Bay

My Beloved Wife,
Greetings and all fine Salutations,
I am forry that I have been gone fo long and Traveled fo far away from You and our Plantation. I pray all is well & Martin is

remembering to falt the Cattle and Sheep once a week as he is fup-
posed too do. The Sheep muft be penned up at night to protect againft
Dogs and Wildcats and bears and fundry other Dangerouf Beaftees
that rome our forefts. I am relying on his Knowleje and Good Intens-
huns to fee these things are done, but you mite find it Convenyunt
to remind Him from tyme to tyme. Worft of all I feer I will not bee
home in tyme to Put In the Tobacco. Thif is hot and sticky work and
I am forry I cannot help but Martin shood be abel to figger out how
to get it all done with ye help of ye others.

My dareft I am Torn in two diff'rent Directions my Desire
to return to You and my Beleef that there is Urgent Busynef that
compells my Presenfe in Canada. I have received Informations of
ye Utmoft Importance which I Dare not divulge in thif Letter when
it could fall into mifchefuf Hands. I pray you Truft I am doing ye
right Thing. If all turns out as I ekspek I am certain Olaf McLeod
and ye rest of ye People of Quality in New Bern will forgive my long
absunce from my Dutees and reward me with their Approval when
they come to learn ye full ftory. I will rite again when I can. Please
convay my love and beft wishes to Mother and Grandfather. And to
Martin and the other Servuntf.

In hafte,

Yr. moft ob. & Loving Hufband, &etc.

James Henry Woodyard

HE FOUND HIS WORDS DISAPPOINTING. AGAIN. HE JUST COULD NOT
find the ones that a clever man with better breeding might use to
say how much he really missed Toby, his two moments of weakness
notwithstanding. And how he longed to return to his own people, his
own country. At the same time, the act of sitting at a writing table and
searching for the right things to say made him think on the distances
that had been growing, year by year, between himself and the people
he considered most his own.

The judge had allowed him glimpses into his world, a place as different from the one Harry inhabited as the two poles said to lie at opposite ends of the earth. Representations had been made. Harry could not honestly call them promises, but certainly they were assurances, founded on the expectation of Harry's continued good behavior, his practice of courtly manners where appropriate, and his accumulation of wealth through canny management of his acres and the acquisition of more. If those things continued to be done, Harry one day would be welcomed into the bosom of privilege and rank, leaving behind for good the brawlers and pranksters and wenchers he previously had kept company with. Their ignorance, profanity, poor table manners, even the places they congregated would be forever a regretted part of Harry's past.

But what then? People of quality might seat Harry at their tables and allow him to join their clubs, but how likely were they to forget his origins? Could those who knew his story ever really overlook the order of events that had sent him off on his path toward respectability?

And what of his own family? To be accepted into the highest circles of Carolina society, would there not come a time when he would need to put fences between himself and them? Neither Talitha nor Natty was likely ever to be invited to a social gathering at the judge's house or the houses of his friends. Could Harry turn his back on his mother and grandfather? And what about Toby? Could the uppermost layer of Craven County society embrace a former indentured servant?

Thoughts of Toby made him wonder again how she was getting along in his absence. Even more worrisome, he realized, was the possibility that she might be getting along very well. Even adjusting to his being gone. He felt a fresh wave of remorse for abandoning her to go off in search of the Campbells' killer and to save Comet Elijah. He longed for Toby's touch, her loving glances. He feared that in his fixation on his own affairs, he risked losing her.

The truth about Comet Elijah came to Harry in a blaze of clarity. When he got back to New Bern, he would have to break the man out of jail.

Maybe he could do it on the sly. Maybe slip in a blacksmith's file for him to use on the window bars. Or bribe a friend on the town watch to leave locks unfastened one night. That would be easier. But he would need to choose carefully. What if he misjudged the loyalty of his would-be confederate?

In all likelihood Harry would have to break him loose himself. The risk of discovery, and thus Harry's undoing, would be great. But he felt more sharply than ever that he held Comet Elijah's life in his hands, just as his old friend once had held Harry's.

He pushed away from the writing table and got out of his chair. It was nearly four in the morning. The taper he had been using, now nearly gone, guttered from the disturbance of air. He stretched his back and looked out a window at the darkened street below, vacant except for a dog-shaped shadow slinking silently down an alley. Despite lack of sleep, his thoughts turned again to his life in North Carolina over the last ten years. Until Toby's arrival it had settled into a routine that varied little from year to year. The passage of writing he had seen in her diary came to mind. He could not remember the exact words, but he had not forgotten the idea. Something about how moments of life flow by in a constant stream. Any one held the prospect of turning the world upside down.

By leaving New Bern, Harry had defied the customary order, the keepers of the rules themselves. That moment could not be relived. And now the stream had become a winding river, flowing ever faster in an ever less predictable direction.

★

The sun was coming up when Harry collected Annie and set out for the docks. He had gotten no sleep but felt wakeful. The innkeeper, an early riser himself, had encouraged Harry's guess that the best way to Quebec would be by ship. Although going by horseback would be more direct, fewer miles, a ship would take about the same amount of time: roughly two weeks, depending on winds and tides. Also, a land route would bring him through enemy territory, where he might be detained, even executed as a spy. A voyage, too, would be easier on Annie. She seemed to have become accustomed to the nautical life, although after disembarking in Boston she had spent the good part of an hour weaving around the street like a drunk. The only drawback of sailing would have been the cost, but with Noah's purse, money was no longer a concern. He remembered the Quebec-bound packet that Browning had said he would be traveling on. The trick, he supposed, would be to convince the captain to let him come along on such short notice.

He arrived at the dock at seven, an hour ahead of the turning of the tide. "I am on my way to join the North Carolina battalion with General Wolfe's army," he lied to the captain, who with his leathery skin, tradesman's clothes, and floppy woolen cap looked more like an aging dockhand than commander of a ship. Harry drew from his pocket a Pennsylvania three-pound note.

"Son, I don't mind if you be going to fight the Turks in Mesopotamia," the captain said, snatching the bill with one hand and touching his forehead with the thumb of his other. "You are welcome aboard my ship."

Harry started away to see about Annie's welfare, then turned back.

"An acquaintance of mine is traveling aboard your ship. I wonder if you can tell me if he has arrived and where I might find him? His name is Browning. Major Browning of the Massachusetts militia."

Harry already had rehearsed what he would say. He would claim he had been so inspired by the sight of American and British uniforms at the ball, and conversations he had heard around the punch bowl about the progress of the war, that he had made up his mind to join the brave men at the final battle of the campaign season. God willing he had arrived in time for it. He would reveal the story of his eavesdropping at a later time, after gauging Browning's disposition toward him.

"I'm afraid Major Browning won't be making this trip," said the captain.

"I'm sorry to hear it. I understand he had some sort of leg injury that had prevented him from joining his militia company earlier. Maybe it has flared up again. How soon will another ship be going out?"

The captain looked grim. "I'm sorry to tell you that Major Browning will never be going to Quebec. We had the news less than an hour ago. It looks like his carriage ran off the road in the dark while coming back from a dancing revel in the country. Him and his driver were found pitched out of the cab. Both necks broke."

CHAPTER 23

82: Undertake not what you cannot perform but be care-
full to keep your promise.

—*Rules of Civility*

THE PECULIAR ODOR OF BURNING HOUSES GHOSTED OVER THE MAIL
sloop *Penguin*. It was late afternoon, cool and river-bottom dank under
a gloomy sky as they drifted past a tip of land identified by a crewman
as Île d'Orléans, the last island on the Saint Lawrence before Quebec.
The smell grew stronger as they continued upriver on a flood tide,
the air taking on a thin, nauseating graininess from the smoke, inky
billows of it rising on either side of the river. Ragged columns that
stretched into the gray distance.

"French farms," the crewman said as Harry put a handkerchief to his nose for a filter. "Seems there's an endless supply of 'em. The lobsterbacks are always coming across new ones to set alight. It's worse like this when there's little breeze, but you get used to it."

The river was the same slate color as the sky, whose ashen light cast passing fields and stands of trees in similar dull shades. They were still twenty-five miles from Point Lévis, where he had heard British soldiers had set up camp across the water from the French stronghold. Close enough to hear faint booms of cannon. The reports coming at leisurely paced intervals.

"Ours," the crewman said, seeing Harry cock an ear to the sound.

"How do you know?"

"The Frenchies are running low on gunpowder. They're saving what they got left for when they really need it."

It had taken the ship twelve days to get from Boston. Winds had favored them, but what the captain originally aimed to be a twelve-hour layover at Louisbourg had turned into three days of recaulking hull seams. The leaks had gotten so bad they threatened to overcome the pumps, which had been manned constantly from the moment of castoff. Repairs involved everyone's vacating the ship so it could be grounded farther up harbor and heeled over at low tide, exposing the bottom for fresh pitch. The process had to be done twice, once for each side. Harry took comfort from the smell of rendered tar, which still infused the ship eight days later. It made him feel closer to home.

He was sure Browning's death was somehow connected to Ayerdale. But it was a puzzle. Browning said he had told no one of his suspicions until the night of the ball. Was it possible that Loring, or even Pownall himself, was involved in some high-level deception? Could one of them have conspired to kill the major to protect Ayerdale's identity as a spy? It beggared the imagination, but nothing was impossible. Nor could he completely rule out the explanation, unlikely as it also seemed, that Browning's death was an entirely unconnected turn of fate.

While in Louisbourg Harry had heard fresh reports from the battle-front. The siege seemed to have settled into a hopeless stalemate. An all-out attack at the end of July, a month after Wolfe's arrival, had failed embarrassingly, with more than two hundred British dead and about as many wounded. Since then Wolfe had busied the army with daily shellings of Quebec City and a campaign to destroy the countryside, torching houses and fields and slaughtering animals. The intention—so said the banquette generals in Louisbourg—was to demoralize the French, goad Montcalm into venturing from his defenses to attack. To fight this time in the open, not from behind barricades as before. But Montcalm refused to be drawn out despite reports from deserters of horrible conditions in the city and outlying encampments, including near-starvation rations to the point that city residents, those who remained, were eating rats when they could catch them. If the British general was the wolf, the experts lining the banquettes agreed, his adversary was the fox, cunningly staying in his hole, biding his time, waiting for winter.

Along with these intelligences, rumors had reached Louisbourg that Wolfe himself was the one who now was demoralized. He quarreled with his brigadiers about strategy. Despaired over the increasing like-lihood of having to leave the Saint Lawrence before winter ice set in with nothing to show for his efforts but a country turned to charcoal, filled with bloated animal corpses. Nothing left but to slouch back to New England, a botch, the wolf more a whipped cur. An inquiry into the question of competence inevitable. Wolfe's mood no doubt was not improved by the fact that he was sick. Reportedly he spent whole chains of days in bed paralyzed by bouts of fever and kidney pain.

They landed near the upriver tip of the island to drop off some mail, then continued a short distance farther to a British camp that had been set up across the water from the fortress of Quebec. Harry formed a silent *O* with his lips as he beheld how the headland loomed up out of the water. It looked like the prow of an unearthly large ship, its leading edge jutting into the place where the Saint Lawrence joined the Saint Charles. The formation was sharply angled and wondrously steep. Easily 150 feet of rock and scrubby vegetation, so sheer as to baffle even a billy goat. Not until that moment did Harry fully understand how apt was the description he had heard bandied about in Louisbourg. It was spoken in an awed whisper or on an angry thrust of breath from the belly, sometimes punctuated by the sharp report of a clay flagon hitting a tavern table.

From the headland at least, Quebec was impregnable.

They had not heard cannon for a while now. Crews done for the day, he guessed. Annie was unsteady on her legs after her long confinement. But happy, Harry could tell, it was over. He arranged for a feed and grooming in the stable attached to the first tavern he saw. It was an old stone building, the French name inscribed on a wooden sign over the door in gold lettering with fleurs-de-lis. *L'auberge Frontenac.* Off to the side stood two tall, slender Indians in buckskin leggings and bleached linen shirts, their heads shaven halfway back in the Iroquois fashion. They were leaning on their muskets while watching a kilted Scotchman show off some sort of jig without benefit of music, his slippered feet nimbly skipping here and there over a pair of crossed broadswords lying flat on the ground. Bolts of color enlivening a gray day.

Harry expected the place to have soldiers inside, it being early evening, but he saw none among the scant gathering of diners. Sitting at a table next to a window was a smartly dressed fat man with a small gold ring in one ear and a glass of beer close at hand. His head was bent over a ledger, a look of concentration on what Harry could see of his face. Harry asked if he could sit. The man grunted, which Harry took as a yes.

"Where are all the redcoats?" Harry said, trying to show a casual manner.

The man looked up. His face was plump, pale, and shiny with perspiration. Graying hair damp and tangled.

"Do I know you?"

Harry said his name and where he was from and offered his hand. The man held onto it, as if not sure what to do next. "I'm Goldie Gott-schalk," he said.

"I'm looking for some of my friends, Mister Gottschalk." Harry got his hand back. "I wonder if you might have seen them. Richard Ayerdale and Maddie McLeod. Also an Anglican minister traveling with them, name of Fletcher. They probably arrived here three or four days ago."

Gottschalk looked at Harry as if at a slow child. "This is a big place, Mister . . ."

"Woodyard."

"My job is to keep track of supplies that come in here. Not people."

"Of course. Well, maybe you could still help me. Mister Ayerdale is a colonel in the Virginia militia, on special duty for the governor of that province. I imagine he will be wherever General Wolfe is."

"In that case, you're out of luck. Far as I know, Jamie Wolfe is with his soldiers. A batch of them went upriver a few days ago to harass the Frenchies."

"Do you know when they'll be back?"

"No idea. And wouldn't say if I did. We just assume around here that anybody we don't know personally is a spy. No offense to you, sir."

"No offense at all."

"Anyway, you're on the wrong side of the water to see Wolfe, even if he was here. He spends his nights on the island." Indicating with a tilt of his head the direction Harry had just come from. "Don't worry though, boats cross back and forth all the time. You can get over there whenever you like."

"It is possible my friends aren't with the general right now, if he is on a patrol."

The big man seemed to be loosening his stern manner. Harry's show of affability paying off.

"If they're moving in the same circles as Wolfe, chances are they'll be staying on the island, too. Jamie has picked himself out a fancy house over there. Belongs to the French overlord—I should say, the French former overlord—of that place. Most of the ranking officers have settled into the same neighborhood. In shouting distance, you might say. And there's been plenty of shouting."

"I heard there've been some disagreements over how the war is being carried on," Harry said.

"We middling sorts hear only dribs and drabs, but it's said his brigadiers fault him for what happened at Beauport."

"That's where the French beat back his big attack." Letting Gottschalk know that Harry was not completely ignorant.

"Unless he can redeem himself at this late hour of the day, the Battle of Beauport will go down as the great shame of Britain during the war for America. And maybe the end of Jamie Wolfe as a soldier."

"Does he deserve the blame?"

Gottschalk took a swig of beer. Sloshed it around in his mouth as he considered his answer.

"I've heard this and that. What I think, it could have gone in either direction. If he'd whipped Montcalm right there, they'd be striking medals for him in London. But it didn't go that way, and the brigs take that as confirmation that he has the military brains of a blowfly. It don't help that they are proper lords, all three of 'em. Aristocrats. Jamie is but a gentleman. So no matter what he does, it's never quite good enough."

"I can surely sympathize with that."

They ordered food and continued conversing through the meal. Goldie doing most of the talking, as if, having gotten over his initial coolness toward an inquisitive newcomer, he was glad to have a fresh set of ears to catch his unhappiness with his current posting.

"This is an evil country. I can't speak for what it's like in winter, thank Providence I ain't been here for that. But the summer has been disgusting. The forest is hot and dark and moldy and lacks air fit to breathe. These rocks and trees are slick with an especially putrid breed of moss. There are places where you can sink up to your knees in black mulch. Clouds of mosquitoes and black flies suck the blood out of you. The fevers make you sweat and shit yourself. I guess only a redskin could actually like it over here." Gottschalk's meaty shoulders gave a quiver. "And French Indians hide behind trees and underneath logs waiting for a British throat to come along for cutting."

"Where are you from?" said Harry.

"Somerset." Harry guessed that was in England.

Goldie took a long pull of beer and gently set the glass back down on the table. "How I long to be back there now."

★

Despite his new friend's assurances, no boats crossed back to the island the following morning. The harbormaster said the next one would not leave until midafternoon. Harry took the opportunity this delay offered to look around.

Walking farther upriver, he came to a grassy hill and on it an emplacement of cannon. Redcoated crews were busy getting five guns ready for the day's dose of mayhem. The pieces were deeply dug in, barrels pointing high. The better, Harry could see, to lob shells all the way across the water, up the cliff, over the stone wall, and into the city. He could see it would do no good to demolish sections of walls, as was usual in the siege tactics the New Bern militia had been taught, since there would be no way to get soldiers up the heights and into a breach. He tried to imagine the damage that already had been done inside the walls by the constant cannonading. Wondered how much was left of Quebec.

Walking up a rise, he came to a ridge, beyond which precise rows of white canvas tents extended into the distance. Outside the reach of French artillery, he guessed. Soldiers in different conditions of dress moved about in the unhurried way of men at routine tasks, some hanging freshly washed clothes on lines rigged between tents, some seeming just to meander. The bits of cloth gave the encampment the flavor of a rag fair.

Harry continued his stroll with no endpoint in mind. His thoughts turning toward the moment he had been anticipating ever since having overheard the doomed Major Browning speak of Ayerdale's treachery. Harry pictured confronting the wretch with his treason. But unsettling thoughts entered Harry's mind. During the sail from Boston he had dwelt only on that satisfying moment when he let fly his accusations. By the strength of evidence he hoped to find, forcing a confession. Now that he was closer to the moment, he began to worry over how exactly the event would play out. His original plan was to act as Browning's confederate in routing out the traitor. But he had no idea how Browning had thought to go about that business, assuming Browning himself had any plan, which, on reflection, Harry guessed he did not. And now Browning was no longer part of the scheme at all. Everything would be up to Harry.

How long could he afford to wait for Ayerdale to make a slip, expose himself to the degree that Harry would feel the time ripe to step in? It might take the rest of his stay in Canada. Too late to head off any mischief Ayerdale might have in mind. He had been good at hiding his deceit for a long time. Years, it seemed, and who knew how far back it really went? And now time was closing in.

It seemed Harry's only course was to confront Ayerdale as soon as possible, with or without convincing proof, and hope to cow him into confessing.

A movement ahead caught his eye. A flash of red.

He stopped. Glancing back, he realized how far he had wandered. No sign of the British guns. The cliff on the opposite side of the river here was considerably lower than the headland, maybe only half as high, and by its appearance not as steep. A small cove at the foot of it. Rising up from that, a subtle crease in vegetation. Possibly indicating a gulley running down the cliff.

He continued walking. At the top of a rise he spotted a lone British soldier. A junior officer, judging from his age, not much older than Harry. The officer's clothing looked more expensive than the ordinary

British issue: knee-length double-breasted overcoat the same intense shade of red that had attracted Harry's eye and without ornamentation other than two rows of brass buttons. Polished black riding boots and black tricorn. He was tall and thin, almost gangly. No trace of the Paunch of Privilege, as Harry had come to think of it: just enough of a swell of belly to signal that the owner never wanted for rich food and never had to labor for it. He was preoccupied with a spyglass, which he held pointed toward the other side of the river, about where Harry had seen the cove.

"Good morning, sir," Harry said when he got within hailing distance.

"Good morning." The officer spoke quietly, as if afraid his own voice might break his concentration. He was holding the glass with both hands, long, almost spidery fingers bracing the leather-bound tube like struts of a bridge. Trying to keep it steady.

"I hear that General Wolfe has gone farther upriver," Harry said, thinking to make sociable conversation. The idea coming into his mind that if he could make friends, this young man might be able to give him the whereabouts of Richard Ayerdale. Assuming that Ayerdale was as well known in the circles of British officerhood as he claimed.

No response. The man briefly took his eye away from the glass, blew a puff of air onto the eyepiece as if to clear some small obstruction, and resumed peering through it.

"I imagine the general is out trying to find a good place to attack the French, don't you think?" Harry said. "Maybe that place you're looking at over there? Do you suppose there might be a pathway up that cliff?"

The redcoat abruptly lowered his glass and gave Harry a sharp look, as if noticing him for the first time. He was not only thin, Harry realized now, but frail, with a pallid complexion and slight tremor about the lips. His face was somewhat rat-like, a receding chin and forehead and an upturned nose too large by about half for the rest of his features. Reddish hair that might have reached his shoulders were it not tied back with a ribbon. His most striking features were his eyes. The rims were red nearly to the point of matching his uniform coat and frighteningly intense against the pallor of his skin.

A soldier wearing the bishop's mitre of a grenadier appeared from behind some brushy trees, musket with bayonet attached casually slung over one shoulder. "Is everything all right, General?" he asked.

"Who are you?" the officer asked Harry.

"A friend," Harry said. Realizing finally who he was talking to.

With a slow, deliberate motion, the sentry swung his musket around until it pointed at Harry.

"Well, friend, I see you are not in uniform. May I ask what brings you before me this morning?"

To his dismay, Harry found himself stuttering, stumbling over how to say he posed no threat. Three more soldiers came up, seemingly out of nowhere. Harry wondered how he had been able to blunder past Wolfe's guard.

"I'm looking for some friends of mine," he said. "Colonel Richard Ayerdale of the Virginia militia and his fiancée, Madeleine McLeod. And a minister of the gospel by the name of Fletcher. I don't suppose you've seen them?" He immediately regretted this last part. Seeming to interrogate the commander of His Majesty's expedition at Quebec.

"Extraordinary," said Wolfe. His bright eyes locked on Harry's with full attention. "I have indeed seen Colonel Ayerdale. And Miss McLeod. Both went missing two days ago, less than a week after they arrived at our camp. Most upsetting. Perhaps you can shed some light on this mystery."

"That is news to me, General. I'm afraid I have no idea. . . ."

"Arrest this man," Wolfe said. He collapsed his telescope with a snap. "I will question him later myself."

Yet another soldier appeared leading a horse. Wolfe grimaced from some hidden pain as he lifted his foot into a stirrup.

"Please inform my brigadiers, wherever they may have wandered off to, that I shall not be dining with them tonight. I have matters to attend."

He wheeled and galloped off in the direction of the camp, trailed by two of the grenadiers at a jog. Leaving Harry now facing two bayonets.

CHAPTER 24

11: Shift not yourself in the Sight of others nor Gnaw
your nails.

—*RULES OF CIVILITY*

HIS ESCORTS WERE NOT INTERESTED IN HARRY'S STORY. ONE DID
promise to try and look up Reverend Fletcher. Harry assured him the
minister could ratify his identity and that he was not a spy. The soldier
sounded grudging, raising doubts in Harry's mind as to whether the
soldier would bother himself any further once shy of his prisoner.

"It won't do yer no good no-how," said the other. "The general
says he wants to question yer, and yer not likely to be let loose 'til
'e does."

The jail was two rooms in the damp cellar of a hulking stone church near the dock. The structure looked ancient and fortress-like. Heavy wooden shutters flanking stained-glass windows. Protection against Indian attack in Quebec's early days, Harry guessed. The larger of the cells contained French prisoners of war. The other was devoted to British soldiers and tars, who, Harry surmised, had run afoul of some regulation or other, and several individuals in civilian clothes. Much of the room was taken up by folding cots, each outfitted with a thick mattress and blanket. Small barred windows let in streams of thin gray light.

One of the civilians had a familiar face. Harry had last seen it smeared with mud and horse droppings outside Cogdell's in New Bern.

"Abel?" Harry said.

"Well, if it isn't Harry Woodyard."

His clothes looked like they had not been washed since court week. His hair was matted and he had a scraggly growth of beard. But he sounded canty, considering his current situation.

"What are you doing here?" said Harry.

"A couple days after you . . . disappeared, old man Dobbs decided it would be a good idea to show the North Carolina standard in Canada for this year's go-round. Judge McLeod had the town watch round up as many militiamen as they could lay hands on in the space of an evening and shipped us off the next morning on a schooner."

"Is Reuben here?"

"He was passed out drunk in the woods at the time of the muster. I knew where he lay but didn't let on."

"How do you come to be in jail?"

"A redcoat lieutenant up here made the mistake of letting me know his view of Americans. Well, me in particular. I'm afraid that's when I pulled him down off his horse and broke his jaw."

"I'm sorry."

"I seen the inside of a jail before, Harry. You have, too. Maybe you were right, though."

"Right about what?"

"I need a course of instruction as to how to conduct myself. Maybe then I wouldn't get into so many scraps. Especially with people I can't really win arguments with." He gave Harry a sly look and said, "And what misunderstanding has laid you up in here?"

Harry recounted his run-in with General Wolfe. "I'm trying to find Maddie McLeod and her fiancé, Richard Ayerdale. And the minister they are traveling with, Reverend Fletcher."

"Can't let an old love go, eh, Harry?"

Harry let Abel's guess go unchallenged.

"I heard Ayerdale and Miss McLeod up and left two or three days ago," Abel said. "Along with a couple of Indians that was traveling with them. Right around the time I got into my scrap."

"I heard about them leaving. But what's this about Indians?"

"I guess Ayerdale had taken them on as servants. Reverend Fletcher is still around. He claims he don't know where they went, is what I hear. Even though they was all staying in the same house."

Harry took another look around. The other prisoners were constantly moving about in the weak light, though slowly, like in a dream and without any clear intent. One jostled Harry. He mumbled an apology and continued on.

"Was there a mutiny here?" Harry asked. "Looks like enough people in this room to fill a couple platoons."

"Mutiny? Not bloody likely. These lads would just as soon jump off a crag as turn against an officer. It's pitiful. You show up late for muster or with dirty breeches, you land in jail. After the whipping, of course. You even look like you're about to sauce one of your betters, you're in jail with stripes on your back. They treat these poor sops like animals, Harry."

Harry nodded. He had heard stories about British Army discipline.

"Seems it don't even enter their thoughts to make a fuss about it. They is more scared of their officers than they is of the enemy. I figure that's why they is such bad news on the battlefield. An officer tells a lobsterback to stand upright and stock-still in front of people shooting at him, and he'll do it. I tell you, it's unnatural the way they act."

"Guess there's no law against locking up Americans."

"I'm lucky they didn't shoot me. They must have decided that killing colonials don't look so good when it come to getting more militia to join the war. Though they don't seem to know what to do with us when we get here. I don't know why they even bother. Look like the only thing to them lower than an American soldier is a red-skinned Indian."

"True enough, on both accounts," said a man who had paused in his wanderings long enough to hear what they were saying. "The only time a Briton respects an Indian is when that Briton is on the sharp side of a tomahawk."

He was tall and bony, in his midthirties, Harry guessed. Cheeks covered with a dark beard about the same state of growth as Abel's. He introduced himself as Ambrose Rutland, a schoolmaster from Massachusetts. He was spending his fourth day in jail for spreading demoralizing thoughts among his colony's detachment accompanying Wolfe's army. The ones that Major Browning would have been joining had he survived his trip home from the ball, Harry guessed. In view of Rutland's polished way of talking, Harry briefly wondered if he should place himself on Rutland's left-hand side to show deference. Instead, he just introduced himself and asked in a sociable way what exactly had gotten Rutland in trouble.

"I made the mistake of openly questioning the harsh tactics General Wolfe is employing against the French. The cruelty of destroying an entire city. We've heard reports that not a house or a shop has been left untouched by cannonballs. And they've laid waste to the countryside by fire and sword. There have been atrocities, Mister Woodyard. Atrocities beyond the bounds of civilized behavior. I found I could not keep quiet about this. I might have escaped censure, for the only people hearing me was other Massachusettians. But word got out I was spreading sedition."

"We is lucky we both didn't hang," said Abel.

"Ah, well." Rutland said something in a foreign tongue. Without waiting to be asked, he said, "Latin. 'Once let out, what you have said cannot be taken back.'"

A disturbance near the staircase interrupted their conversation. In the poor light, Harry could just make out two soldiers struggling to haul down a large cooking pot.

"Wonder what kind of soup they have for us today," said Abel. "The food ain't that bad here, if you like soup."

"By the way, Abel," Harry said a few minutes later as they stood in line, "I've given some thought to what you told me when I came in."

"What's that?" said Abel.

"About you needing lessons on how to behave yourself."

"Well, if you're not too busy sometime."

"I was wrong. You don't need any lessons from me."

★

It rained all night and continued past daybreak. The soldiers who had brought in soup came back and set out hard biscuits and buckets of water that smelled of river, then a sergeant called the names of five Britons to be quick-stepped upstairs and back to their units. As soon as they were gone, six more offenders made their way down. All gathered around them to hear the latest news. The young general had left on a frigate to join a redcoat host several miles upriver, where they were keeping an eye on a large French camp on the opposite side. Wolfe still seeming to brood on where to make his second and final attempt of the year to bring down Montcalm. The bearer of this tiding was a middle-aged corporal who seemed to be taking his four-day sentence for filching rations from an officer's kit as just another unfortunate episode in a soldier's life.

"If he has any ideas on where to attack, he ain't sharing them, even with his brigs, is what I hear," said the corporal. "I heard it said he's all but given up and is ready to sail out of this putrid hole. Can't be soon enough for me. But I'm sure he'll make one more try, just to satisfy honor." He said the last words with a snigger.

Harry thought this valuation of Canada, which jibed with Goldie Gottschalk's, too harsh. He generally had found the surroundings pleasant enough except for the smoke, which lay over the land like a shroud. Certainly that was not Canada's fault. He wondered what Noah would have made of the landscape here. It was far more varied than the flatness of coastal North Carolina. Harry also liked the weather. Though rainy, it was cool for the time of year. People made fun of Governor Dobbs's complaints about New Bern's climate, especially in summer, but in truth summer was not Harry's favorite time, either.

About midmorning, he heard his name called out. He was surprised to see one of the soldiers who had taken him to jail.

"Well, I asked around and found the place you said your man Fletcher was staying. He weren't there, so I scratched out a note, said you were here in the church jail, and wanted to see him. Just wanted to let you know."

"You don't know what this means to me," said Harry. And, in fact, the man likely had no idea how it was to have every hope pinned on the whim of a stranger who had no reason to go out of his way.

"Oh, and here's a letter for you. Just got here yesterday. A friend in the mail office heard me talking about you and your name sounded familiar. He remembered seeing this, but he didn't know where it was supposed to go."

Harry was already opening the envelope. It was Toby's handwriting.

CHAPTER 25

9: Spit not in the Fire, nor Stoop low before it neither Put
your Hands into the Flames to warm them, nor Set your
Feet upon the Fire especially if there be meat before it.

—RULES OF CIVILITY

August 14, 1759
New Bern, North Carolina

Dearest Husband,

I was Glad to get yr. Letter of August 8th inst. & was hoping you
would be back before I could reply. May you be safe & well Home
again before this finds its way into yr. beloved hands. But if not, I
hope it finds you in Fair Health and Good Cheer. Wee planted out
our Colliflowers soon after you left and sowed Carrots and Turnep
Seed laft week, and transplanted Brocoli to ftand. Yesterday Wee

sowed some lots of Onion feed and Rhadish & Lettuce, Garden
Cresses & a little white mustard. Martin says you fo much like Peas
in the Fall so Wee will fow fome of them bye-and-bye. Also fome
Fpinatch. It has been very dry here. Don't be worried but wee had a
little excitement ye other night when a Lightning Bolt fet a Tree afire
in the Turpentine Orchard down near ye Creek. It was full of fap
and burned like a torch & might've burnt down ye Whole Orchard
except Martin had posted fome Men to keep a Watch for just such
a Thing and when they faw it there they blew their horns and got
fome Neighbors over to help our boys put it out before it did too much
Damage. Martin expects Wee will have 1 or 2 hundred barrels of
turpentine ready to ship before long and more before ye Season is
thru'. He is overfeeing the diftillery at ye Creek himself, which he
says takes every bit as much care as making a Good Whisky.

I fuppose you have no way of Knowing what a Difturbanfe your
leaving New Bern without ye Blefings of Judge McLeod and his Court-
house Circle has Caused. No need to Dwell on that now, but there can
be little Doubt that ye longer you ftay away, ye more Trouble there is
likely to be. I am not Upbraiding or intending to Upfet you, my Dear,
but only Letting You Know how ye land lies here. I am certain that
whatever decifions you are Making, are ye Correct Ones.

Longing for yr Safe Return. Every Day is a Misery without You.
Yr. Loving Wife, Toby Woodyard

SHE HAD ADDRESSED IT TO HARRY IN THE CARE OF PETER BURKE IN
Boston, whose name she must have gotten from someone in New Bern
who knew Noah. Somehow it had passed from hand to hand, ship
to ship, followed in Harry's wake all the way to the Saint Lawrence.

"You see? You see?" Harry said, waving the letter in front of the
soldier. "This letter proves who I am. It is addressed to me, Henry
Woodyard, and it's from my wife, Toby Woodyard, of New Bern, North
Carolina."

The soldier shrugged. "That's something you need to take up with the general. If we're not at war by the time he gets back. Good luck to you, mate."

Reading by the cold light of a cellar window, he felt injured by Toby's words. Especially the endearments. They were reminders of how he had betrayed her, both physically with Jacqueline and mentally, in the case of his feelings for Maddie, confused as they might be. He knew that Toby could only be wondering what he was up to, dashing off on the trail of an old love. He felt suddenly unworthy of the woman who waited for him and had a renewed longing to be back at her side.

His efforts to expose Ayerdale as a liar and a spy were no further along than that night at the ball in Massachusetts Bay. Now that he considered the matter, they had come to less than nothing, except a possible explanation for Ayerdale's disappearance from camp. It fit the pattern of his previous perfidy, leaving suddenly on the eve of a fight. As for Maddie, her fate was almost certainly out of Harry's hands. What remained was the mystery of why she had gone missing along with Ayerdale. Could she somehow have become entwined in Ayerdale's crimes? It had been ten years since Harry had seen her, and in the intervening time she had traveled the length and breadth of the European continent. Met many sorts of people, including Ayerdale himself. Even spent time in France. Maybe she had even gotten involved with the Scotch would-be prince, the one reportedly planning his second invasion of England, possibly with the aid of the French king. Could Maddie herself somehow have turned coat? Whatever the case, the reality was that Harry was now cooped up in a cool, damp, poorly lit church basement in Canada. Powerless to do anything but complain.

He folded the letter, handling it as gently as holy writ, and tucked it into his pocket. There his fingers rubbed up against a metal object.

The badge.

Harry had time on his hands. Nothing to do but wait until General Wolfe returned from his scouting expedition upriver.

Time to work on a puzzle.

Ambrose the schoolmaster had some writing materials in his knapsack and was happy to lend them out. In the watery window light, positioning the brooch for as good a view as he could get, Harry began scribbling. He continued until daylight faded, then resumed at sunup. Crumpling sheets and dropping them to the floor as he filled them up with chains of letters that spelled nothing.

★

"I didn't know you could write Latin," said Ambrose, stopping by at midmorning to see what Harry was doing. Harry was just about to throw away another sheet decorated with crosshatches and random-looking letters.

"I don't," said Harry.

"Well, you've written out a proper Latin phrase." Pointing a finger at Harry's latest result at the bottom of the paper. "*LEVIUSQUAMAER*. It means 'lighter than air.' Except your Latin is all run together. No spaces between the words."

Harry stared at what Ambrose was looking at. It was the same group of letters he had made three weeks earlier using the name of Ayerdale's plantation as the key word. He had just gone through the exercise a second time using *Rosewood*, thinking he may have made some mistake in his previous attempt, since what it had produced looked like nonsense.

He now remembered where he had seen the phrase before. *Levius quam aer* was the family motto cut into the stone pillar at the entrance to the Ayerdale plantation. Though *light* and *airy* were not what came to mind when Harry thought about Rosewood.

His thoughts flew back to the night he and Noah had sat inside the Campbell house. The bodies of Edward and Anne Campbell on the floor, resting in caked pools of their own blood. Little Andy Campbell's lifeless form outside in the yard. Harry recalled his guess-work, his invented account of how the crime might have unfolded.

A storm-battered traveler seeking shelter. The Campbells opening their home, as was the custom. Then, trouble. A dispute or something discovered that the traveler needed to keep secret. Violence. The turmoil so unexpected that the Campbells had had no chance to defend themselves. Edward the first to die, since he was the most able. Throat slashed. Then Anne stabbed. Last, little Andy, shot in the back outside as he tried to escape. The baby spared, maybe out of some speck of humanity buried deep inside the killer despite the horror he had just committed. The bodies positioned to make it look like Indians' work. Then, bad luck for the murderer. A piece of finery he was wearing, a Freemason's pin, separating from his clothing during the struggle. Sent skittering, unnoticed, across the floor. Coming to rest underneath the baby's crib.

And now a name to go with the badge.

"It has a pretty ring," Ambrose said. "'Lighter than air.' Does that phrase have some special meaning to you?"

"It bloody well does," said Harry.

★

Another batch of prisoners made a clatter on the steps as they marched out. A single replacement came in and, needing scant urging, revealed the latest subject of discussion in the camps. Wolfe had finished his scouting upriver and was now back in his island quarters. Still no word as to when or where he might decide to attack.

Harry climbed the steps and banged on the door until a guard opened it to see what was the matter. "I have to talk to General Wolfe," he said. "I have urgent information for him."

The guard promised he would let General Wolfe know. Leaving Harry once again to marinate in a puddle of doubt and impotence.

That afternoon he had a visitor. It was the friendly soldier who had left the message for Fletcher. "I brought something for you," he said. He reached into his rucksack and pulled out a piece of salt pork. "Try not to show it around. This lot would trample their granny for a taste of bacon."

"Have you heard from Reverend Fletcher?"

"No, no word."

"Listen . . . what's your name?"

"Baker. Sergeant Baker."

"Baker, something big's afoot here. I need to talk to General Wolfe. It is a matter of the utmost importance."

"I'll make sure he knows."

"There was an American here in the camp, his name is Ayerdale. An officer in the Virginia militia. He disappeared several days ago. I have proof he is on a spying mission for the French. And that he is a murderer besides. By now he may have crossed over to the French side to tell them what Wolfe is up to."

"I don't think even Wolfe knows what he's up to."

"We've only been led to think that. Maybe he made up his mind days ago, and somehow Ayerdale found out. Or maybe Ayerdale has some other piece of vital information. Anyway, the general needs to be made aware of this without delay. Ayerdale is a traitor. It could affect the success of the whole campaign."

"That sounds very serious, Harry. I'll see that he gets this information immediately."

"Wait a minute." Harry began talking faster, sensing he had not made his case well enough and, in fact, may have sounded like a mad man. "I am the constable of Craven County, North Carolina. I have spent the past six weeks chasing Colonel Ayerdale for a murder I am now certain he committed there." He reached into his jacket pocket and took out the Masonic badge. "I found this at the place where the crime took place. It was dropped by the killer. Do you see this inscription?" Harry pointed to the markings, trying to keep his fingers from trembling with anxiety. "This is code for a Latin phrase, 'lighter than air.' That's the Ayerdale family motto. If you don't believe anything else, please take my word as a sworn officer of His Majesty the king that this proves Ayerdale is a criminal, and he may be consorting with the French army at this very moment."

He watched Baker climb the stairs. Still unsure if he had been persuasive but satisfied he had done as best he could.

The day wore on. Inmates milled about in the gloom. More soup, improved by the pork, which he shared with Abel and Ambrose.

He felt strangely tired when he finally lay down on his cot for the night. Wondering why so exhausted. As darkness set in and he slipped off to sleep, he realized he had been prowling the room the whole afternoon.

Sergeant Baker woke him the next morning, shaking his shoulder.

"You've been sprung."

"Am I to see General Wolfe?"

Baker put a finger to his lips and beckoned him to follow. Harry said quick good-byes to Abel and Ambrose, promising to do what he could to get them freed, then trailed Baker up the staircase. He passed the guards, who nodded to Baker. Through the wooden doors of the church they went, then outside onto the elaborately carved two-story stone porch.

At the foot of the entrance steps, looking like a herald of the underworld with his black robe and unsmiling face, was Reverend Fletcher.

CHAPTER 26

10: When you Sit down, Keep your Feet firm and Even,
without putting one on the other or Crossing them.

—*Rules of Civility*

THE MINISTER'S BORROWED QUARTERS BACK ON THE ISLAND PROVED
to be a handsome two-story white stucco house surrounded by flowers.
Harry had seen others very similar in New Bern, Bath, and Edenton.
He had never been to France, but somehow this one looked peculiarly
French. He could not say why.

During the boat ride under a misty rain, the minister had made
clear that any questions would have to wait until they arrived at their
destination. Whether it was wise to go along with someone who had

been in the steady company of a murderer passed through Harry's mind. Though Fletcher was of smallish build, now that Harry had a chance to see him moving about for a longer period, Harry guessed that underneath the robe might be the body of an athlete. Harry took comfort in Fletcher's apparent association with the sturdy Sergeant Baker and also the fact that the guards had given back Harry's blades.

Harry and Fletcher settled into chairs in the front parlor, which was expensively furnished though covered with a fine veil of soot. Fletcher's face remained hard. But not particularly menacing. More like a man with a toothache.

Harry spoke first. "You must have good connections here, to get me out of jail. I thought I wasn't to be released until General Wolfe questioned me."

"There are few things in this world that cannot be purchased, including freedom. But set that aside. An interview with the general would not be the best idea at this time." Before Harry could judge his meaning and whether it contained a threat, Fletcher said, "I understand you've been asking after the whereabouts of Colonel Ayerdale and Miss McLeod. You've been quite insistent."

"I believe Colonel Ayerdale is spying on General Wolfe for the French army. And that he is a murderer." May as well come to the heart of it and gauge Fletcher's reaction as to whether Harry should be going after his weapons.

Expressionless, Fletcher got up from his chair, walked to the window, and looked out. The rain had stopped and a fog was drifting in off the water.

"And I suppose you want to inform General Wolfe of these suspicions," he said.

"They're more than suspicions, Reverend. I have strong evidence. And, yes, that is my intention. If you are somehow involved in this business, it would be to your advantage to say so now."

Fletcher looked at Harry, this time with what could have passed for a smile. Harry thought it wise to get onto his feet. At the same time he moved his hand toward the side of his belt where his blades hung. Fletcher, taking note of Harry's posture, gave a short, joyless laugh.

"Young man—may I call you Harry?"

Harry nodded.

"I do have a confession. I am not a minister of the gospel."

"I have doubted such from the beginning."

"My name is Giles deSavoy. I am a colonel in His Majesty's army."

It took Harry a moment to absorb this, consider the possibility it was a lie.

"Your name sounds French."

"Norman, actually. One of my ancestors was among the duke's knights when he gave the usurper Harold his comeuppance at Hastings. One of my now long-dead cousins was Richard Coeur de Lion. My personal favorite out of our rather large family."

Harry found himself blinking, trying to take it all in. Staying at the ready. Every muscle charged with stored-up energy. But Fletcher's— deSavoy's—demeanor remained peaceable.

"You may have some French ties yourself, if you go back far enough. William wasn't called 'the Conqueror' for battlefield exploits alone, as my numerous kin like to say. One of his female offspring somewhere in the line may very well have married a good native Saxon by the name of Woodyard."

"Let's say I believe any of this," said Harry. "Why have you been keeping such close company with Richard Ayerdale?"

"You are correct in your suspicions about Richard. He is a spy. I congratulate you on your powers of perception. But now, he is our spy."

★

They were seated again. Harry relaxing his guard as the story unfolded. It seemed too rich to be made up. At least, if this man Giles's intention were to deceive, he could have used something simpler.

During his career, he said, which mostly had consisted of fighting the French army in France or elsewhere on the Continent, he had been drawn to a particular specialty: catching enemy agents. He had made a name for himself in this field. So when the government began suspecting a highly placed turncoat in America, the ministers turned to him for advice. Of several notable indications of treachery, the best evidence was the same that had gained the attention of the Americans whom Harry had overheard in Boston: a run of unexpected French victories near the beginning of the war.

Early suspicions had fallen on Governor Shirley. But surprising French successes had continued after he had been recalled to London. Finally, Giles had been dispatched to America personally by the new strongman in Whitehall, a fiery-tongued package of energy named William Pitt, to investigate. Giles himself thought up his disguise as a senior clergyman looking into the status of the church in the provinces. A good excuse for his travels and inquiries, even when those verged beyond strictly religious matters.

The same logical path taken by Browning had led Giles to Ayerdale. The name began cropping up during conversations with different officials in both the American and British military. It became a common thread: Ayerdale's supposed taskings to gather information on the progress of the war and report back to the governor of Virginia. Giles sent Ayerdale's name back to London as one of several possibilities. There, a fellow specialist in ferreting out such activities undertook some of his own investigating and discovered the truth about Ayerdale's financial condition. Broke as a Methodist parson.

"I also discovered that despite his outward shows of patriotism, Ayerdale has long harbored deep resentments toward His Majesty's government," Giles said. "Especially the army."

It was Harry's turn to share. He told Giles what he had overheard about Ayerdale's quarrel with the redcoat captain at the Monongahela.

"I'd not heard that, but it fits with the rest of the picture. He is an important man in America, among the elite in your society. Many of them deeply resent being treated as anything less than full-fledged British citizens, with undiluted political and social privileges of such. In all honesty, I have to say I sympathize with their feelings. As colonists, you Americans in fact do not have the full rights of natural Britons. You even lack representation in Parliament."

"Our governor says the king represents our interests in Parliament."

"Yes, and I am sure His Majesty puts nothing above the welfare of his loyal subjects across the ocean and works tirelessly every day in their behalf."

Harry briefly weighed the man's sincerity, and it came up short.

Giles resumed. "When I caught up with Ayerdale in North Carolina, I confronted him with the evidences I had. This was only the day before you and I first met in the tavern. He denied everything, of course. But I informed him I had no choice but to put him under arrest and send him to London for trial. A board of British officers in Virginia would undoubtedly have had no qualms about convicting him if the allegations were proved, but I feared there might be interference on the part of the locals, since his family is so revered in the area."

"The Ayerdales are much admired, I can vouch for that." Harry thought it might be too distracting to mention just now his own family's long-ago connection with them.

"In all frankness," said Giles, "had it been I facing these accusations, I might have maintained my innocence and demanded a trial. But the more we discussed the prospects of a military court, the more unnerved he seemed to become. I think he recognized he could never live down the accusation, even if he were found innocent. His name would be forever tainted. He certainly would be exposed as a financial failure, maybe even land in debtors' prison. The alternative was to accept my proposal to become an agent of the Crown. My orders from Whitehall were to discover the turncoat and either imprison him or flip him to our own use. I proposed he continue giving the French information about our operations. But we would choose the information to be delivered, and it would be intended to mislead and confuse."

"And he accepted this?"

"He didn't reject it. I'm not even certain he realized in the tension of those moments that just by remaining mute in the face of my accusations he was admitting guilt. His silence, as he pondered his choices, was tantamount to a confession. I believe he saw his future as resting in my hands. Before he had a chance to say no, I began laying out some of the benefits that would accrue to him. He could continue collecting his salary from the French. To this day I don't know how much that is nor do I care, since I would have only his word for it anyway. But however much, it would be supplemented with rather handsome payments from the British treasury. This offer finally proved irresistible. Especially when the alternative was a probable encounter with the hangman."

"But why are you so determined that I not expose him to General Wolfe? Surely, if what you are saying is true, the general should know."

"Wolfe must not be made aware of any of this for now. General Amherst himself has no knowledge even of my presence in America, and he is commander-in-chief of all British forces here. When I set off on my mission we had no idea who the spy was or how well connected. A casual remark by a high-ranking British officer might have found its way to the spy's ears, alerted him that someone was on his trail."

"But now you have your man."

"Yes. But if he is to be of use to us now and in the future, the fewer who know of it the better. And I am relying on your loyalty to your king and your country not to speak of it. I hope you can appreciate the trust I am putting in you just by explaining all of this. The only reason I am telling you is because it seems clear you will not stop until you expose Ayerdale. I had only one alternative to taking you into my confidence, and that was to kill you. And that is not the British way—at least, not if it can be avoided."

Harry laughed but noticed Giles was not joining in. Making Harry think of the two recent attempts on his life. He decided to put that matter aside for the moment.

"I will do nothing on purpose to hurt the British cause," Harry said. "That I swear. But there is something I must know."

"You want to know where Ayerdale is now. And Miss McLeod."

Harry nodded.

Giles gave him a long look, as if judging the sincerity of his promise. "I will tell you this: Richard is on a new mission. He is under my orders to deliver a report in person to General Montcalm. He is to say that Wolfe has finally decided on a course of action, that he intends to attack the Beauport shore again, and the attack will come within a matter of days. And I fully expect it will. But not at that location."

"That was the site of Wolfe's earlier attack, the one that failed so miserably?"

"Yes. It is the gateway to the city."

"But that is not to be his target now?"

"I would not say, even if I knew, the exact place Wolfe has chosen. In fact, no one knows for certain what is going on inside Wolfe's mind right now. We just know he intends to risk everything, the lives of thousands of British soldiers and tons of munitions and his own career as a soldier, on one final assault before giving up for the winter. But of a certainty it will not be at Beauport."

"And how do you know this?"

"I have my own sources in Wolfe's high command who know he has definitely ruled out a second go at that place. The most likely target is the French camp twenty miles upriver at Cap-Rouge. So it would be in the best interests of Britain if Montcalm were to keep a substantial contingent of soldiers committed down here at Beauport."

Harry remembered hearing about the three officers serving as Wolfe's brigadiers. Aristocrats all, just like Giles. One of them might well have shared information with an old friend wearing peculiar garb without asking questions.

"By now Ayerdale will have made his way through the lines and delivered his lie to Montcalm. The general will make his own judgment as to Ayerdale's credibility on this, but he will not be able to ignore it. If the ploy draws even one extra battalion of French soldiers away from the site of the actual invasion, it could spell the difference between success or failure."

"But where is Maddie McLeod? And what does she have to do with any of this?"

Giles's eyebrows arched in what could have been a genuine expression of regret. "I am afraid Miss McLeod, through no fault of her own, has become involved in this intrigue."

"How is that possible?"

"The French officer to whom Richard has been reporting all along is a notorious spymaster. All I know is that his name is d'Brienne, and he is in this country, and he moves in the shadows. Richard said he would reveal his identity later, but for now it would be better he did not. This information is not critical to me at this moment, and in the treacherous world we inhabit, sometimes ignorance is preferred. On the evening Richard was to make his way to the French side, Miss McLeod stumbled upon a letter from d'Brienne with detailed instructions for the crossing. Unfortunately, Miss McLeod is not only bright; she is also fluent in French. She recognized the purpose of the letter. Richard made an effort to explain himself without actually divulging any secrets, telling her that things were not as they seemed, but he quickly saw that he could not risk discovery at this critical stage of the game. He had no choice but to take her with him."

"If I know Maddie McLeod, she would not have gone peaceably."

"By heavens, she did not. It took the combined efforts of Ayerdale and his two Indians to convince her that she had no choice."

"What is this about Indians?"

"A pair of warriors were supplied to him by d'Brienne soon after Richard's arrival here. It took all three of them to bind Miss McLeod and get a handkerchief into her mouth. Even then, she broke a fine setting of tableware with her feet on her way out. The heart of a wild highlander beats beneath that lovely breast, I assure you."

"You speak as if you were there when this happened."

"I am sorry to tell you that I was. I hated to see it, but Ayerdale had to be allowed to complete his mission."

Harry considered breaking open Giles's skull on the spot. Seemingly unaware of his anger, the officer continued. "I believe that Miss McLeod will come to no permanent harm and will be rescued in due time, when our forces are successful. Montcalm is quite the gallant when it comes to women. Especially attractive young ones."

"Maybe he is, but I've heard he allows his Indians privileges with their prisoners. By the way, are you aware that Richard Ayerdale murdered the Campbell family?"

"What makes you think that?"

Harry reached into his jacket pocket for the badge. It was not there. He tried the other pocket. Nothing but clutter Harry had picked up in his travels. The folded-up chart of Pamlico Sound also was missing.

A sickening feeling came over him. Both objects must have somehow slipped out of his pocket. Or someone took them.

He pressed on.

"Do you remember the medal I found in the home of the people who were killed? I passed it around at Judge McLeod's breakfast table, if you recall. The inscription on the back is a Freemason's cypher, and I have discovered its meaning. It is the Ayerdale family motto. Ayerdale was inside the Campbell household. The only explanation possible as to why he did not admit this fact that morning and claim the medal as his is that he killed them. Probably because they had discovered something about his mission as a spy, just as Maddie did."

Giles gestured impatience with his hand. "When we made our bargain he told me about stopping at the Campbell house to get out of the storm while on his way to New Bern. He didn't come right out and admit he killed them. Maybe he just didn't want to say the words. He did say he later discovered he had lost his medallion somewhere, possibly there, and it might cause complications if it were discovered at the place of the murders and the inscription somehow were to be deciphered. He also mentioned that he was missing the nautical chart you showed around. But he would speak no further on this matter of the killings. And I did not press the issue."

"You did not *press the issue*? The murder of three British subjects?" Harry felt his gall rising again. But before declaring open hostilities, he decided to get as much information as he could. "And why would he have a chart of Pamlico Sound?"

Giles took in a long breath. His imperious manner further infuriating Harry.

"I suppose it will do no harm to tell you this now. Colonel Ayerdale was in North Carolina in the service of Monsieur d'Brienne. His real mission was to survey the ever-shifting depths in the sound for the purpose of picking out a channel between Ocracoke Inlet and New Bern through which French frigates could pass."

"French ships? In North Carolina?"

"It seems that Louis is actually contemplating sending a fleet to invade your southern coastline."

The thought came to Harry that Giles might not be just a liar but also a maniac.

"It is his *stratégie du sud*, as he calls it. It's not quite as far-fetched as you might think. The theory is it would take the pressure off Louis's forces up here in the North. He proposes to cut your nation in half, disrupt supply lines, maybe even spark an uprising among your slaves. But the French court is terrible at keeping secrets. We knew about the scheme almost as soon as it was hatched. Also, our agents in Paris say the French Parliament is all but fed up with this war, nearly as much as our own. It seems doubtful they would ever approve funds for such an expedition. Which could be a mistake. The scheme sounds a bit harebrained, but it is bold and could even make a difference, given proper execution."

Giles had been relating all of this in the manner of a professional soldier coolly analyzing the tactics of his enemy. Now he leaned forward and fixed Harry with a purposeful, nearly menacing stare.

"So, I hope you can see that it would not do for this whole business of the badge and the chart to come to light just now. If it did, Richard could not continue functioning as an agent of the Crown. I simply cannot allow that to happen."

"But he will be called to account for his crimes someday, yes? He will be punished for slaughtering a family?" Harry tried to keep his temper in check. Inwardly, he was boiling.

"I am afraid that is not likely. As an officer of the British Army, an agent of Secretary Pitt, and a peer of the realm, I am empowered to bind my word on behalf of the king and his government. I have promised Richard that he will never come to trial, neither here in America nor in England, for anything illegal he has done up until now. It is part of our bargain. I understand this will be hard for you to accept, Constable Woodyard, but we must keep matters in perspective. The fate of British America must take precedence over the extinction of one North Carolina family, as lamentable as that certainly was."

Harry was thinking fast, looking for reasons why this arrangement would not work.

"Your entire undertaking now depends on me not making it public," was the best he could come up with.

Giles leaned back in his chair, the half-smile returning to his face. He looked relaxed, not at all like someone who had just been threatened with exposure. He looked confident, in fact.

"And what proof have you that there is a scheme afoot?"

"The people of New Bern have seen the medal. They may have a different understanding of the matter when I show it again and demonstrate how the code works, what the inscription means. The badge is all the proof anyone needs that Ayerdale was at the Campbell house."

"Harry, I know that you no longer possess the object of which you speak. Or the chart. They both were lifted from your pocket this morning by Sergeant Baker before he awakened you. Baker is an old friend from campaigns on the Continent. I am quite sure the chart has already been burned and the badge melted down for its gold. I am allowing him to keep the proceeds as compensation for his efforts."

"And what of the attacks on me?" Harry spoke evenly, trying not to let his outrage show.

"What attacks?"

"I was set upon by three men during my ride from Williamsburg to Philadelphia. It resulted in the death of a dear friend. I was attacked again aboard a ship by a man who clearly intended to kill me."

"Richard told me nothing of this. You must consider another explanation. D'Brienne has overseen Ayerdale's activities ever since he was recruited. D'Brienne may have caught wind of your mission. Perhaps these attacks were made on his orders, without Richard's knowledge."

Harry had been sitting in the same position for so long that a leg muscle was making a painful complaint. He stood and walked about, stretching his tendons. And reminded himself of the issue that mattered most.

"And what about Maddie? You say you hope she will be rescued when Wolfe storms the city. But surely she will speak out against Ayerdale as soon as she is free to do so. Your promises will mean nothing to her."

"No one, either here or on the Continent, thinks this will be the final battle of the war. I hope that as a loyal subject of the king, Miss McLeod also will see the need to preserve Ayerdale's usefulness."

"And if the French decide on their own that they can't take any chances of her ruining Ayerdale's usefulness to them? Might not they kill her to keep her quiet?"

"It is not in Montcalm's nature to kill prisoners. But the reality is that Miss McLeod's fate is out of our hands. Nothing either you or I can do or say in the next twenty-four to forty-eight hours can possibly alter the course of events. As for you, you do have a choice to make. You could raise a commotion. March yourself into Wolfe's house and, if you're not arrested again, try to unmask an agent of the Crown as a turncoat and murderer. Even though you have no proof. You can't even show that Ayerdale has defected. For all anyone knows, he might simply have slipped aboard an outgoing ship and returned to Virginia with his bride to be. I predict that if that is your choice, you would go back to your home under a cloud, if not outright disgrace, for making unfounded charges against a prominent American from a storied family."

Giles got out of his chair and squared off in front of Harry. What came next sounded rehearsed. The final words in a scene that had been blocked out in advance.

"Here is the other possible outcome, Harry. I am the one person in the world at this moment who has any idea of how brilliantly you have conducted your pursuit of the Campbells' killer—and, subsequently, your determination to unmask a spy. Now I ask that you respect the trust I have placed in you during this interview and remain loyal to the British cause, as you swore a few minutes ago you would. You will do nothing to interfere with the playing-out of events that already have been set into motion, and you and I both will place our trust in heaven that all will work out for the best. If you follow this course, I will see to it that you'll return to New Bern a hero. You will receive a letter of praise from Secretary Pitt and a commendation from the king himself attesting to your fidelity and service. The particulars not specified, of course, but I can guarantee the language of these letters will be fulsome, because I will write them myself. It will take a few weeks for these documents to cross the Atlantic, but I swear they will be forthcoming. Your standing in your community, in the colony of North Carolina and beyond, will be uplifted to an extent that you could never have dreamed. I wouldn't be surprised if they didn't name a government building for you. And one more thing: in my experience, I have found that suitable financial rewards inevitably follow such honors."

Giles had his back to the window so that Harry could see only his silhouette. A black form wearing the caped robe of a cleric. Underneath that masquerade, the power of the British Empire.

"So, Constable Woodyard," said the black shape. "Which will it be?"

CHAPTER 27

44: When a man does all he can though it Succeeds not
well blame not him that did it.

—*RULES OF CIVILITY*

HARRY MADE HIS WAY TO THE DOCK A LITTLE AFTER MIDNIGHT.
Searching under a quarter moon and patchy clouds, he chose an unat-
tended flat-bottom rowboat and fell in with a flotilla of larger vessels
making their way upriver on the slack tide. The others sat low in the
water, burdened with supplies for the big redcoat encampment a few
miles in that direction, he guessed. He got as close to the last one as
he dared, hoping to appear part of the convoy without inviting special
scrutiny. An unseen shore-side sentry at the cannon emplacement

issued a challenge. One of the sailors gave a one-word response, low and solemn, and they proceeded unmolested.

When they came to the hill where Harry had seen Wolfe two days earlier, he held back, watched the others continue until they were little more than dark specks, then veered off toward the opposite shore. He judged the river here to be less than two miles wide. The cliff on the other side was a featureless black mass lying between pewter-colored water and a matching sky. Recalling a trick taught to him by Natty, he scanned the top of the tree line for some distinctive shape to steer on. He found a shallow V that he thought could be the cove Wolfe had been looking at, and headed on that.

Pulling patiently on the oars, trying to muffle their entry into the water, and constantly adjusting for the gathering current, he thought of what lay ahead. He had only the broadest outline of a plan. Find Maddie, bring her back. If the French still valued Ayerdale's services, unaware of his betrayal, they would not allow her to live to expose him, whether or not they lost Quebec. If Harry did nothing, Maddie would die, of a certainty.

The odds of a successful rescue seemed long. His best chance was they would be in disarray due to the shellings and constant anxiety over a final, all-out, do-or-die attack. He would need to enter without being noticed, and, against all reasonable expectation, somehow find Maddie and spirit them both away.

He did not fear being hurt, even dying. Never had, so long as his death was not a shameful one. What bothered him was his inability to imagine how it might happen.

His rowing position had him mostly staring at the British-held shoreline whence he came, convinced he was not making much progress. But this proved an illusion. When he next looked over his shoulder he saw a small dark beach, surprisingly close, sloping upward from the water.

The boat set up a startling clatter as it drove onto the bottom. Wood against gravel. Harry hopped out. He had hoped to secret the vessel somewhere along the shore for use in an escape but now feared the noise of pulling it any farther would give him away. After brief consideration of how long it would take to swim back, he eased the boat into the river to drift away.

He took his time getting off the beach. Walked erect, as if he belonged there, rather than proving he did not by skulking. Just a man out for a nighttime ramble. The shadow cast by the moon preceding him among the pebbles. Finally he came to the trees. His way past was blocked by a wall of underbrush.

Maintaining an attitude of innocence, he clasped his hands behind his back as thoughtful people do and veered left. Moved his head from side to side as he proceeded, taking in the nighttime scenery as if enjoying a leisurely stroll.

From a small opening in the scrub came a sound of rushing water. Trees and shrubbery all but hid the stream as it coursed down the bluff at a steep crosswise angle. Alongside one bank was a trail. Or at least an irregular break in the vegetation that might pass for one. It was rocky and narrow, boulders slick with lichen and rotting leaves. A challenge even for a member of the goat clan, which Harry was not. Comet Elijah had once told him his Tuscarora spirit animal was a turtle. Not helpful here.

Starting up, his feet immediately slid from under him and he pitched forward onto all fours. His right hand caught the brunt of his attempt to break the fall, sending shards of pain through his wrist.

But no broken bones.

Barely able to see beyond the length of his arm, inch by inch, yard by yard, he continued the upward track. Grasping at bushes and saplings on either side to help haul himself higher. At intervals the solid rock gave way to shale, making footing all the more unstable. He lost track of time, thinking at one point he would never reach the top and be stuck here forever doing penance in a Canadian purgatory, at long last being made to answer for all the sins of his youth.

After a while the foliage became lower and scrubbier. Then, a glow of moonlight. Redoubling his care not to make noise, he slithered the rest of the way to the crest and peeked over.

A stone's throw away stood a double row of tents. Twelve in all. Beyond them, an open field stretched into the distance.

He ducked his head. Waited for a challenge. Hearing nothing, he took another peek. From its puny size and apparently unguarded status, it did not seem to be an important outpost. He supposed the idea of any sizeable number of British soldiers storming up the path he had just climbed, especially at night, had been considered and deemed ridiculous.

Adopting the same casual manner he had used on the beach, he stepped onto the plain and started walking back in the direction of Quebec. After a short time, he came to a cornfield angling out between the field and the bluff, its withered stalks about head high.

Thankful for this cover, he entered it. But too late. Someone behind him called out a single word. It sounded like French, with the tinge of a question. Harry kept walking. Then, another word, more insistent this time. He wished he had taken the trouble to learn a phrase or two of the Gallic language, as his childhood tutor had urged. A simple "good evening" might have sufficed.

He turned around. Nothing visible but cornstalks and open field. Then a man stepped into view. It was a young Indian, probably in his teens. Bare from the waist up except for a chest plate of beads hanging from his neck. Deerskin leggings. Shaved head, a knot of hair at the very back.

"*Canadien?*" he said with a questioning tone. He sounded friendly enough.

Harry smiled and nodded. "*Canadien,*" he said, imitating the accent.

The Indian said a string of French words. Harry smiled and nodded some more, then turned to continue along his way.

"*Anglais,*" the Indian said. More a statement of fact than a question.

"No, no." Harry turned back again, wondering what had given him away. Maybe his clothes, which were wet and bedraggled. As if he had just climbed a cliff. "*Canadien,*" he repeated, throwing in one more reassuring nod.

The Indian came forward. A knife, big and ugly, appeared in one of his hands as if by magic. Harry managed to sidestep his lunge, at the same time grabbing his own blades. A bronze wrist blocked Harry's ax chop, colliding with the wrist Harry had injured. Bone on bruised bone. The jolt loosened Harry's grip and his ax tumbled away.

Without pause, the Indian drove forward, knife aimed at Harry's gut. Harry made a half turn to avoid the weapon while aiming his own knife toward the same region on the Indian. Both connected, but at glancing angles. The Indian's blade ripped through Harry's shirt, drawing a ragged line across his stomach. Then came the warmth of seeping blood.

They each stepped back and surveyed their injuries. From a quick glance Harry judged he had not been cut too badly. The Indian was wounded in his midsection as well, also bleeding, but not a torrent.

This will be over soon, he told himself.

The fight had spilled into the open field. They began circling each other. The Indian treating Harry with respect based on their encounter. Harry felt every bit of Comet Elijah's training flowing back. Endless practice with wooden weapons, lessons drilled into Harry's sinews. Had it not been for his throbbing wrist and missing ax, they would be about evenly matched. But that they were not. He knew that to survive the night, he would have to be better than an Indian at Indian fighting.

They had gotten an audience. Five or six of the Indian's mates had stepped out from the cornfield to watch. From their looks of anticipation, they seemed to be enjoying themselves as Harry and his opponent continued circling. Each making feints, then dodging away, judging the other's reaction.

Harry settled his mind. After one more feint he would drive in, knife pointed straight ahead, like a spear, toward the man's heart. Let his momentum carry him through, no matter what, like a mounted knight in a joust. They might both die in the clash. But it seemed his only chance to prolong his life at least for a few more minutes.

Then someone called out his name. Gave it a musical twist, emphasizing the second syllable. The way he first had heard it in Williamsburg and again in Boston. Only deeper, more authoritative.

French words followed, apparently aimed at the warrior. The Indian gave Harry a murderous look, then, slowly relaxing his pose of belligerence, backed away. From his expression, still not convinced the fight was at an end.

As soon as Harry judged himself out of striking range, he turned to look. Against all probability expecting to see the Baroness Contrecoeur.

Instead, what he saw was simply impossible.

Like a portrait painted in moonlight, a French officer in a white uniform jacket with blue facings sat atop a gray mare. He wore a black tricorn with cockade raked at a jaunty angle. Sword hanging from his hip.

"I can't say I'm surprised to see you," the man said. Harry thought he caught a wistful note. "I do hope you're enjoying your stay in New France, *ma chéri.*"

CHAPTER 28

1: Every Action done in Company, ought to be with Some
Sign of Respect, to those that are Present.

—*Rules of Civility*

HIS NAME WAS RENÉ-ROBERT D'BRIENNE DE BEAUMONT. KNOWN AS THE
Chevalier d'Brienne, he explained as they walked toward the city,
the officer leading his mount. A major in rank, detailed since early
in the war in America to spy on the British and recruit spies, adopting
whatever disguise he thought suitable, even the one that he practiced
in his private life in France. A few weeks previously he had received an
urgent message calling him back to his regiment in Canada to resume
his role as a regular officer of infantry, every man needed immediately

at the front. He was returning by horseback when he stopped off in Boston to mingle business with pleasure just once more at a gala ball. Tonight he had been sent to inspect a position in the French defensive line, a spot that had been weighing on General Montcalm's mind in recent days, even though it seemed an unlikely avenue of attack.

Harry was still getting over his shock. Something bitter boiling up in his throat. "But . . . you and I . . ."

"And you did not know. But where is the harm? You found me attractive. And I, you. Affairs of the flesh, like those of the heart, take place mostly in the mind, *n'est-ce pas*? But I see you are wounded."

"It's not serious," Harry said, as much out of hope as conviction. His attention remaining fixed on adjusting to the new reality. Trying to rid his mouth of the rancid taste that had come into it. The resemblance to the person he knew as Jacqueline was, by turns, tantalizing and stomach turning. The fair skin and slender build. The voice. Now a somewhat more masculine version of the one he had half fallen in love with. A matter of inflection. There was even a suggestion of lilac in the air on this mild, breezeless night.

Harry felt cheated. There would never again be such a woman as Jacqueline Contrecoeur living in his mind. Or would there? The thought made him shudder. Then it entered his head that this Chevalier d'Brienne might try to kill him in order to safeguard the secret of his pretended sex. Whether guessing at Harry's thought, or just continuing his story, like a new acquaintance chatting up his life's history, he said, "Oh, those who matter know all about my charade among the *Anglais*. We French are more accepting of unusual forms of human expression, especially such as mine."

Continuing to anticipate Harry's train of thought, d'Brienne said, "You need not think I am concerned you will expose my professional activities to the British. My work on your continent is done. I am returning at first opportunity to Paris to refute certain jealous lies that are being spread by my enemies in court. Whatever the outcome, I have grown weary of this business, anyway. I intend to retire from service to the king and live out my life on my small estate fully and openly as the person I was born to be: a woman."

To his surprise, Harry found he was getting used to the idea.

"Then it must have been you who's been trying to kill me. And you must have murdered Major Browning. To keep Ayerdale's secret safe."

As soon as the words were out, Harry realized his blunder. D'Brienne stopped walking and faced Harry.

"You know about our mutual friend? The one from Virginia?"

Harry's lack of reply confirmed it.

"So, you, too, heard the conversation on the night of the ball," said d'Brienne, an expression of received truth coming over his delicate features. "I thought you had returned to the dancing after our tryst. How stupid of me not to realize. You must have remained on the balcony. I myself had returned downstairs, then sometime later followed the governor when I noticed him and the others going up. I was listening at the door. Not the best vantage point, but I heard enough of their suspicions of Monsieur Ayerdale and Major Brown's purpose to expose him."

"So you had the major killed. And you must have tried to kill me. Twice."

D'Brienne brought his shoulders up in an exaggerated shrug. "If you recall, I tried to dissuade you from your quest before any of that happened. I have done only as I was bound by oath to my king, *chéri*. I had to protect our Richard from discovery. It had nothing to do with my affection for you, which I assure you was genuine. I hope that you, as a man of the world, can understand that."

They fell into silence. Harry ruminating on their shared past as they continued walking and d'Brienne, he supposed, on Harry's future. The likelihood that this headstrong American would expose Richard as a French spy at first opportunity.

If you only knew the whole truth about your Richard.

Trying not to appear too obvious, Harry glanced around, took notice of where the Indians were. They were close behind. Alert, he reckoned, for any attempt at escape.

"I thought the Contrecoeurs were enemies of the pope," Harry said after a while. "Huguenots. Or was that another lie?"

"The Contrecoeurs were indeed Huguenots. The entire family was executed in secret several years ago. A cunning deception for me to take on the lady's identity, you must agree. But perhaps it would be best if we spoke no more of these things." He touched Harry on the arm. A tender touch. "You may find this hard to accept, Harry, but I bear you no ill. You've done as you've felt you had to do and I the same. As a trusted member of the general's staff, I shall try to keep you from being shot."

★

Three soldiers took charge of him at the city gate. They were all but lost in their uniforms, which might have fit them during fatter times. Still, they were strong and not at all gentle, despite d'Brienne's brief and, given the circumstances, charitable explanation of Harry's case, which he translated for Harry's benefit. He was a native-born American citizen who had blundered into French territory by mistake. D'Brienne commanded them to treat him well while the case awaited disposition. They were roughly shackling his wrists behind him as the major spoke. Not seeming to pay much attention.

D'Brienne mounted and said good-bye, until later, go with God, and added a small bow with a flourish of his hand, which Harry thought a little fancy. Then d'Brienne rode off into the night, leaving Harry to wonder what the Frenchman would really say to Montcalm.

The city looked dead. Smoke and the dry smell of blasted stone hung heavy in the air. Streets devoid of people. Torches unlit, windows dark. Almost every building he saw showed some kind of damage. In extreme cases, what might have been houses or shops or government buildings were little more than piles of rubble. He had heard that the lower town, the village at the foot of the cliff, had suffered even worse treatment. By his guards' manners, pulling and shoving as they walked along, he gathered they considered him personally responsible for it all.

They came to a squat one-story stone structure, comparatively unscathed, with barred windows. A proper jail. One of his escorts went inside. Harry took what he guessed would be his last opportunity and bolted.

Despite his shackles, he was able to get two streets away before being brought down by the soldier who proved swiftest of foot. This one was immediately joined by the other two, and they all began punching and kicking but with such a fury that at first only a few blows landed squarely. Harry curled up. His last conscious thought to protect his knife wound from more damage.

Sensing daylight through his eyelids, he cracked them open. Hovering over him, as if in a dream, was Maddie McLeod. A look of concern on her beautiful face.

★

"What are you doing here?"

"I've come to save you." Still groggy, sore in numerous places.

"Well, you're doing a first-rate job. That's a horrid cut on your stomach."

"It's not as bad as it looks. At least I don't think so."

He lifted his head enough to look around. He was stretched out on a mattress consisting, by its uneven feel, of straw sewn up in a muslin sack. About a dozen others were stacked in a corner of the stone-walled cell. It was spacious and, except for them, empty. A single outside window secured with iron bars.

Maddie looked disheveled in a thin cotton gown on top of a petticoat. At-home lounging clothes, the same ones she was kidnapped in, Harry guessed. Her hair looked as if it had not seen a brush since about then.

Before Harry could clear his head enough to ask any smart questions, a soldier admitted into the room a middle-aged officer who looked not much better-fed than the rest. He had courtly manners and a good knowledge of English. A surgeon, he said, sent at the request of the Chevalier d'Brienne. He cleaned and dressed Harry's wound, inquired about the lady's well-being, then bid adieu, bowing and edging toward the door, backside first.

The soldier returned with discs of hard biscuit and a bowl of water with a dipping ladle. He said something that Maddie interpreted as, "We regret that we are out of wine at the moment."

"Richard Ayerdale has turned into a beast," Maddie said as soon as they were alone again. "I'm afraid your instincts about him were correct."

"I'm not one to gloat. But I am rarely wrong about judging people." The words were beyond recall by the time he remembered about d'Brienne.

Maddie said, "On our voyage from Boston I confessed to Richard about my grandfather's financial condition. I had been wrestling with this and concluded that we should begin our marriage on a truthful footing. At first he seemed only stunned, but then he began behaving like a wild animal. I honestly was afraid to be around him. If the lack of a dowry was to be the deciding factor as to our wedding, he could have just told me and departed in peace when we landed. But he was so angry that I could barely even make out what he was saying. Mostly accusing me, in the most impolite terms, of dishonesty. He threw in a few nasty remarks about the Scotch race as well."

"Did he hurt you?"

"As it turned out, no. After several minutes of abusive language, he rushed out of our cabin. When I saw him an hour later, it was as if nothing had happened. He was a perfect gentleman again. It was the oddest thing."

"Before you go further, I have something to tell you that I guess you still don't know."

Harry enlightened Maddie about Ayerdale's finances. The news left her speechless but only for a moment.

"So we were each looking to the other for salvation. How perfect."

"You shouldn't be too hard with yourself. If I've learned anything during these past four weeks, it is that we all do what we have to do."

"Harry, that is so brilliant. You really should find a publisher. Share that wisdom with the world."

He made to get up off the mattress, but the movement revealed new areas of pain. He gently let himself back down.

Maddie continued her tale. Their arrival on Île d'Orléans. Assignment to a handsome house not far from Wolfe's own commandeered mansion, a gesture of deference to a distinguished American visitor. Her discovering a letter among Ayerdale's belongings that exposed him as having secret dealings with the enemy.

"Reverend Fletcher also must be working for the French," Maddie said.

"Why do you think that?" Just wanting to hear whatever story Giles might have told.

"He made no effort to prevent my being carried away. He did seem a bit embarrassed to have me watching him watching me being trussed like a Christmas goose by two redskinners. Before they were finished he left the room. When we get back to the camp we must report him as well."

"It's more complicated than that, Maddie."

Harry told her of Fletcher's real identity and how he had recruited Ayerdale to betray his French masters and work for King George. This second revelation seemed to take the rest of the wind out of her.

"But what game is this Giles deSavoy playing now? Why did he permit Richard to cross over to the French, with me as his captive?"

"Your fiancé has been tasked to give false information about where General Wolfe intends to attack, in hopes of drawing Montcalm's forces to that location and away from the real place. He almost certainly has delivered this message by now. The battle could begin at any moment, if deSavoy is guessing right about the timing. But not where Montcalm now has been led to believe."

Harry tried to get up again. This time, with Maddie's help, he pressed through the pain and gained his feet. After walking around, trying out his limbs, he remembered that in the excitement of the previous evening, he had forgotten to eat supper.

He plucked a biscuit from the metal tray and took a tentative bite. It was strangely pleasing. Not as hard as it looked, at least not on the inside.

Maddie screamed. Harry looked up in time to see her spitting and throwing a biscuit across the room, causing a small explosion of crumbs in the corner where it landed.

"Worms," she said in a quivery voice.

Harry took a closer look at his own biscuit. A severed half of a weevil was wriggling underneath the top crust. As if waving hello.

"The people of Quebec are starving," Harry said. "Wolfe has burned all their farms."

"Well, this is the first time I've been served worms. I'd rather take my chances on starvation."

Harry continued eating, trying to set a good example. After a few minutes Maddie got over her revulsion enough to pick up another biscuit and begin picking through it, flicking away moving pieces. Despite Harry's continued assurances that the worms would be good for her.

"About Richard's new identity," she said after some further reflection. "Does this mean I have to start thinking of him as a hero again?"

"No."

★

The rest of the day passed quietly. A light drizzle settling outside. Harry slept fitfully. He got off his bed again around midafternoon and asked Maddie what she did for a toilet. She pointed him toward a wooden door, smaller than the main one to the cell, and in the shadows at the far end. It opened into a narrow, oblong chamber ventilated by another barred window. A single wooden bench ran along the length of one wall, three holes about the size of watermelons cut into the top. The smell was not too bad.

That evening the surgeon came back to check on Harry's dressing. The man was in a mixed mood. Friendly enough but not trying to hide his unhappiness over what had been done to his city, which, as it turned out, was his place of birth. He likened Quebec to a broken shell. Hardly any residents left; most either dead or run away. And the few that remained no better off than those living in ruined houses and makeshift shelters in the countryside. Dreading the onset of winter. Only one company of *troupes de terre* occupied the citadel, a place of last refuge should Montcalm's army have need of it.

"Where is the general?" Harry said in a conversational way. Thinking to get some idea of where Ayerdale might be.

"Montcalm is sleeping with his boots on and horse saddled at his house just down the river at Beauport, along with more than half his army. The rest are upriver at Cap-Rouge. Though I have noticed Beauport has been reinforced over the past twenty-four hours."

"You needn't tell us all this," Maddie said.

The officer waved his hand. "By the time you are released it will be over. God willing, all of this misery soon will be over."

He pronounced satisfaction with the way Harry's wound was healing and made another gallant exit. Harry waited until he was sure he was gone and what he had to say could not be overheard.

"You know, Maddie, it's not so much what we know about the French and their deployments that's the problem. It's what they know about us. They know we know Ayerdale is working for them. At least that's what they think he's doing."

Fear rose in Maddie's eyes as she caught his logic.

"And how can they let us go free to spread the knowledge of Richard's treachery?" she said, completing his thought. "It would be simpler just to kill us."

★

They were up at sunrise the next day. Hungry again by the time their keeper came around with more biscuits and water.

Harry spent the morning trying to figure a way to get out. He went over every inch of the cell. Digging through the stone slab floor was out of the question. The bars over the window were thick and by all appearances indestructible. The tiny door window was not even large enough for a head to pass through. But through it Harry could see part of a guard desk. A set of keys hung tantalizingly from a spike in the wall.

He parsed the latrine in detail, thinking it might empty into a sewer outside. Or have another ventilation opening. If so, he would be willing to give it a try. There was a good chance Maddie would not go along, but this drawback proved not to matter. As best as he could make out, there was nothing below but a deep, dark, and entirely enclosed pit. Not completely odor free but surprisingly inoffensive: a tribute to either French engineering skills or the cell's present low occupancy condition. All the scoundrels having been let out to fight, he guessed.

The rain outside stopped but the sky remained sullen. It was noticeably colder, prompting him to wonder what inmates did for heat in the winter. He was thankful he had taken his wool jacket for the river crossing.

Someone had given Maddie a blanket. Standing idly underneath the window, eyes downcast, she pulled it close around herself, then looked up and caught him staring at her.

"What are you looking for, old witch?" She smiled.

Harry briefly wondered if she had slid into madness. Then he remembered. It was a game she had made him play when she was a child and he a self-conscious teenager. They would take turns being the witch.

"My darning needle?" he said, wondering if he recalled the reply correctly.

"Is this it?" She parted the blanket, pulled her petticoat up to her knee, and displayed one foot.

He shook his head.

She showed him the other foot. He shook his head again. She put forward one of her palms.

Harry said, "Somewhere in here, I think I'm supposed to say yes and start chasing you around the room."

"And what if you caught me?"

He felt his face flush and tried to think of something entertaining to say. Something friendly, playful, but not presuming too much.

"Dance with me," she said, getting him off the hook. Before he could complain there was no music, she said, "I shall sing."

Letting her blanket fall away, she curtseyed and began humming a brisk tune. Harry made an awkward bow, trying to remember how to begin. The last time he had danced had been at his wedding. Several eras ago as it now seemed.

She offered both hands, which he grasped without thinking. He bowed and she curtseyed again and motioned for Harry to drop one of his hands but keep hold of hers with the other. They turned and faced the pretend orchestra, he following her lead. Some of the judge's drills coming back. A skipping step to the left, one to the right. His unpracticed stepping more of a series of stumbles. She lifted his hand, did a twirl under his arm, and motioned for him to switch hands and perform his own twirl. And so they went, circling and turning and stepping forward and back to the rhythm of Maddie's silvery vocalizations. Harry got better as they went along. He even remembered the name of this dance. The Allemande. But he had forgot how it ended until it did. With him holding Maddie. Both of them slightly out of breath. Lips close enough to touch.

She relaxed her arms and turned away.

"It's too bad our times didn't match up," said Harry.

Maddie made an ambiguous sound in her throat.

"I was in no position to marry anyone, much less somebody like you," he said.

"Like me?"

"You know. Above my station."

"'Station?' Oh, Harry. When did you ever begin talking like that?"

"Since your grandfather taught me how the world really works. It's not anything like what I was raised to think."

"I liked how you used to think. We could have been happy together." She sat down on her cot. "We could have made our own station, if that's what you want to call it."

"That's not the idea I got from you when we last talked, at Natty's house. Besides, you were only thirteen."

"My love for you was all grown up."

"Then, why did you go along with leaving North Carolina?"

Maddie took a big breath, as if getting ready to make a speech. "It's all a tangle," she said and let the breath out.

"Untangle it for me. I'd really like to know."

"Where to start?"

Good question, Harry thought.

CHAPTER 29

26: In Pulling off your Hat to Persons of Distinction, as Noblemen, Justices, Churchmen & etc make a Reverence, bowing more or less according to the Custom of the Better Bred, and Quality of the Person. Amongst your equals expect not always that they Should begin with you first, but to Pull off the Hat when there is no need is Affectation, in the Manner of Saluting and resaluting in words keep to the most usual Custom.

—*Rules of Civility*

HARRY HAD JUST TURNED THIRTEEN. TOO OLD TO BE PLAYING WITH children. But Talitha had business in court that day. She made him stay outside with the dozen or so others whose parents were likewise occupied. The game, organized by one of the grandmothers, was one that Harry had played many times while growing up. They were marching in a circle around a randomly chosen child, in this case a red-haired, big-eared nine-year-old by the name of Anthony. They chanted as they tramped along:

> *King William was King James's son,*
> *From the royal race was sprung,*
> *Wore a star upon his breast.*
> *Go choose your East, go choose your West;*
> *Choose the one that you love best.*
> *If she's not here to take your part,*
> *Choose another with all your heart.*

With that, Anthony, blushing deeply, reached out and tapped the shoulder of a pretty little girl Harry had never seen before. She looked about ten years old, with skinny arms and curly hair the color of late wheat. Though the boy's performance was familiar, part of the game, it brought a burst of giggles and catcalls from the other children.

At the grandmother's direction, the girl stepped out of the circle and joined Anthony in the center. The marching resumed, the girl looking bewildered.

> *Down on this carpet you must kneel*
> *Sure as the grass grows on the green.*
> *When you rise upon your feet,*
> *Salute your bride and kiss her sweet.*

They stopped marching and began chanting, "Kiss her sweet! Kiss her sweet!" Anthony looked here and there as if to find a means of escape. But the longer he put it off, the worse the harassment became. He finally did as commanded—to a renewed outburst of giddy derision. Then, under the guidance of the old woman, who seemed to be having the best time of anyone, the children again took up their circular trek.

Now you're married you must be good.
Split the kindling, chop the wood.
Split it fine and carry it in.
Then she'll let you kiss her again.

This time, Anthony grabbed the little girl by both arms, gave her a hasty kiss on the cheek, and retreated into the circle, looking relieved and thankful the ordeal was over. The girl, who seemed dazed, began to follow, but the grandmother said, "No, dear, you must stay where you are. Now it's your turn."

The marching started up again with the children chanting from the beginning but changing the words to suit a girl. By the time they came to the end of the first stanza, "Choose another with all your heart," she knew exactly what to do. She had been sizing up the boys with a critical eye. As far as Harry could tell she had not given him a second look. But she stepped forward with unsettling boldness and poked him square in the chest.

The giggling and taunting began, though this time it had a different timbre. It was more tentative, as if the children recognized that Harry's advanced age put him on the borderline of familiarity. Harry, who for some time had been paying close attention to girls of his own age and older, the way they looked, and their sometimes mystifying behavior, was not pleased at all. Until now he had felt his presence in the children's circle merely undignified. Now he felt ridiculous. But he was trapped. No choice but to go along.

Standing on tiptoes, grasping Harry's shoulders to pull him down within reach, she kissed him full on the lips. She held it for what seemed a long time, allowing the scent of a girl-child flushed with exertion to fill Harry's senses.

Her name was Madeleine. Maddie, as she preferred. She was the
granddaughter of the county's chief justice of the peace, recently
arrived in New Bern from a city across the ocean called Edinburgh.
Her father had died unexpectedly and her mother taken ill. As weeks
passed, then months, Harry somehow kept finding himself in her
company, usually but not always in the vicinity of other children or
adults. She introduced him to riddles, a pastime of hers in Scotland.
She taught him those she already knew and some she was learning
through new friends she was making among the better families of
New Bern. Families that did not include the Woodyards. Harry was
flummoxed by the sly logic of such brain scramblers as:

Nebuchadnezzar, king of Jews,
Sat down on the floor to put on his shoes.
How do you spell that with four letters?

Harry liked solving puzzles. People said he had a knack for it. But
he was not fond of riddles, which depended on tricks with words and
phrasings. He could not think of an answer to the Nebuchadnezzar
one that he imagined would come anywhere close to correct. Finally
Maddie leaned over and whispered in his ear, "T-H-A-T! Four letters!"
She rocked back, convulsed with laughter.

Despite the joy she took in baffling him, Harry found that he
enjoyed Maddie's company. He was sure she was much smarter than
he, and that made him nervous, afraid she would tire of him. He kept
assuring himself that he felt no physical attraction whatsoever. But
with the passage of months, the barest hint of breasts became visible
underneath certain types of clothing and angles of light. And she was
growing hips.

He tried to avoid even thinking about thinking in such terms.
Having sex with girls before they were physically ready was not
unheard of in North Carolina. From time to time such a thing would
come to the attention to the Court of Quarterly Sessions, especially

in the case of orphans. Harry's instincts told him that such thoughts, the thoughts themselves, let alone any actions that might flow from them, were against the laws of nature. But to his distress he found he could not stop wondering what she looked like without clothes. He had the sensation of standing on a slippery ledge overlooking an uncharted and possibly dangerous bottomland. Flattered by her attentions but aware of where they might lead without constant vigilance. He fancied that she thought of him as one might of a big brother. He returned this by making himself think of her as a little sister. A very affectionate little sister.

She continued her practice of kissing him on the mouth whenever they said hello or good-bye, as if they were grown-ups, each time delivering her sweet, musky bouquet. This behavior struck him as both childish and strangely mature, like dressing up in adult clothing. But, then, he was discovering a great many peculiarities about feminine behavior overall.

It was three years before they made love. At age sixteen, Harry felt fully grown. Old enough to be turning out for militia musters. Maddie, at thirteen, was the same age as the new bride of the sixty-eight-year-old governor of North Carolina. They moved gradually toward it, with laughing tussles during outings in fields and forests within the town gates and beyond as opportunities presented themselves.

Harry's mother's suspicions were stirred up one afternoon as she was finishing some business in town and getting their wagon ready for the trip back home. She noticed Harry and Maddie walking along a shady side street, playfully pushing and poking at each other. A little too playfully for her satisfaction. She went directly to Judge McLeod and told him what she had seen. The result was that the two were forbidden to spend time together alone. Harry was willing to accept this outcome but not Maddie. Soon she was figuring out ways to be together secretly, with the added sense of drama their clandestine meetings brought.

One warm afternoon in early fall, in the shadow of a haystack in a field belonging to an old man named Rollins, a wrestling match became a halting exploration of the unknown. For Harry it was a stunning revelation, how well men and women fit together in actual fact, compared to what he had only heard. Unfortunately, Rollins came riding by before they had finished putting their clothes back on, and what had been a journey to heaven became a long and sudden fall in the opposite direction.

Harry's mother was feverish with anxiety over possible consequences. Harry had no doubt he would be hung. But days passed and no posse came to their doorstep. After a suspenseful week, they learned from friends that McLeod had decided his granddaughter had seen enough of America and would be returning to Scotland to finish her education at a proper academy. Though everyone in New Bern knew exactly what had happened, the judge stuck publicly to the fiction that nothing had actually happened, that his flesh and blood remained unsullied. That meant, miraculously, no punishment for Harry, for the reason that no offense had occurred.

Maddie's leaving left a wound that would not heal. He even considered following her to Scotland, reckoning he could figure out what to do then after he got there. Those thoughts faded with agonizing slowness until at last Maddie was no longer a burning scar on his heart, the first thing he thought of in the morning and the last thing at night.

Having had a taste of heaven, he spent the next year looking for more. He found he was one of those blessed few who could bed just about any unmarried girl he wanted and a few married ones as well. Another discovery was that his mother no longer could call his tune. He could do as he pleased. Of the men in Harry's life who counted, Natty had no objection to youthful adventure. Nor did Comet Elijah, who was busy teaching him about other things, like how to throw a tomahawk.

The time of freedom came to an end just before his eighteenth birthday. Harry was arrested for nearly burning down Speight's Tavern, whose owner's face, Harry's crowd had decided, reminded them of a pig. Besides the fact that liquor was involved, the trial established that Harry had not intended to destroy the place, just see what would happen when the object of their ridicule came from the kitchen to see a bonfire in the tap room. Harry suffered a pang of regret when he saw the look of bewilderment on Speight's plump pink face. It took the fun out of it.

Nevertheless, Harry's reputation as a hellion had become established, and it seemed that somewhere in the upper reaches of the town leadership it had been decided this was as good a time as any to bring him to heel. The county solicitor recommended a penalty of twenty strokes, time in stocks, and a fine of fifteen pounds plus damages. Of these punishments, the prospect of the lashes was the most daunting. People were known to be permanently maimed by such treatment, to the point that the rich never were made to suffer them, no matter how serious their offense. They were always let off with a fine.

But, to everyone's surprise, in light of the family's otherwise good standing in the community and Harry's father's faithful, and probably fatal, service to the Crown at Cartagena, McLeod offered an alternative. Harry would become his ward and part-time servant for the period of a year. He would submit to the judge's authority in all respects, undertake any course of instruction, and carry out all services required, with the intention of making of the now grown-up Harry an upstanding citizen of New Bern. If the project succeeded, his name would migrate from the liability column of the community ledger to the asset side.

The tasks turned out to include emptying slop jars for McLeod and several of his neighbors, working on repairs to the town fence, rounding up stray animals off the street, and occasionally assisting constables and sheriff's deputies in serving writs and escorting prisoners. And dancing lessons. The judge said one could not be a proper gentleman without knowing how to dance. All of these activities to be performed after Harry had put in a full morning's work at his family's plantation.

In addition, he had to sit through a daily lecture on some aspect of the importance of honor, duty, and the rules of proper conduct as observed by the better sorts of people throughout the world. Rooted in some ancient Italian court, later written out by an elderly Frenchman, they recently had been translated into English as *Rules of Civility & Decent Behaviour In Company and Conversation*. These directions covered every social situation a person of refinement was likely to encounter in a lifetime. They included guidelines for polite conversation, appropriate dress, manners at table, conduct on the street, and the respectful treatment of one's betters. This last thing, as Harry learned, was a whole subsidiary set of extensively evolved rules concerning where one should sit at a table, when to initiate speech and when to remain silent, the finer points of cap doffing, and even on which side of another person one should walk, depending on the social rank of each. Despite the tedious nature of the rules, McLeod assured Harry they were indispensable, that no matter where he might travel in the future, whether to London or Paris or Rome or Vienna, he would recognize the application of this code of behavior when among courteous society. And they would recognize it in him and know he was a person of good breeding. One of them.

To help it all stick in Harry's mind, he had to buy himself a small ledger book in which to paraphrase the judge's lectures and memorize these shortened versions, two rules per week. He found many of them ran contrary to his upbringing and some just flat-out strange. He avoided as much as he could sharing any of it with Natty so as to save himself the trouble of having to explain why Harry was going along with it. When Natty heard the outlines of the judge's program, he said he would have preferred the lashes.

Harry's new way of life was a source of unending mirth among his friends and past confederates in Craven County waggery. But as time went by he embraced the fresh start he was being offered, if for no other reason than to satisfy Talitha. She regarded the program as a gift from God, an astonishing opportunity, something that could lead, over time, to the elevation of the Woodyard name into the highest places of Pamlico society. Harry was not convinced this was a realistic expectation, but he was infected by Talitha's enthusiasm, her constant harping on what she called the family's rightful destiny.

Harry came to suspect the judge took some dark satisfaction in having such power over his granddaughter's despoiler. In any case, McLeod's apparent willingness to let go of the unfortunate past and take on the remaking of Harry Woodyard seemed only to raise the judge's already lofty standing in the community. The verdict on the streets of New Bern was that McLeod had handled his predicament with wisdom and grace.

But Harry never lost his fear that this forbearance someday would run its course.

★

Maddie picked up her blanket and pulled it around her shoulders again.

"In the days after we were found out, Grandfather hardly would let me out of his sight. When he did, he made his housekeeper keep her eyes on me and the manservant to watch the both of us. They kept me from slipping off, finding you, asking if you wanted to run away together."

"I would have gone. It's all I ever thought about."

"Me too. But Grandfather made me a promise."

Harry nodded, anticipating. "He said he would make you return to Scotland."

"He did, but first he promised that if we tried to run away, he would send men to chase us down. No matter where we went, even into the swamps, they would find us. They would kill you on the spot and bring me back to New Bern. He stated that quite matter-of-factly. The choice was between staying here, maddeningly close to you but with no possibility of our ever being together, or going back to Scotland and finishing my education. It was no choice at all, really."

In the gray light of the barred window, he caught a look at her eyes. They were red rimmed, but dry.

"It's a cold, ugly world out there, my love. At least it can be. And I am not as beautiful or as rich or as brilliant as I once thought."

"But you wrote poems. And a play. I can't imagine writing a play."

"It was never produced on the stage. Despite endless promises. I've come to understand that people led me on for their own selfish purposes. Especially men. They are unreliable, Harry. Changeable. With the exception of a certain gentleman from North Carolina, of course."

★

He woke up in the middle of the night to the sound of cannon fire. It was faint. Somewhere beyond the city walls. Maybe more harassment from the British in preparation for an assault in the morning. Or maybe the battle had begun.

For the first time, Harry felt sharply uneasy about being in a locked room. He disliked the idea of dying in an enclosed place. He tried to think about something else. Someplace outdoors. Roanoke Island would do. Digging into the wet sand with Comet Elijah, picking through the past.

CHAPTER 30

22: Shew not yourself glad at the Misfortune of another though he were your enemy.

—Rules of Civility

AN HOUR AND A HALF AFTER SUNRISE, A CLAMOR ERUPTED OUTSIDE their cell. Rushing footsteps and excited voices. After a short spell all became quiet again except for a patter of rain on the street outside.

"I couldn't make out all of what they were saying, but it seems the British have made their move," said Maddie. "Our guards are going to help fight them off."

Harry said he guessed that meant there would be no biscuits this morning. Maddie acknowledged his go at humor with a half-smile. She seemed nervous.

A few minutes later there was a rattle at the door. Two men entered. One was an Abnaki Indian dressed in buckskins and carrying a pistol. The entire lower half of his face was painted a ferocious shade of red, the upper half black with white stripes. The other man wore unremarkable civilian clothes and was armed with a hanger.

"Hello, Richard," said Maddie.

"Good morning, my dear." To Harry he said, "Welcome to our little *auberge*, Constable Woodyard."

The Indian's eyes darted back and forth between the two prisoners. He looked ready to shoot without much provocation. Ayerdale had a demeanor of forced calm.

"What's happening?" Harry said.

"A miracle. Last night the redcoats somehow figured out a way to get up a cliff and onto the plain behind Quebec."

"Where did this happen?"

"It seems that there is a poor excuse for a pathway next to a nearly vertical stream somewhere upriver between here and Cap-Rouge. If that makes any difference to you."

Amazing, Harry thought.

"They've planted themselves on the field about a mile away, a long red line stretching from the Saint Lawrence side of the peninsula to the Saint Charles. They're just standing there, waiting to see what Montcalm will do, I suppose."

"What will he do?" said Harry.

"He is rushing his army out to try to chase them away before they can entrench. Once Wolfe gets cannon into place, Quebec will be doomed. But that is no concern of yours. I am afraid it is time for you and your sweetheart to leave these prison walls. But not the way you came in."

Maddie caught her breath.

Thinking to put down his last card, Harry said, "Look, Ayerdale, I know you've been spying for the French. I also know that now you're working for our side. Your secret is safe with us. I've already given my word to your man deSavoy, who has taken me into his confidence."

A grin divided Ayerdale's face, giving Harry a good look at his teeth. Harry had guessed right. At least half were rotted.

"You lie so prettily, Mister Woodyard. I wish I could rely on your word, but I have the rest of my life to consider. I will not let it be overshadowed by the threat of exposure that I once betrayed my country. Your miserable lives are simply not worth the risk. For all anyone will know when they discover your bodies, you will have been killed by your French captors."

"But surely you are already suspected of something," said Maddie. Her eyes were wide, but if she was frightened she was hiding it well. She seemed more angry. "How to explain your sudden disappearance from Wolfe's camp?"

"Thank you, my dear, for your concern on that score. The question of my whereabouts for the past several days will be of little interest to anyone in light of what is happening now, no matter how it comes out. If anyone is curious enough to ask, I left camp to make my own survey of the French lines. With Colonel deSavoy to vouch for me, I have nothing to fear on that score. As for you, I will be heartsore, and completely bewildered, over how you managed to get yourself killed inside a French jail."

"I guess you intend to follow your usual practice of skipping away just before the fight," said Harry.

"Not at all. I will simply appear on the battlefield and fall onto the ground as soon as the firing begins, as if to reload. It will take me a very long time to perform that task. When the firing stops, I shall get back up and join whichever side has won. I will be welcomed as a hero in either case. A solvent one too, thanks to the generosity of both parties, now and into the foreseeable future. Who knows how much longer this tiresome war will last? Or how many more occasions for profit may arise? The truth is, I have begun to like this game of spying."

Ayerdale seemed to enjoy taunting them with his view of his own cheerful future. Or maybe he was just indulging himself. How many others were there with whom he could share his happiness?

Maddie said, "Did you love me once?"

"In fact, I rather fancy I did. I have long yearned for a partner, someone to share my life, help me bear my trials. Love me for myself, despite my shortcomings. Which are many, I'll admit."

"Richard, for the sake of what we had, don't do something you can't undo."

Ayerdale walked over and put both hands on Maddie's loosely covered shoulders.

"Milady, I could have chosen any of a number of beauties to marry, either here or in Europe. Wealthy ones. Some with titles. Unfortunately, I chose you. A liar. But such a damned pretty one."

One hand crept down toward her bodice, as if no longer obliged to follow any rules.

She knocked it away.

"Bitch."

He grasped the top edge of her gown and yanked downward. The cloth was surprisingly strong. It stretched but did not tear. Half exposing her front.

Harry lunged. But before he could cause any damage, the Indian clubbed him with his pistol butt. Harry's legs gave out and he felt himself going down.

"We should have played like this more often," he heard Ayerdale say through the ringing in his ears. "Alas, now we have no time."

"We can do it when you get back," Maddie said. Her voice was ragged and breathy, as if in a passion.

Harry lifted his head enough to see that Ayerdale was now holding her from behind, gripping her partially uncovered breasts with both hands. All but lifting her off her feet, and giving the Indian a good show. On his face a twisting together of anger and desire. And maybe surprise over what he had just heard from Maddie.

"A damned nice thought. And a way of extending your life for a few more hours, I suppose. But if our side wins this thing, the British, I mean, I'm afraid it would not do for them to discover you here. Hear your story."

He let her go with a shove that nearly knocked her down.

"I would like nothing better than to tarry, my dear," he said, "but that is not possible. So, as the French say, adieu. Please convey my respects to God."

★

The Indian took his time. Maybe waiting for Ayerdale to be far enough away that he would not have to hear the shots. As the minutes passed and the Indian continued staring at Maddie, it occurred to Harry that he might have gotten the idea of doing some of his own business with her first.

Harry made to get up. See what he could do. But a rush of dizziness interfered. The Indian walked over to him as he slumped back. Put the pistol barrel to his forehead and pulled back the hammer.

"Monsieur," Harry heard someone say. The voice seeming to come from the far end of the world.

Harry caught a glimpse of a French uniform. The Indian twisted around to see who it was, then seemed unsure of what to do next. Before he could make a plan, the newcomer shot him.

"D'Brienne," said Harry. "You are just a bag full of surprises."

"I believe it is bad luck to kill a man from behind." He stepped through the smoke and stood over the still twitching body. "I was on my way to join my commander on the field but decided to make a detour to see after your welfare. Harry, I find I cannot bear to see you die."

Questions danced on Maddie's face. Harry said he would explain later. Wondering how much of the story he would be willing to tell.

"When I arrived at the door I was surprised to hear Richard's voice inside. My protégé has become quite the celebrity among Montcalm's inner circle, you know. I paused to hear what he might say. And I'm glad I did. For shame, playing a double game like that. When the spawn of a dog came out of your cell, I hid myself. Maybe I should have killed him then, but I felt it more prudent to deal with them one at a time."

They followed d'Brienne outside, Harry pausing to steal some things from the deceased. His pistol, a kit containing ball and powder, his knife and tomahawk. The ax looked old and well used. The wood at the business end stained almost black.

The Frenchman mounted his horse with liquid grace.

"*Au revoir, mes amis.* The next time we meet may be in heaven." He made a flourish toward Maddie and went away at a gallop.

CHAPTER 31

82: Undertake not what you cannot perform but be care-
full to keep your promise.

—Rules of Civility

MORNING SHOWERS SEEMED ENDED BUT THE SKY WAS DENSE WITH
clouds. They could make out the sound of gunfire beyond the city wall.
Sporadic musketry and an occasional boom of cannon.

Harry said, "You stay here. I'm going to find Ayerdale." She
nodded, but a minute later he looked around and she was still there
as he moved down the street. Her gown more or less restored to
proper fit. Looser than before but passably decent as long as she
kept it pulled up.

"Maddie, there's nothing you can do. Just find a place around here and keep yourself hidden until this is over."

"All right," she said. But she kept following.

The horse gate was closed. Through the pedestrian door civilians streamed into the city, seeking protection behind the walls. The guard had multiplied since Harry's passage. No one interfered with two people struggling against the noisy incoming tide. Possibly thinking they were mad for trying to go out.

They walked at a brisk pace, feet making sucking sounds in the wet ground. There was no pathway, only patches of wild grass and scrubby underbrush. The thinning clouds exposed a hazy white disk of sun. At the crest of a hill, a broad plain stretched out below them. The same field Harry had first seen in moonlight. Swathes of knee-high grasses with stands of brush and weeds wore patchy autumnal shades of brown and tan and yellow. Amid the vegetation, standing in thick formations, hordes of French soldiers.

The closest bunches were but a stone's throw away, oblong clusters three and four and five men deep stretching out in either direction. Thousands of men. Mostly regulars in their white-and-blue uniforms, but, interspersed throughout, gangs of men in civilian clothes. Canadian militia. Looking like bumpkins who had wandered into a dress ball.

A half-mile farther along stood men wearing coats the startling color of fresh blood. They looked like painted lead toys in the distance, extending in a thin line from one side of the plain to the other. The whole thing had a fragile look. Only two men deep instead of the usual three or four. The ranks stretched out, Harry reckoned, so as to cover the entire width of the field, discourage flanking attempts. Short intervals separated platoons, wider spaces between battalions. Harry counted seven battalions in all, though smoke from a cluster of burning houses at the right end partly obscured that section.

He made a quick calculation from what he remembered about the strength of redcoat units. There must have been as many as four thousand men there. About as many as the more densely clustered

French. Men on both sides ready to die in a place where they did not live for men they almost certainly had never met, the kings of Britain and France.

French crews busied themselves about several cannon they had wheeled into place, firing and reloading with the practiced poise of court dancers. Otherwise, both sides stood motionless, or as still as men can hold themselves for extended periods. As if waiting for the gods of war to make up their minds. Say what should happen next.

Rifle fire was coming from a stand of trees to the right, where the burning houses were, and the cornfield on the left, the same area where Harry had fought with the Indian. The shooting was intermittent. Sudden thin gray stalks of smoke belching from barrels here and there at random intervals. The occasional redcoat dropping as a ball found flesh or a twelve-pound globe of iron from a cannon went bounding through the line like a bowler's ball, taking off limbs or heads or cutting men clean in two. Or when an explosive charge sent up a spray of fire and dirt and bits of iron. The redcoats stood impassively through it all, seeming to ignore oncoming death as one might disregard a minor distraction, a buzzing of flies. Harry recalled what Abel had said about what he had seen of British army discipline. *They is more scared of their officers than they is of the enemy.*

Ayerdale was nowhere in sight.

"We'd better go back," said Harry.

"And miss this? You must be joking." Craning her neck as if that might help her see better.

He spotted a stand of bushes grown up around a pile of small boulders. There they would be at least partly hidden but still able to see what was afoot. They could duck behind the rocks if the firing became too worrisome.

They had no more than settled in when a motion went through the British line. The redcoats seemed to be melting into the grass. In groups. Not falling, Harry realized, but lying down. Making themselves less visible to riflemen and cannoneers.

The miracle of the ascent of several thousand Britons up a cliff seemed not to have extended to horseflesh. The only mounted men in view were a dozen or so French officers grouped together off to the right. Harry did spot two small brass cannon on the British side. He tried to imagine how they had managed to get them up. And he recognized why Montcalm was concerned. Once the redcoats dug in, they could begin zigzagging their trench line forward to a place where those two cannon, plus as many bigger brothers as they cared to hoist up at their leisure, could murder the walls of the citadel.

The mounted Frenchmen were deferring to an individual toward their center, a portly officer with heavy eyebrows who was wearing a clean white uniform and black tricorn and sitting atop a finely muscled black horse. Starvation might be stalking Quebec, but this man and his animal seemed not to have suffered.

"Montcalm?" Maddie said into Harry's ear, following his gaze.

"That would be my guess."

The cluster broke up. Riders headed off in different directions. A few minutes later, commands went up and down the line. Muskets came unslung. The general made his way smartly into the front of the ranks. He wheeled and began riding back and forth, shouting angrily as he went and gesticulating toward the British. Harry looked to Maddie for translation. She made a shrugging motion. Too far away, she said, and suggested he use his imagination.

After a few minutes of this, Montcalm wheeled and faced down-field. More commands passed through the lines, this time triggering a clatter of drums. Syncopated, blood quickening, boasting of deadly purpose.

Montcalm raised his sword. His mount began stepping forward at a stately pace.

A cheer swept through the ranks and they too began to move. Their pace matching the relentless cadence of the drums. All the formations moving together with precision, as if one giant machine. Bayonets pointing forward.

"Come on," said Maddie, getting to her feet. She looked flushed and excited. "I want to get closer."

"This is a pretty good spot. I think I'll stay here. But you go ahead. You can tell me about it later."

She hesitated, gave him a disgusted look, and sat down again.

Although the masses of men were moving away, their shouts grew louder. A long, sustained sound of many voices but no longer what Harry would call a cheer. He remembered what the physician had said, his talk of British actions over the summer. He had put the matter politely but pointedly. "Depredations," he called them. Harry recognized the voices of angry men. Their thirst for revenge held in check beyond endurance by leaders who kept saying they were not strong enough to ride out of their fortress, challenge the enemy. And so the anger had festered. Especially, Harry guessed, among the militia. The regulars, those that survived whatever happened, could expect to return to France and find their homes and families intact. It was the Canadian fighters who had seen their farms and houses and shops turned to ash, wives and children going hungry, living like outcasts in their own land. Though Harry had never experienced anything like this himself, he felt he understood. Now, finally released from restraint, the militiamen especially must be burning for retribution, determined to expel the foreigners from their midst, as a human body might heave up a dose of poison. All their stored-up bitterness and frustration now focused on this feeble streak of scarlet etched like a taunt across the plain. A scab begging to be torn away.

He had seen this kind of anger before. When it settled over men of quality, it could be resolved in only one of two ways: with pistols or swords. Passions on both sides of the matter bridled by an ancient, strictly prescribed ritual. Appointed hours, attendants, chosen weapons, measured steps. God would choose which cause was the more just. As for the rest of humankind, the ordinary sorts of men, there was little ceremony. Just spontaneous maiming contests of fists and knives and axes or whatever weapons came to hand. Now

Harry understood he was seeing something new to his experience: the virtuous anger that underlies duels and brawls multiplied by thousands.

In their eagerness, some of the militia began to run ahead. The regulars quickened their step, and orderliness began to suffer. Defining spaces between battalions blurred. The wrath of each individual Frenchman flowing into a gyre, a whorl of ferocity that fed on its own energies like a piney-wood fire or one of the violent summer storms that come in from the ocean. The voice of this human tempest not that of many but as if from one. A slavering beast hungering for slaughter.

The charge now took the form of a coiling line, its contours changing with each passing moment. Muscular and fluid as it fumed and howled and boiled across the grass and scrub. Driving unremittingly forward.

The leading loop overtook Montcalm. He responded by surging ahead, gesturing with his sword. Trying to restore order, Harry guessed. Whatever commands he was shouting surely lost in the uproar. Some of the soldiers responded by running faster. Maybe thinking he was urging them on.

The redcoats rose from the grass. Still in their perfect double-row formations. Battalion by battalion, on command, each front rank dropped to one knee. Rear ranks remained standing.

And the French throng kept coming.

Harry tried to imagine what the redcoats were seeing as they stood shoulder to shoulder, barrack mates on either side, each soldier facing his own destiny. Close enough to make out the face of its agent, the tone of his flesh, whether light- or dark-skinned, the shape of his beard. Each life about to hang on the whim of a hot, fat ball as it made its wobbly way through the morning air. The brainless gob of metal having not the slightest care where it landed.

Maddie tugged at Harry's sleeve. "Why don't they shoot?" Urgency in her voice, as if ready to shout a warning to General Wolfe. Explain that in another minute it would be too late.

Before Harry could offer a guess, the French units that had surged the farthest ahead, the ones on the left and right sides of the field, stopped, took aim, and fired a volley.

It was more ragged than their officers probably would have liked for the sake of military display as well as lethality. But it had an effect. The report took several moments to reach Harry's ears, by which time a few tiny red-coated figures had crumpled.

Another platoon fired on command, then another. More British went down each time. The survivors remained all but motionless, only shuffling from one side to the other to close up gaps. Seemingly indifferent to the death visiting their ranks as randomly as a scatter of summer hail. Ritual slaughter the way Harry was given to understand they did it on the plains of Europe. Insanity, to Harry's thinking.

Then he noticed something odd. Although not a single shot had been fired from the British side, men in the French ranks were dropping. But not the whitecoats. Just militiamen in their civilian clothes.

"What's happening?" said Maddie.

"I think the Canadians are falling on to the ground to reload. If the French army is like the British, their regulars are trained to stay upright."

It came to Harry that Ayerdale was likely among those now on their bellies. If in fact he had even shown up.

The advance resumed. Firing and reloading as they went, mostly by platoons but some individually. Their eagerness to dispatch redcoats still plain. Organization suffering even among the better-trained regulars, who, Harry figured, might have been getting thrown off their pace by the sight of militiamen collapsing around them. Maybe not sure if they were being struck by unseen British fire or maybe just had decided to abandon the fight, hunker down until it was over. The Ayerdale strategy.

The left and right sides of the field now bore little resemblance to an organized army. Some haphazardly strewn clumps of men were going ahead faster than others. Only those in the center, where Montcalm likely had put his most experienced warriors, retained their definable formations, though even they had lost some of their crispness.

Thin though it was, the red line looked as unmovable as if each soldier had been screwed into place. Within minutes, a few knots of French soldiers were so close that Harry imagined they could have exchanged greetings. Or insults.

Finally, the forward line of a redcoat platoon on the left leveled muskets and fired.

"At last," said Maddie.

The precisely timed volley made a flying wall of metal. The result was gratifying. The closest host of Frenchmen collapsed as neatly as grass cut down by a scythe. A visible shudder passed through the rest of the ranks.

Moments later, a squeal of bagpipes reached Harry's ears. Maybe they had been playing before and the sound was just now arriving on the breeze. At the same time, British platoons on the left and right commenced firing volleys. With each flight of lead and each resultant row of newly dead or crippled French soldiers, the advance faltered. Only the center formations continued at the same deliberate pace, still stepping to the drums.

The center of the British line had not yet fired. For an instant, Harry wondered if they had been standing in one place for so long as to have fallen asleep. The idea had barely entered his head when both rows of men, the ones standing and those kneeling, leveled their muskets. The maneuver as precise as that of a high-born lady snapping open her fan.

In his twenty-eight years of being alive, Harry had seen many noteworthy things. Mysterious balls of light playing through swamps on moonless nights. A panther killing a bear. The top of a sap-rich pine tree exploding like a bomb when struck by lightning. But he had never seen anything close to what he saw next.

A simultaneous flash of fire and smoke issued from hundreds of Brown Bess muskets. A single tremendous clap of thunder. Smoke billowed over the field so thickly that Harry could not see who was still alive on the other side and who was not.

By the time the smoke had drifted enough to allow vision, the British had reloaded. All were on their feet now, stepping forward, their own drums beating time. The hay-colored grass to their front turning red and flattened by the weight of bodies. The Frenchmen who remained standing looking dazed.

Then, with the precision of fine clockwork, the redcoats stopped, leveled their muskets, and fired a second volley.

Madness, maybe. And yet, he had to admit, convincing proof of why His Majesty's enemies, from snowy Prussia to the steaming lowlands of India, feared his soldiers. What was left of a distinguishable French line dissolved. Men dropped their weapons and ran in the opposite direction. First just a few, then many, as panic infected those still standing. The entire army suddenly was scurrying away like a pack of beetles caught in a light.

The last of the low-lying clouds had melted away. Under a bright mid-morning sky, the sight of fleeing Frenchmen seemed at last to awaken passion among the Britons. A faint roar reached Harry's ears. War cries. A detachment of kilted redcoats broke away and gave chase. Claymores twirled and glittered in the sunlight, in the distance looking like shiny needles. Straggling Frenchmen, either wounded or just exhausted, disappeared underneath the swarm of highlanders. Huzzahs went up elsewhere across the plain as other battalions surged forward, joined the chase.

Running men filled the field. All headed more or less in the direction of Harry and Maddie.

He weighed their options. They could stay in the bushes or hide behind rocks, but they could not become invisible. They could put their arms in the air and try to explain to the first British soldier that arrived what they were doing there. Or a shortened version of the story. But the redcoats did not look like they would be interested in listening to explanations just now. In fact, they seemed focused on a simple purpose: making holes in every living thing not wearing red.

His other thought was to join the retreat, flee to the safety of the French citadel, temporary though that safety might be. But that carried its own risk: discovery as British subjects and not in uniform. The definition of spies. Someone might even remember that when last seen they had been in the jail.

Before Harry could decide which would be the less dangerous choice, the British charge itself began to falter as firing resumed from the cornfield on the left and the forest and buildings on the right. Numbers of redcoats paused to shoot back. But the fleeing Frenchmen were not slowing for anything. The first group flowed around their bushy stand like a herd of panicked cattle. The nearest ones gave them no more than disinterested glances, the men's gunpowder-stained faces complicated maps of anger and fear.

"Look over there," Maddie said. Pointing to the right. Montcalm, pale in the face and bloodied from the waist down, sat slumped in his saddle, kept from falling off by several men trotting alongside, guiding his magnificent horse at a good clip in the direction of Quebec. Harry looked among the fugitives for d'Brienne. There was no sign of the chevalier.

As soon as the first Briton, one of the kilted ones, came into shouting distance, Harry stepped from the bushes. He waved his arms back and forth in the air and hollered, "American! American!" Thinking it over later, he reckoned that what really saved them was Maddie coming up from behind, waving her arms and shouting, "Scotch! Scotch!" Allowing her badly stretched gown top to droop just past the point of modesty. The highlander paused for a good look, then continued on his mission.

The bulk of the soldiers passed them by. And then, bringing up the British rear practically all by himself, there was Ayerdale.

He trudged toward them at a steady pace, pistol in one hand and hanger in the other, glancing warily from one side to the other. When he saw Harry and Maddie, he stopped and gaped. Harry drew his stolen pistol from his belt, aimed, and walked forward.

They were too far apart to have much chance of either hitting the other. But Harry felt a rush of confidence. He was certain that somehow at this critical moment the supreme judge of just and virtuous retribution would seize control and give him victory. Not a well-considered feeling, he realized, but it emboldened him. At the same time he realized this was the closest he had ever come to taking part in a proper duel. Not a rowdy punching contest in a tavern or a street among drunken hooligans, the kind he was used to, but a true contest of honor between men of breeding. As convincing a proof as any that the Woodyards and the Ayerdales at last had come onto equal footing.

The last thing he expected was that Ayerdale would turn around and run.

Harry gave chase, wondering how this was possible. Then realizing that even assuming the best outcome for Ayerdale, Harry dead, Ayerdale's pistol would have been spent, and he still would have had Maddie to deal with. He might be hard-pressed to explain to any remnants of the army that might still be around to witness it why he was trying to kill either one. Or maybe he was just unnerved by the sight of Harry and the murderous look Harry supposed was showing in his eye. Better for Ayerdale, Harry guessed, if he just disappeared. Sorted things out later. Possibly with the help of his protector, Colonel deSavoy. A coward to the end.

But first he would have to get away from Harry.

They were heading toward the pine forest on the north side of the field just cleared of Indian and militia sharpshooters by a redcoat platoon. Ayerdale was thirty paces or so ahead but with every step losing ground to the younger, more physically capable man.

They crossed a carriage road. Off to the left, a riderless horse stood chomping on a roadside stand of grass, its muzzle moving methodically from side to side, ignoring its former owner, who lay lifeless a few feet away. The animal was too far off to offer Ayerdale a means of escape, though a momentary interruption in his stride indicated he briefly considered it.

When he reached the edge of the trees he stopped abruptly, turned, and discharged his pistol. Harry felt the ball chitter past his left ear. He returned the shot. Screaming, Ayerdale dropped both pistol and sword and clutched his right hand.

"You son of a rat whore, you've shot off my finger." He held up the bloody hand like an accusation. Harry tried to remember if Ayerdale was right- or left-handed, thinking it might have a bearing on what would follow.

He recovered his hanger and jumped into the forest, Harry not twenty paces behind.

The darkness was sudden and complete. His eyes protested the abrupt switch to thickly canopied forest by withholding vision. But nothing interfered with his ears, which picked up the dry sound of a body colliding with a tree off to his left. An outcry followed, by its sound equal parts annoyance and hurt. Harry turned in that direction, thrusting his arms in front of himself in the posture of a boxer to detect obstacles before he ran into them, as Ayerdale apparently had.

Harry's eyes began to adjust. These northern trees were more closely spaced, and the thicket of top boughs denser and more light-repelling, than the long-leaf variety Harry was used to. Below the canopy, bare and partly broken-off limbs, relics of years of previous growth, girdled each tree like spikes, almost all the way to the ground, making rapid movement hazardous. Harry wondered if Ayerdale had managed to impale himself on one of these. But the sounds of vigorous footfalls indicated he was still alive and in good health, aside from the condition of his right hand.

Not so the Indian whose body Harry tripped over. Harry looked around the ground for a fallen firearm, hoping for one of the newer models with rifling worthy of a sharpshooter. But if the warrior had owned one, it must now have been in the hands of a British soldier.

Partly on instinct, and partly in response to the sound of a crackling twig, Harry ducked. Just in time to avoid Ayerdale's sword, which parted the air overhead and embedded itself in a tree. But he couldn't avoid the toe of Ayerdale's boot. It struck him in the jaw and sent him sprawling. By the time he regained his footing, Ayerdale had wrenched his blade free and was lunging forward, aiming for his chest. Harry leapt aside and swung his Abenaki tomahawk.

Ayerdale cried out again, an anguished yelp as if badly wounded. But he was still on his feet, now clutching his sword arm with his injured hand. Harry had not had the time or the fetch to make the strike fatal or even very disabling. But he had inflicted pain.

Now they stood looking at each other, both catching their breath. Ayerdale seeming to recover his composure. Keeping a wary eye on Harry, he examined his finger, which had not been completely blown off. It was a pulpy lump hanging by a piece of skin. With some deliberation, as if having reached a disagreeable but necessary conclusion, he got the loose part between his teeth and tore it away, spat it onto the ground.

"Now see what you've done, you cockroach?" he said. Heat in his voice, in contrast to the ghostly cast of his skin. The scar along the side of his face from British steel now a sickly shade of purple.

They tangled some more, dodging around trees, trying to avoid the spiky branches. The advantage of reach that Ayerdale had by virtue of his sword, compared to Harry's tomahawk and knife, was cancelled to a degree by the obstacles that prevented a full degree of motion and the fact that Ayerdale was wielding the blade with his weaker hand. He kept the injured one lifted to minimize blood loss, giving him the aspect of a gentleman fencer. Droplets flung from the wound with every twisting motion.

All Harry could do was dodge and retreat, waiting for him to tire, make a mistake, offer an opening. But the opportunity did not come soon enough. Jumping back to avoid a slicing, Harry found himself wedged between a splay of bare branches. He quickly found they were too thick to break. He could move in only one direction: forward. Right into the tip of the hanger, which was now almost touching his belly. The blade slightly quivering, as if in anticipation.

Ayerdale paused as if to savor the moment. Both of them breathing hard. The golden man seemed to be composing some farewell remark. Rather than allowing the satisfaction written on his face to be the last thing he saw, Harry considered looking up into the treetops. Accepting divine judgment, however mistaken it might have been, and going to heaven with visions of pine needles. Instead, he blew a glob of phlegm into Ayerdale's open, about-to-speak, mouth.

Suddenly Ayerdale was no longer there. In his place was Maddie holding a dead branch like a club with both hands. A look of wild animal in her eyes.

Ayerdale was a few feet away, still on his feet, still holding his sword but turned partly from them and groaning. He made a jerking motion, which was accompanied by the dry sound of cracking wood. He lowered his head and looked. A broken-off piece of limb protruded about six inches from his side. It must have gone into flank meat only, missing vital organs.

"Bollocks," he said. More of a grunt than a full-throated curse.

Harry stepped out of his woody trap, knife and tomahawk at the ready. But before he could strike, Ayerdale swung his sword, not at him but at Maddie, who was closer. She made a sound like someone having her breath sucked away. Her hands flew to her neck and at the same time her knees gave way, and she spilled onto the ground.

Ayerdale remained standing but looked all done in. Instead of pressing his attack, he took a few staggering steps backward, then turned and started off. Clutching his injured side with his ruined hand and with the other hand using his sword as a cane. Heading back out of the forest.

Harry rushed to Maddie's side. She lay on her back, clasping her neck, a mix of shock and fear on her face. Harry gently pried her hands from the wound. It had an angry look but did not appear too deep. From the moderate flow of blood, he guessed the blade had missed the big vein.

"I'm not going to die," she said in a shaky voice. More a question or a declaration of hope than a statement of fact.

"I don't think so," he said. "Not from this."

"Then go and kill the bastard."

He stripped off his shirt and tore a sleeve away. This he knotted and padded around her neck as best he could, taking care not to choke her. He advised her to keep her hand pressed against it. Then he set off after Ayerdale.

By the time he got clear of the trees, Ayerdale had managed to reach the horse they had seen and had begun riding away. Glancing back, he caught sight of Harry. He shouted in a voice surprisingly strong, considering his various injuries, "I'll see you hung as a spy, Mister Woodyard. Or assassinated. You and your whore of a lady friend as well, if she's still alive. Who do you think they'll believe about all this?"

Harry judged the range. At least thirty feet, as he made it, and the distance rapidly increasing. Already at about the limit of anything he had ever hit before. A moving target to boot. Impossible, really.

He grasped the ax toward the bottom of its handle with both hands, as if holding a sledge hammer. Lifted it as far back over his head as he could, bringing it almost level with the nape of his neck. And threw. Uncoiling himself like a spring, putting his whole body into the effort. Timing the release to give the instrument a high arc. Aiming for it to intersect with a point a good bit ahead of where Ayerdale was at the moment. He followed through as Comet Elijah had taught him, the energy of the throw bringing him forward until he was hunched over, bowing like a Catholic. But head up. Watching as the tomahawk took its twirling, arcing path through the air. Magically tracking the movement of Ayerdale's borrowed horse. The horse moving at a moderately brisk trot. Heedless of anything unusual taking place, right up until the moment its rider slipped from the saddle.

The animal slowed, came to a dignified stop, and looked back. It looked ahead again, then back once more at the new body lying on the ground. Hesitating, as if awaiting further instructions. Finally, it ambled back onto the grass beside the road. Resumed its interrupted meal.

CHAPTER 32

110: Labour to keep alive in your Breast that Little Spark
of Celestial fire Called Conscience.

—*RULES OF CIVILITY*

IN NOVEMBER THEY MADE APPLE BUTTER AND APPLE CIDER AND
sorghum molasses to put on their biscuits. The peach tree bore a
generous crop, so they set aside some of the fruit to run through the
knob mill, bruise it up just right before pressing. When it was all done
Natty judged the cider "peachy," a play on words he never seemed to
tire of from one year to the next. Talitha taught Toby to make soft
soap and candles using grease and fat left over from the season's main
activity, butchering enough meat to get them through the winter. The

tobacco-curing barn still smelled wondrous of giant leaves turning golden as they had hung from floor-to-ceiling rows of sticks.

Toby had been on a shopping trip in New Bern when Harry arrived back from Canada. It was the first Friday of October. Her diary was lying open on the kitchen table, the date as yet blank. She had coped very well during his absence, he gathered as he paged back to the time he had ridden off for Williamsburg. He skimmed through days of risings, weather reports, chores done, meals cooked, visits from neighbors, and bedtimes. On July 18 she briefly noted a visit from Constable John Blinn to check on her welfare. Harry found three more such visits over the following two weeks. Finally on August 2, Toby stated that she asked him to stop coming over. No elaboration. Harry's first thought was to ride over to Blinn's house and see what he would have to say about this. But he realized that Toby would likely find out he had been looking through her diary and would be upset. Since she seemed to have taken care of the matter, whatever it was, he decided to leave it alone. But he was not happy. Especially when he found out Toby was pregnant. The first chance he had, he added up the days, based on their best guess as to when she would deliver, and figured she must have caught the seed two or three weeks before Harry had left for Williamsburg. It was not until the matter was settled in his mind that Harry felt like celebrating his soon-to-be fatherhood.

He was not shy in saying he wished for a boy. New Bern's militia captain, a bookkeeper by the name of Tatum, joined him in that wish, though he noted that the unit would have to wait sixteen years before welcoming in its new recruit. Harry wondered if they would still be fighting the French by then.

The other big surprise was that Olaf McLeod had died. His summer cold had advanced to pneumonia, and he had crossed over without much fuss. It happened around the time Harry and Maddie had been locked in their cell in Quebec. He wondered how Maddie would react to the news or even when it would reach her. When he last saw her, she was at Point Lévis recovering from her wound under the supervision of the Scottish soldier who had paused to admire her on the battle-field. This individual turned out to be the colonel of his regiment, a titled highlander, recently widowed, with a great pink harled castle in the Grampian Mountains. Which, Harry could see, might fit in well with a dream Maddie had shared with him the night before he left Canada: to return to Scotland and write a play based on her experiences. She had tentatively titled it *A Highland Girl's Wild Adventures in America.*

DeSavoy had disappeared by the time Harry got back to Point Lévis. Ayerdale's death was ascribed to combat after his body was found with multiple wounds. With him dead and deSavoy missing, Harry pondered what to do with the information that the man was a spy and a murderer. He had promised to keep these things secret. Maybe death had freed him from this obligation. But to expose Ayerdale would have required Harry to admit that he killed a person the world still believed to be a prominent American patriot. He had Maddie to vouch for Ayerdale's guilt but otherwise not a jot of real evidence. He finally decided the effort, and the complications it might bring, were not worth whatever gratification he might gain from posthumously destroying Ayerdale's reputation. Harry had better things to do with his time.

But what to do about Comet Elijah? How to save him from hanging if Ayerdale were not exposed?

As he discovered from a second letter from Toby that caught up with him before he left Canada, he need not have worried. The old Indian had made good his second attempt at escaping. People were still talking about it when Harry arrived back home, how Comet Elijah must have grown wings and flown away or crawled up twelve feet of warehouse wall like a fly, over the open top, then finally melted through one of the sealed bullet-glass windows to the out-side. Tuscarora magic. But no one seemed much interested in trying to recapture him. All assumed he had fled the district and by now was beyond their reach.

Harry recalled that his original purpose in setting out to catch a killer was to save Comet Elijah's life. As it turned out, he might as well not have bothered. Comet Elijah wound up rescuing himself. At least Harry had saved Maddie McLeod from a disastrous marriage. Who knows how that might have played out had Harry not gone to Canada. And maybe by not exposing Ayerdale, Harry had played a small role in helping the British cause against France.

He took comfort in these thoughts, though he would never get over his sorrow that his actions had led, though unintentionally, to the death of a gentle spirit.

Conversations on the streets and among the town commissioners had shifted to other matters, like who would take over as their new chief justice in Olaf McLeod's stead. Governor Dobbs had approved the council's nomination of an interim, a good Anglican property owner by the name of Hastings, and the town was now awaiting Dobbs's pleasure as to a permanent replacement. The matter was somewhat complicated by the fact that Dobbs had finally made good on his threat to relocate to Wilmington. Though even farther south, it was closer to the ocean and its cooling breezes. New Bernians were beginning to despair that their town would ever again be the seat of government. The hopeful consensus was that eventually the old man would either retire or go keel over, maybe while pleasuring himself with his now fourteen-year-old wife, and the next governor could be persuaded to come back. There was even talk of offering to build a palace, something to match or even exceed the grand edifice at Williamsburg.

No one seemed to care much about Harry's recent willful behavior, running off to chase the "true" killer of the Campbells when it seemed perfectly clear who that person was. As near as Harry could figure, he had not been replaced as constable of Craven County, even though he had not arrived back home in time for peacekeeping duties at the September Court of Quarterly Sessions. He received a notice from Hastings that Harry's services would be needed for the upcoming meeting of the Superior Court.

★

One of Harry's first stops after he got back to New Bern had been the parsonage of Christ Church, where he gave Reverend Reed a leather pouch. As the cleric was opening it, Harry explained that during a stopover in Philadelphia he had visited the parents of Noah Burke. At their parting, the senior Burke had given Harry all the money Harry had returned from what Noah had given him, plus a liberal contribution from Peter and Martha. To be invested and used, Peter requested, under the supervision of Reed and the vestry, to operate a free school for parentless children.

★

The week before Christmas, Harry received a letter from the prime minister of England.

He knew something was afoot as soon as he entered town that morning on his way to du Plessis's store to buy spices for a new syllabub recipe Talitha wanted to try out. People he saw on the streets stared and pointed at him as he rode past. The clerk at the store, which also served as the town's post office, said there was something there for him, but he needed to get du Plessis to come over from his house and deliver it in person. Which he did with great formality, refusing to just hand the letter over but instead placing it on a silver tray for Harry to pick up with his own fingers.

The language was flowery and inked in an ornate style of script. It would take Harry several readings to fully understand everything. Even du Plessis, who read it out for all to hear, confessed that he had never seen a more impressive document. The signature was that of Thomas Pelham-Holles, First Duke of Newcastle, First Lord of the Treasury and Leader of the House of Lords. It extolled Harry's virtues as a loyal subject of the Crown and a British patriot in the finest ancient traditions of the realm. It thanked him for his "Courageous

& incalculably valuable Services to ye British Army in Canada during ye late War with France." The letter did not go into specifics on this point. Despite the persistence of du Plessis and other citizens of New Bern who now crowded into the store, the best Harry would deliver up was that he had been on a secret undertaking for the government at Whitehall, one whose nature he still was not at liberty to discuss. An admiring murmur went around when they heard that. But no amount of pressing could persuade him to go further.

Du Plessis allowed him to leave with a free batch of spices.

★

Abel and Reuben were having ale with friends before the fireplace at Speight's when Harry next saw them. Though only midafternoon, it was nearly dark outside owing to the early winter twilight and a thick cover of clouds that hinted at snow.

"Is that Constable Henry Woodyard at the door?" said Abel, squinting to see.

They shifted around their table to make room. The serving girl brought a wooden flagon topped with a mound of foam.

"I don't know what your fine friends over at Cogdell's are going to make of you coming in here," said Reuben. "Have you forgot where you belong?"

"Wherever I want to drink a health to old friends, that's where I belong," said Harry. "I'll still go to Cogdell's, but if they don't like me coming in here, too, it's not my concern."

This statement was met with a surprised silence.

"Well, that don't seem to have stopped you from wanting to get rich," said Reuben. "Or, should I say, richer. I heard you bought some more land."

"A nice piece of acreage came up for sale on the north end of our place. The turpentine was good this year, so I was able to get hold of it. I already signed contracts to bring over three more indentures to help me clear some space for planting. Might have to build another tobacco barn, too."

"These new workers you're getting, any coming over from Wales?" Abel asked with a mask of innocence. Knowing chuckles around the table.

"The best bargains these days are coming from up toward Scotland, the borderlands in the east, if you want to know."

Reuben said, "I'm seeing more and more Africans working these fields, just like the big operators have up in Virginia. Seems like the easiest thing now is just buy them right off the ship and have done with it."

"I will never own a man, no matter how much cheaper it might be. The idea makes me sick."

Abel lifted his wooden cup and said, "Well, here's to our old mate. Welcome home, Harry boy."

★

Riding through his new holdings a few days later with a map, trying to figure out where the boundaries were, he caught a whiff of roasting chicken.

Comet Elijah was on his haunches at a makeshift spit. The carcasses of two small animals turning a nice golden brown before him. He was wearing woolen trousers, mismatched boots, a woman's dirty pink overcoat, and a beaver hat.

"Come sit beside me, Harry," he said without looking up. "I put on an extra bird for you."

Harry hitched Annie to a tree. The mare was looking frayed. He wondered if she would last out the winter. He had chinked up cracks in the plank siding of the barn and banked the outside of the north wall with brush and dirt and whatever else he could find lying around to block out the wind. But the return from Canada, which involved long stretches aboard ships and two storms, had worn her out, and her old energy had not come back.

Though in a cheerful state of mind, the Indian was not helpful when it came to satisfying Harry's curiosity about how he broke out of jail. "That kind of thing calls for special knowledge that you don't just pick up anywhere," he said. "Maybe someday you'll be ready to have it but not just yet. You might hurt yourself. I'll see if I can teach you later on, if you're still interested." After a reflective pause, he added, "If I don't die first."

"You've been talking about dying for a good while now," Harry said. "The idea doesn't seem to bother you."

Comet Elijah lifted the sticks from the fire and put the chickens on two tin plates he got from a knapsack. It was a handsome outfit that looked like something one of the better-heeled members of the militia might bring on muster day. Harry let pass an itch to know how he came to have it.

"I've died many times, always come back. I thought I told you that before. Pretty soon you learn not to make a big to-do about such things."

He got out a tin flask and two cups and poured out a pinkish brown liquid that smelled like old apple brandy. Harry put away his reluctance, gulped his down, and accepted Comet Elijah's insistence on another.

They talked some more while they ate and drank. Harry told him about Canada, giving an especially detailed description of his fight in the cornfield. The whole time feeling he was just confirming what Comet Elijah already knew. When they were finished they got onto their feet and stamped out the fire.

"You know, you should really leave the Pamlico," said Harry. "They're not making any effort to find you now, but that could change. And if somebody happened to catch up with you in these woods . . ."

Comet Elijah interrupted. "I've already decided to go away. I have people in the south, where the Spanish are."

"Florida?"

He nodded. "They stay warm the whole winter long down there. To tell the truth, I'm tired of cold weather."

"Well, it's a good idea to leave here. I'm the only one who knows who really killed the Campbells."

Comet Elijah had been adjusting himself, arranging the kit he had loaded onto his back. Eyes moving here and there over the ground, looking for stray property. Now he stopped and looked at Harry.

"And how do you know that?"

The question startled Harry. Maybe he had wounded the old warrior's pride by seeming to suggest he was no longer able to hurt anybody.

"Since you asked, I'll tell you. But it is something you must swear never to repeat."

"That's fine."

"No, you must swear to me. Because if this got out, it could complicate my life very badly."

"I swear I won't tell anybody, even if they torture me."

The thought came to Harry that if Comet Elijah was so good at poking through peoples' minds, he should know about his finding the medallion and the nautical chart of Pamlico Sound on the floor under the crib. His thoughts went back to that first gleam of gold. How he had got up from the table, gone down on all fours to look. The medallion of the Freemasons, sitting atop the chart of Pamlico Sound. Stacked so neatly. Harry recalled now that he had wondered if someone had placed them there, instead of their having skittered across the floor haphazardly. He had puzzled over this but only momentarily in his haste to have a better look at the objects. After that, things had moved so fast he had forgotten about this little piece of the puzzle that did not quite fit. This small nattering voice, so quiet that it had been all but drowned out. Only now he realized it never really had gone away.

"I guess I never told you about the monster," Comet Elijah said.

"What monster?"

"The one I had a fight with. I thought I told you already. The truth is, it's getting harder to remember what I said in the last few minutes, much less days or weeks ago. But that's not important now." He looked up at the sun through the filter of pine tops. It was beginning its long downward slide in the southwestern sky. "Anyway, it's getting late."

Harry put a hand on Comet Elijah's arm as he turned to leave.

"Tell me about the monster."

The Indian got fussy, tried to shake him off. Said he needed to get started so he could find a place of shelter before nightfall. He could discuss the monster episode later on, if Harry was still interested.

Harry kept his hold. Half coaxing, half demanding. He needed to hear it right now.

They sat down again. Comet Elijah seemed to warm to the subject as he talked. Maybe a little flattered by Harry's interest. He made hand gestures, furnished descriptive details, filled in color and the illusion of movement as a painter does to make a canvas come alive.

It seemed like Harry could see it unfolding.

★

It was an hour or so after the rider had passed by. Still well before dawn, the murky part of night when spirits are about. The storm had tapered off to almost nothing. Sleep ruined anyway, he thought to go into the town, see if he could find some dry, safe place to recollect himself. Someplace where he would not draw attention until returning to the forest at first light.

He was moving at a good pace down the new-cut road when he saw a light ahead. A farmhouse. He sprang onto the porch like a cat and peeked into one of the windows. Inside was a woman, young and good-looking, with red hair. She was staring straight at him. He ducked back down and got ready to run, then realized she must have been looking at her own reflection in the glass. He stole another glimpse. She was touching up her hair with her hand and messing with her blouse, all in a sly way, like she did not want anyone to notice. The way women sometimes do when they are around men who are not their husbands.

He lowered his head, waited a minute or two, then looked again. Now her back was turned and she was facing a table where two men were sitting. One was wearing dirty breeches and a loose-fitting hunting shirt made of coarse material. The other was better dressed, but everything was damp, including the man's matted yellow hair. A fancy robin's-egg blue jacket was drying out on a chair next to the fireplace. A baby's crib in a corner. The only other person he could see was a little boy standing near the chair. He was looking at the jacket.

The yellow-haired man was eating and taking draughts from a metal cup and talking between mouthfuls, going back and forth in conversation with the other man. Comet Elijah could not see what was on his plate, but watching his jaws work made him hungry. He had a thought to knock at the door and ask for something for himself. He had not eaten in three days. But before he could act on the idea, he noticed the little boy reach inside one of the jacket pockets. The adults were tangled up in their conversation and not paying attention.

As he watched, the boy drew something from the pocket. Comet Elijah caught a glimpse of gold. Then the boy reached back in and pulled out a folded-up piece of paper. He looked back at the table where the adults were. Seeing he had not been seen, he squatted and put both objects, the gold piece and the paper, underneath the crib. Maybe thinking to look at them more closely later on.

By and by, the men got out of their chairs and shook hands. The yellow-haired one pulled on his jacket, shaking his head no. Likely turning down an offer to stay the rest of the night.

Comet Elijah crept to the side of the porch and jumped down onto the ground and stayed there until he was sure the man had gone. Then he circled back around to the steps, walked boldly up, knocked on the door, and asked if he could have some food.

The man and woman looked surprised but got over it. In a short time he was at the table having a meal of roasted corn, red beans, and collards flavored with pork bits.

That is when the monster showed up.

Comet Elijah had seen such things among his own people. A child will be going along just fine, acting normally, like children do, when all of a sudden something will get into it. It will start yelling and screaming for no reason or twitching or talking in some unknown language. Just like a demon had got hold of it. And that is exactly the case. The child acts like whichever type of devil has come inside of it. It can be a dangerous proposition if the child is older or big for its age or if the parents just let it go on without doing anything. Like these parents were. Either they were afraid or just being too lenient, letting the little boy get away with whatever came into its little monster head to do.

The parents seemed like good people. Comet Elijah could see they would appreciate having somebody step in and show them how to handle the situation. He got out of his chair and walked over and picked the child up and threw it nearly all the way across the room.

The man was upon Comet Elijah in an instant. Clearly he had misjudged him. Suddenly aware he might lose a combat with a younger, stronger person, he had no choice but to finish it quickly with his knife. The woman started in on him next. He figured he might be able to fight her off without hurting her too badly, but in the uproar he accidently stuck her in the side. She fell back to the floor bleeding like a pig in a chute, then started dragging herself off into the next room.

While that was happening, the little boy demon recovered enough from its injuries to run out the front door. Comet Elijah pulled the man's rifle down from over the fireplace—he already had noticed it was primed and ready—and shot him in the back.

The baby was awake and squalling now but offered no threat.

The woman finally finished breathing. Regretting what had happened, though none of it had been his fault, as a gesture of respect he arranged the family in dignified positions. Even plucked a sprig of rosemary from the garden and put it at the boy's nose to emphasize his sorrow over the outcome of his fight with the monster. An apology to the dead people's souls.

Comet Elijah stopped talking. Finished with his story. He stared at the ground in silence. Harry also stayed quiet, trying to take in the enormity of what he had heard. He looked into Comet Elijah's thickly lined face, wondered what was going on inside that dark, all-but-bald head. Maybe now that he had relived it fully, maybe for the first time, the experience weighed him down as it had not before.

"You may be right," Comet Elijah said finally, once again correctly reading Harry's thoughts. "Maybe I acted too quick. Some of my own people used to criticize me for that kind of thing. But a lot of it was just jealousy of my bold leadership style."

He struggled to regain his footing as old men do when they have been sitting for a while. He came onto all fours, straightened his legs, tried to push off with his arms. That did not work. Finally, he accepted Harry's offer of a hand. Then there was the chore of recovering his kit again. Several pieces of flatware, and who knows what else, had spilled out of it.

Harry's mind raced as he helped restore order. Was the story believable? It seemed too detailed and too close to what Harry knew to be true to have been made up. Unlike riddles, whose answers were arbitrary and depended on wordplay, solving puzzles demanded the use of logic. In this case logic ruled out every possibility except that Comet Elijah had just confessed to killing the Campbells. Albeit with the occasional embellishment. Harry did not believe the business about jumping around like a cat, for example. But he could not have been describing just some elaborate dream, some vision he'd had, with himself inserted into it. Comet Elijah killed the Campbell family. And Harry could not rule out the possibility that he might do something similar again if allowed to go free.

As he sifted through pine needles, pretending to look for lost objects, Harry sorted out the ramifications. It would seem that duty demanded he bring Comet Elijah back with him into New Bern to stand trial. He tried to imagine just getting him there. A struggle was possible. Harry weighed the odds of being overpowered by some Tuscarora conjuring, the kind that had allowed Comet Elijah to escape prison. But logic again intervened. It seemed more likely he had stolen away through some dereliction on the part of his guards, not by climbing up a wall like a fly and melting through a bullet-glass window. For all the posturing about strength and agility, given equal combat without the advantage of surprise, Harry was sure he could whip Comet Elijah. At least he was passably sure.

He pictured in his mind the trial and its certain outcome: hanging from the gibbet in front of the old courthouse. The man who, with Natty, had raised Harry. Taught him everything he needed to know about life and survival in the world outside the genteel haunts of colonels and judges and young cadets and all their rules of civility. Sheltered him from the cold.

He wondered what Natty would do.

Although absorbed by these thoughts, he had not failed to notice that Comet Elijah had begun to wander away. There was less and less of him to see, as the trees and patches of underbrush were breaking up the picture. Harry realized that by not acting, he was making a choice. Maybe he already had.

He walked toward the place he had last caught a glimpse of dirty pink. When he got there all he could see was more forest. Something moved off to his right, and he started in that direction. He had not gotten many steps along when he saw another pink patch, this one even dimmer, still farther to the right. He turned that way. Then realized that if he continued on like this he would be going in circles.

He looked back at what he took to be his original position. There was no sign of Annie. The pine forest seemed to have closed in behind him. It was quiet except for a woodpecker hammering at a tree, short bursts of stutterings so close together they sounded like the swinging of a rusty hinge. That, and a low babbling that somewhat resembled human laughter, but was probably coming from the creek.

Suddenly, there was Comet Elijah. Or at least his face. It was nestled among some fully leafed pine limbs thirty feet off the ground. Smiling down at him.

Harry stood there for a while trying to ignore it. Tired of tricks. Or maybe it was just the apple brandy. He took deep breaths to help resettle his mind. Remembered a snatch of what Toby had put down in her diary, something about pieces of time forever flowing by. His own life had taken a sharp turn over the past four months. He had not been aware of it while it was happening, but now he could see it as plainly as a hawk can make out a twist in a river from high in the air. Another marked change of course had occurred ten years earlier, when old man Rollins had caught him and Maddie in a hayfield. He could bring back neither of those times, make them turn in a different direction. And it would do him no good to wonder if he and Maddie somehow ever might have had a future together. Those moments were locked in the past.

What he saw ahead was life with a woman he knew he loved, Toby, and fatherhood. And years of working in the tobacco fields and pine orchards of what might be an ever expanding Woodyard plantation. He looked into a future of being a good friend to his neighbors, the people of Craven County, in whatever ways he could. Lending food and livestock and tools and hours of his time when needed to help them through hard stretches. Certain these favors would be returned when needed. And keeping up his volunteer service as a constable. Maintaining order at public meetings. Serving writs on people who needed to answer for skipping Sabbath services or missing militia musters or making drunken fusses in public. Arresting those who would do more serious harm to his countrymen or the Crown.

These waters looked somewhat familiar and yet fresh and new, full of unforeseen moments. As for Comet Elijah, Harry contented his mind. Florida seemed as good a place as any to die again.

THE END

ACKNOWLEDGMENTS

THE GODS OF WRITING ARE KIND TO PRACTITIONERS OF HISTORICAL fiction. They allow us to fill as many gaps as we wish in the written record of whatever bygone day, for whatever reason, catches our attention. The only limits are imagination and some measure of the laws of plausibility. Many of the characters in this book are based on real people, including a few historical figures like George Washington and a gangly teenaged Virginia fiddler named Thomas Jefferson. Several key characters with made-up names were suggested by real people, including the French spymaster, who readers may find the most remarkable of any they meet here. Such a person did exist, and after the war did retire to France to live out his life on his own terms. As for the constable himself, I had an ancestor in that part of North Carolina just around that time who served in the same kind of position, a volunteer constable, and later as a militia officer. The real Henry

("Captain Harry") Smith exists today as no more than the faintest of shadows formed by two brief lines in a 1930s family genealogy, and his birth and death records. Harry Woodyard's story, with his family's roots in the swampy back country around Albemarle Sound, and his efforts to fulfill his mother's ambitions for him and her family name in the up-and-coming Pamlico region, is imaginary. But it is entirely plausible. All I did was fill in some gaps.

I'm indebted to the authors of more than one hundred histories, journals, and travel logs I've digested about old North Carolina and, more broadly, America, in this crucial but much under-appreciated period of our history, when foundations were being laid for the American Revolution twenty years later. Prominent among my history sources was Fred Anderson, University of Colorado professor and author of *Crucible of War: The Seven Years' War and the Fate of Empire in British North America, 1754–1766.* (When I told him I was writing a novel about a constable in colonial North Carolina during the French and Indian War, he observed, "You are entering virgin fictional territory.") I based much of my point-of-view depiction of the climactic Battle of the Plains of Abraham on his account, the most detailed and nicely written one I have seen. Also especially useful were Noeleen McIlvenna's *A Very Mutinous People: The Struggle for North Carolina, 1660–1713* (University of North Carolina Press, 2009); Alan D. Watson's *A History of New Bern and Craven County* (Tryon Palace Commission, 1987); Gertrude S. Carraway's *Crown of Life: History of Christ Church, New Bern, N.C., 1715–1940* (Owen G. Dunn, 1940); Dwight C. McLemore's *The Fighting Tomahawk: An Illustrated Guide to Using the Tomahawk and Long Knife as Weapons* (Paladin Press, 2004), and the marvelous four-volume series of North Carolina folklore collected by Duke University Prof. Frank C. Brown between 1912 and 1943, in collaboration with the state's folklore society, which he founded. Many of the oral traditions he came across in his wanderings have unmistakable origins in the period of this book and earlier.

Of course, as with all historians whose works have formed my understanding of these times and events, I take responsibility for any inaccuracies—or, as I might prefer to call them, artistic licenses.

I also owe an untold number of novelists whose works I've read in a lifetime, including recently David Liss, who assured me (when I needed assuring) that a good story will find readers no matter the era in which it is set; James Grady for his riveting story lines and painterly writing; James W. Hall for his mysteries set in the weirdness of South Florida, and Charles Frazier for the lessons he teaches in, among other subjects, narrative voice. As is true concerning factual content, though, any shortcomings in the literary department are entirely my own.

My thanks to the first person in the New York publishing world who gave me any reason to think I could write a novel that people might want to read: my agent, Jennifer Unter. Thanks to the creative team at Pegasus Books, including the sharp-eyed, deft-handed editor I was lucky enough to have, Maia Larson. Also to Maria Fernandez who came up with the typography, and Kara Davison for her brilliantly conceived and executed cover art, with its circlet of stars suggesting an independent America just beginning to emerge from the mists of the future.

I can't thank enough three friends who read early manuscripts for their encouragement and wise counsel along the way: Barbara Mathias-Riegel, Punch Wray, and Cathy Healy. Thanks to my two lovely daughters, Hillary and Jessica, for being the delightful people they are; and to my older brother Kendall, who as a child experienced bits of a rapidly disappearing old North Carolina that I, growing up mostly in Northern Virginia, did not.

And finally, the most thanks of all to my wonderful wife, Pat Durkin, an estimable writer herself, and student of natural history, who read earlier drafts, and who has supported me for so long with love, encouragement, and kindnesses large and small. My gratitude to her is beyond measure.